ORANGE LAUGHTER

ORANGE LAUGHTER

LEONE ROSS

Farrar, Straus and Giroux
New York

Farrar, Straus and Giroux
19 Union Square West, New York 10003

Distributed in Canada by Douglas & McIntyre Ltd.
Printed in the United States of America
First published in 1999 by Angela Royal Publishing, Great Britain
First published in the United States by Farrar, Straus and Giroux
First edition, 2000

Library of Congress Cataloging-in-Publication Data
Ross, Leone, 1969–
    Orange laughter / Leone Ross. — 1st ed.
        p.   cm.
    ISBN 0-374-22676-8
    1. Homeless persons—Fiction. 2. Civil rights movements—Fiction. 3. New
York (N.Y.)—Fiction. 4. North Carolina—Fiction. 5. Mentally ill—Fiction.
6. Subways—Fiction. I. Title.
PR6068.O836 O73   2000
823'.914—dc21   00-034091

For Daniel and Benjamin

Children get used to restriction, so they don't venture far; then, when they try to, they feel like they've crossed the world.
—Paula Rego

Let man fear woman when she loves . . .   —Nietzsche

ORANGE LAUGHTER

1

I stooped over the child and looked at him for a long time but I felt nothing I wondered if he was garbage I hunkered down a foot away and stared at his body at first he looked like a sack then a mattress torn apart I stretched and I could see his arm and the tilt of his pelvis I stared hard WAS it a child you know the darkness plays with all our minds down here I didn't want to touch I tried to decide not to know but I'm not an animal baby so I reached out for the pathetic coat he wore I couldn't see its colour and I wondered where the sound was coming from a raw sorrow song I wondered who was crying over his crumpled face dang I saw the tears falling onto his little arm I watched them fall and I was thinking *there are so many leaks down here* then I realised the leak was me

it was me

someone was screaming there were bruises going purple on his cheeks his skin was ashy he was raven lips and ebony cheekbones a coal jawline his tight jet hair cupped his forehead and his ink eyes were open wide he had deep sable nostrils and I thought *did somebody love you before you died* I realised the scream was coming from my throat God I held him he was cold all I had was a thin coat but I wrapped it around him I hugged him to me and thought *if only he would cough and struggle like the end of any good book everything would be alright* his head was soaked with my tears how old was he why did he die alone down here in this stinking place *did the trains get you child*

Agatha laughed at my tears I looked up and there she was sitting on the steel beam above my head smiling down at both of us you know you don't know fear until you look straight into Agatha's eyes they are

1

diamond full stops you could bang them against concrete Agatha laughed and she laughed and I hugged the boy to me *leave him alone* I yelled *leave him alone he's dead* I looked down into my arms and there was no child anymore all I'm doing is hugging myself in the green coat I wear the tears drying on my arms the little boy lost gone like the sea

I got to my feet and Agatha was gone too there was nothing but darkness and me sucking the salt water off my arms

so the bitch is back with her head games

I call Agatha a bitch because that's what she is a bitch in heat I thought she'd gone that she'd left me alone but now she's back and it will be the same old story her swishing her tail in my direction throwing her thick hair over her shoulders wanting me to see her she will peek out at me from behind the trains and I will hear that luscious heavy laughter once again she is tall enough to break a man there are snowy strands in her dark hair but you wouldn't believe her age with those breasts bullet nipples and though I know I have never kissed the dark discs around them I still imagine that if I did she would make sounds so good I'd go mad she leaves pools of energy behind her as she walks streaming yellow from the soles of her bare feet her lips are naked she has a midnight face her Momma must have started to paint that skin on then got scared and tried some funky New Age design rippling and freaking out one side of her face where the skin is scarred but she's still beautiful and each time she laughs I see it light up this place her laughter is a flash fire in the distance

you want to know where I'm at I'm under the Noo Yawk streets that's where and I know the trains like they're brothers and you know down here we call where we're at Underneath and the rats are as big as cats and five times as scary staring at my ass with antique eyes and all of us down here call where you live Topside I thought I'd escaped down here but no trust the bitch to come back with that stunt that little boy is just her style *let me give him a corpse* she must have thought to herself *let me see if my Tony is still human*

I haven't been Topside and watched the breeze for over a year but I went out the other night after the boy lay dead in my arms I had to mail an important letter and there was wax on my fingers it dripped from the candle and made hot white circles on my skin pattering one

2

two one two burn baby burn I need a candle because it's dark down here the dark is thick like oatmeal like nothing you've ever seen and I can hear the A train in the distance sometimes it freaks me out big time because you feel like it's coming to get you even when you know it's not scheduled you know down here we all dream that the trains will get us and run us over or the third rail will fry us one strange night when the balance goes when you're stepping over the tracks you know what I mean about the third rail right the rail that they run all those million watts through that's right Chaz is always saying that one day she's going to drop kick it like a stupid motherfucker and deep fry herself on that rail YOU CAN RING MY BE-E-ELL RINGIN MY BELL MY BELL DING DONG DING OW

I was writing the letter under the candle the wax making my fingers white and I wanted to ask Chaz to mail it for me when she went Topside she goes to pan-handle but she's a jealous bitch too WHY am I surrounded by all these bitches so I made a decision that I had to do it myself and I ran my thumbs over the letter that I'd written and thought about Chaz telling me how she gets her letters from her sister who thinks that her fine ass self is working as a dancer but really she's living Underneath here with me Chaz said *yeah Tony you could get mail at the gas station they cool like that they got a fine brother across the counter and he be giving me free Hershey's and those cigarettes you smoking* all I know is she wanted me to cop an attitude because she called the brother fine but I don't give a good goddamn I like Chaz and the pussy is good but I can't love in a place like this

jealousy is for Topside it's for real life for 42nd street and McDonalds and Queens and the Statue of Liberty whenever I tell Chaz about the Lady she asks me *who she ever give liberty Tony not to me yo* and I tell her she's just a cynic because this is the land of the free and the home of the brave and she thinks I'm serious you could never say that Chaz had an ear for irony or sarcasm I knew Chaz would ask too many questions if I asked her to mail the letter so I took the few short paces up the ladder yeah up to Topside

I wanted to fall when the night hit me it wasn't dark enough and the moon was so bright I hadn't seen it for a year and the silver shadows were merry *goddamn I still got a turn of phrase* and I crushed

3

the envelope in my hand I kept saying *this is the only way a man has to admit that he needs some help sometimes not a lot of help just a little you know a man needs to ask a friend for a favour sometimes* and the moon laughed down at me

the letter is going to Michael Abraham Tennyson PhD and when he gets it we could have a great reunion yeah class of North Carolina 1965 so he could remind me that she's DEAD Agatha's dead I know she's dead but I need him to tell me the whole story of how we came to be best buds I know she's dead but I saw her yesterday and I know you think I'm crazy but her face was so sweet I swear when she laughs it's orange and there are yellow pools at her feet and her arms are red with blood so I wrote him and now I'm sitting Underneath in the subway tunnels where I live nobody knows I'm here I'm waiting because Mikey was the best friend a man ever had and I know he's going to come through for me it's a damn shame we haven't spoken so long how old were we twelve thirteen nine when we first met that would be 1962

I've written him and told him I can't get the Soul Snatcher out of my mind

2

The black boy picked pecans every day at nine o'clock. Mikey started worming his way under Miss Ezekiel's house at half past eight. His bulk made the venture difficult, but he pulled his stomach towards his backbone and crushed the small breasts on his chest against the rough dirt. The best way was to lie on his stomach and shuffle backwards. Once he'd wedged his legs and hips as far as they could go, he braced himself on his hands and pushed against the ground. Inch by inch, his body complied. When he was in position only his fingers showed, and he was trapped until the black boy left. Getting out was harder.

Each time he hid under the house, Mikey spent a few minutes in prayer. He prayed that Miss Ezekiel would not discover him. Above him he could feel the tremor of movement inside the building - she and Agatha walking in the kitchen, frying meat and making biscuits. Agatha stepping through, sweeping the floors. In his most horrific imaginings he could actually *see* the moment his grandmother spotted the big moving lump that was him, bending the floorboards. She would call Agatha and she'd say, 'What in all hell is that? Agatha, come over here, watch out fo' snakes and jes' you see what's the cause of this hump!' Then they would find him - stuck, dirty, too slow and too big to scramble out. The black boy would turn around and finally speak to him, and the words would be damning: 'Whatchoo doin' watchin' me?'. It would all be out and he would have to raise his eyes to heaven and die.

Mikey blinked as sweat trickled into his left eye and sighed as the back door opened. He heard the boy's soft footfall on the front steps.

Miss Ezekiel told him that you could smell niggers before they came up on you, if the wind was blowing right. She said she was surprised people didn't just lay down and die when all of them got together, that was probably why intelligent folks didn't encourage them to gather. She said when she passed them nigger gin joints in town she smelled them on the air. All drink and sinning. She said she was surprised that these silver-rights goings on didn't kill the police with the stench. Mikey had never smelt anything special on the niggers. Just sweat and a Sunday afternoon, like him. Except Agatha.

Mikey smiled, thinking about her. Agatha. Miss Ezekiel's daily help, who came six days a week, at seven in the morning. Agatha, who always, always smelled good. Even when the heat blistered the porch walls and a man could drink shade like lemonade, she smelled good. He shifted, thinking about the way she made ice cream, cranking the old machine. One day her sweat had dripped onto his arm as she handed him a bowl. It was all the best smells in the world. Her skin was like hot butter in a pan. He could imagine her pouring herself over biscuits.

He'd been in Edene for eighteen months, ever since Miss Ezekiel brought him over from his home town in Georgia. Two days after they arrived, Agatha came to the back door looking for work. Mikey watched the tall, brown-skinned woman duck her way into the house and then looked away. He was more concerned with his own lingering disorientation. It had only been four months since his father had died, and he didn't like Miss Ezekiel. The house his grandmother had rented - with his father's money, he was sure - still looked unknown and empty, despite the boxes and bags strewn in the front room and across the porch. Miss Ezekiel hadn't let him bring anything that belonged to him. She bought him all new clothes. She said his daddy's things smelled like death.

In Georgia, the people on the street had respect for his daddy, so they didn't exclaim about Mr Tennyson's fat son. But in Edene, each new person widened their eyes, as if they were trying to squeeze him into them. Mrs Jenkins - Miss Ezekiel's neighbour, who had her up in all the sewing circles, all the church meetings - took one look at him and proclaimed him as wide as he was tall. She said it in a loud voice.

6

Mikey dipped his head and scurried inside himself. That was where he lived.

Agatha was different. When she saw him, her eyes had widened too, but there was something warm there. She looked at him thoughtfully, as if she'd been about to say something but changed her mind. When Miss Ezekiel turned away, Agatha put out one hand and stroked the damp hair off his forehead. She wrinkled her nose at Miss Ezekiel's back, a conspiratorial gesture that made Mikey smile.

Agatha was six feet tall if she was a mile, and her hair wasn't like any colour Mikey had seen before. It fell from a widow's peak into slender black ropes, past the bright cloth in her hair and down across her shoulders. When she held her head just so, secret strands went blue. Her skin was high yellow-brown and her feet were small. When you got up close your eyes were drawn to a surprise in her face: thin lines that crawled across her right cheekbone, around the eye socket, scattered across half of her forehead, crept under her chin and down her neck. It looked like a pattern. She saw him looking and smiled, as if to say yes, I see you looking, I see you've seen it, now what? He blushed and looked away. On that ice cream day he sat down with his dried, sweated-on arm, smelling her, until Miss Ezekiel asked him what the hell he was doing. He'd sniffed the Agatha-smell all day. It was the smell of love.

Four months ago, as July's weight bore down upon them like an old man with a burning, nearly-lost dream, Agatha had introduced the black boy. His name was Tony. She came to the back door holding his hand. Mikey wanted to hate him: Tony was as beautiful as a girl. The sunshine made his skin glossy. He had a new haircut. Agatha explained that when Tony arrived at the bus station from New York, his head was all rat tails. She couldn't untangle it, so she sheared it off.

Tony raised his bowed head as she spoke and Mikey was punched by the full force of his face. The boy was pretty, but he was going to be a man. Thick eyelashes framed bottomless eyes that stole too much space and saw too much pain. Blackberry eyes. He looked at Mikey looking at him while Agatha explained chores: Miss Ezekiel wanted the lawn cut and she wanted the silver cleaned and boy, we've got to move on now. Her voice was firm and peaceful.

Tony didn't speak. He nodded to show that he understood. Agatha said he never uttered a word. Mikey wondered if the black boy was a retard. He knew that Miss Ezekiel didn't like the lack of yessum, no-um. He'd realised early on that words like that made his grandmother happy. But there was nothing Miss Ezekiel could change about the silent boy in her house all summer. Mikey listened to her comfort herself out loud in the evenings as he did his homework at the dinner table, knees together, hands flat on the table top like he was told, doodling around the edge of the paper when he couldn't get the work right: the boy was clean, Agatha was a decent coloured and the Lord, well He did send things to test a body.

Mikey avoided Tony, as he avoided most. When the school holidays started, he'd found once more that he had no friends, and needed no more enemies. There wasn't much to do except go into the woods, avoiding the swamp, lest Miss Ezekiel start hollering, his niggershooter in one hand and food in a bag: quarter of a watermelon, some biscuits, a handful of peanuts and one of Miss Ezekiel's chickens fried up brown and smelling good, in case he needed to keep his strength up. He tried fishing in the creek, but the fish just seemed to laugh at him, and he was tired of that, so he kept walking, looking at squirrels and shooting at them. He knew he'd miss but it didn't bother him. He liked squirrels. It was just that he couldn't take any joy in the summer, like a nine year old boy should. He wasn't good at anything and eventually when the sun became merciless, he decided to go home. It was like this every day, and before he knew it, school was in again and the teasing began again and this, he decided, was his life. Yells of disgust in the hallways and no-one ever talking to him without contempt. Until October came, and the pecans began to fall. It had been another long day when he happened upon Tony in the yard, picking pecans, and talking.

Mikey wriggled, trying to get comfortable as Tony walked forward into his range. He grinned to himself, then frowned. It would soon be over. The pecans were only good for a couple more days. When Tony had started picking they were nearly three inches thick on the ground. Miss Ezekiel was mighty proud of the pecan trees on her new land.

8

Tony shook out the first sack and began to pick up nuts.

When he first heard the black boy's voice, Mikey had been too shocked to make out the words. He'd paused, excited, debating the wisdom of dashing out and saying hey, or running into the house and telling Agatha, to let her praise the Lord for a miracle. He would have given his whole lunch and a lot more to be responsible for a light in her face. He moved behind a tree and listened, his stomach churning. It was only a murmur, but the words were unmistakable.

'And Elimelech, Naomi's husband died, and she was left, and her two sons...'

Mikey guessed that it was the Bible. He wondered whether it was such a good idea to run inside and tell Agatha. If the boy was talking damnation maybe that would make her sad. He leaned against the tree and listened. His daddy once told him he had good ears.

'And they took them wives of the women of Moab, and the name of the one was Orpah, and the name of the other Ruth, and they dwelled there about ten years,' said Tony, picking up pecans.

Mikey had seen the coloured all hollering and shouting up in their churches. Agatha's grandaddy had been a preacher. Maybe she knew. Maybe she'd been teaching Tony the Bible. Maybe it was the only thing he could say. He listened to the pleasant voice and decided that he liked it. It was soothing. His daddy's voice had been good too, cutting through noise like water. Mikey crouched behind the tree for a long time, hearing about Ruth's life, until Agatha called for Tony and the boy went inside.

For three days Mikey hid under the house, waiting to hear Tony speak. He didn't know why he was doing it. He only knew that it distanced the self-consciousness in his belly. It was their secret, even if Tony didn't know. Agatha was tearing out her hair about why this boy don't speak, but he, Mikey, could see Tony doing it every day, words running out of his mouth into the deep afternoons. It was like watching a miracle. He thrilled to himself when he saw Miss Ezekiel muttering under her breath, cussing how this little nigger better not be sassing her with his buttoned-up lip. He knew that Tony was more than silence.

9

Mikey smiled as Tony took a breath and began.

'The song of songs, which is Solomon's. Let him kiss me with the kisses of his mouth, for their love is better than wine...'

It was a good secret for a little boy who couldn't hit the house with a rock if he tried. A boy who had comics on his shelf until Miss Ezekiel found them and burned them, watching Superman and Spiderman go up in flames. He wanted Spidey to jump out of that big old fire and give Miss Ezekiel a hiding. Then they would be friends, he and Spidey, go up North on Greyhound and no-one would think he was a sissy boy then. Spidey would teach him how to use his Spidey sense and he'd know who was a bad 'un and he would leave all them bad folks alone.

'I am black, but comely, o ye daughters of Jerusalem, as the tents of Kedar, as the curtains of Solomon. Look not upon me, because I am black, because the sun hath looked upon me...'

When Spiderman declined the offer and continued to burn, Mikey wasn't surprised. Nothing good had happened since his daddy died. He saw Agatha shaking her head. Later she asked Miss Ezekiel in that fancy voice of hers - better, Mikey admitted, than his grandmother's or his own - why the woman felt the need to be burning up the boy's only pleasure. Miss Ezekiel turned her back on Agatha and there was nothing more to be said. He noticed that Miss Ezekiel didn't give Agatha any of the leftover clabber milk that evening. Agatha's fancy voice fascinated him almost as much as her face. Almost as much as Tony's incorporeal murmur.

'I have compared thee, o my love, to a company of horses in Pharoah's chariots. Thy cheeks are comely with rows of jewels, thy neck with chains of gold...'

Mikey strained to hear, hoping snakes wouldn't eat his knees.

'We will make thee borders of gold with studs of silver. Thy lips, o my spouse, drop as the honeycomb, honey and milk are under thy tongue and the smell of thy garments...'

'Michael Abraham! Michael Abraham? Where is that boy?'

Mikey banged his head against the floorboards above him. He bit his bottom lip to suppress a yelp. Bruised air exploded from his lungs in a sharp hiss. Miss Ezekiel was yelling from the house. He glanced back

10

at Tony. The boy was still talking. Panic began to hum through his body. Surely Tony would hear her calling and shut his mouth. There must be a reason why Tony could talk and wasn't. There must be a very big reason.

'I said, Michael Abraham, where you at, boy?'

'Thy plants are an orchard of pomegranates, with pleasant fruits, camphire...'

Mikey wished he would stop talking about campfires. Tony's voice was getting louder. There would be hell to pay if Miss Ezekiel heard him, but he was talking and talking, picking up pecans with his nimble fingers. They were nearly gone.

Mikey listened to the footsteps moving through the house above him. Miss Ezekiel had called to him from the inside and now somebody - Agatha, he prayed it was Agatha - was heading for the back door facing Tony. They'd both get a whipping if Miss Ezekiel heard him. She would know that Tony had been fooling her. She'd know that he, Mikey, had been listening. She might say it was a plan. That Agatha knew all along. She might tell Agatha to get going. The thought made him bite his lip even harder. And Tony was still talking, as if he couldn't stop.

'...with spikenard, spikenard and saffron, calamus and cinnamon...'

Miss Ezekiel was shouting at the top of her voice. Why couldn't Tony hear?

'Michael? I said, Michael, where you at, boy?' His grandmother's voice cracked with impatience.

Maybe this was a punishment. He was going to be found out, lying and watching a nigger talk out the Lord's words like he was somebody. Like he was black and comely like Solomon said. Mikey had asked his teacher what comely meant and she said it was another word for pretty. Miss Ezekiel was going to find out and Tony was going on and on, as if he was in a trance, squeezing the plump nuts in his small fists, dropping them in yet another sack, using his enchanted, pained voice. He had to distract her. He could hear her at the back door.

'Mizz Ezekiel! Mizz Ezekiel!' Mikey yelled.

Tony jumped like the devil was coming and peered over the sack in his hand. He looked alarmed, furtive, embarrassed and angry all at the same time.

'*Michael?*' Miss Ezekiel's voice sounded even more annoyed. The back door opened.

Mikey scrabbled at the ground in front of him, hoisting his weight forward. He had to get to his feet. Miss Ezekiel walked down the steps and began to move around the house. He could see her long feet and cracked toes in the sandals she wore. He gripped at the ground. His nails scraped against stones that cut into his palms and fell away, seeming to chuckle at him. She was going the wrong way, heading around the left hand side of the house, peeping, arthritis making her joints rustle. Any moment now she was going to be standing over him, yelling out that he should be afraid of snakes and ha'ants under the house, how you put yo' fat self up under that porch anyhow, boy, is you a fool? A panicked tear squeezed itself out of his eye as he tried to lever his feet into a position from which he could push. He was stuck.

A pair of brown legs appeared in front of him.

A brown hand reached out. Mikey gaped up in astonishment as Tony grasped his hand and pulled. He felt as if his gut would rip. A nipple scraped against splinters. Tony braced himself and pulled again. Mikey felt himself sliding. Tony flailed and lost his balance and the two boys fell to the ground, Mikey almost in Tony's arms. They could hear Miss Ezekiel's patterned footfall coming back around - 'Boy, where you at, looka heah, don' be playin' with me now!' - and Tony tugged again. Then they were both on their feet, panting. Tony's face was solemn. Miss Ezekiel turned the corner of the house just as Agatha came to the back steps.

'Tony! Why you not picking those pecans? Get on, now!' Agatha said. Her hand clenched and unclenched her skirt.

Miss Ezekiel stared at Mikey's shirt. Dust painted the front and a rip hung sadly on the sleeve.

'Boy, you a fool? I need you to be inside these books! What you out here doin'? What you do to yo' shirt?'

Mikey looked down. Out of the corner of his eye he saw Tony hurrying back to the nuts, picking faster than ever.

'Nothin', ma'am,' he said.

'Then get in the house, boy!'

He smiled up the steps. He looked at Tony but the boy had his head down again. Mikey decided that he didn't care. Now they shared the secret. It was out in the open and he didn't care about the fussing. Everything was fine.

3

I passed out when I was Topside with that letter for Mikey don't ask me why I guess my body couldn't take the shock and when I woke up the sky was blue and light above me I put my tongue over my teeth and there was so much scum and the sun hurt my eyes like a drill through jelly I rolled over and put my hand in rotting cabbage it felt like bad pussy wet and soft I was near the Chinese restaurant so I knew what breakfast would be I looked down and there it all was across my shirt a buffet for the fucked

I was in an alley and a man came round the corner with his arms full of garbage he wasn't happy to see me he threatened me like I couldn't take him in five minutes it doesn't matter that I've been on a Underneath diet that rich bitches in LA would envy I told him I was sorry and he dropped the bag and trotted away and my leg hurt so I rolled up my jeans yeah if you want to call them that they're rags now I looked at the dried blood and the gash in my leg and tried to decide when it got put there said fuck it and limped out to look for breakfast I thought it would be a treat for Chaz to have breakfast from me you know her rough ornate hands seem to help keep the bitch away but maybe things will change now that I saw the bitch the other day night whatever I haven't seen the bitch for a long time I thought I'd lost her since I was Underneath

I limped on with my hollow belly and I saw a garbage man so I asked him if I could see what he had there and he stared at me I had to ask because there was a time when Chaz found fifteen pounds of prime chicken breast in a bin and it lasted us for nearly three months packed away in her ice box you don't think we have ice boxes Underneath well

14

Chaz hooked us up to the third rail ha who ever said a woman was only good for one thing and Chaz looked so fine sitting on blankets with fried chicken grease running down her fingers

the garbage man stuck out his bag and he looked sick when I found two and a half burgers and a whole apple pie wedge and half a milkshake but I threw that back because ants were partying in it and the man jerked the sack away *gimme that* he said and his lip curled I tried to stare him down but my leg hurt too much so I bent at the knees instead and I could hear the joints pop and see the cut gouting fresh liquid I picked up the pie and the burgers and the garbage man told me to stop he asked me how I got like this there were fat beads of sweat on his brow he was a fine brother as Chaz would say and I would say so too you know not cute just honest hard working and RIPPED I put the food in my shirt and the trash man was on my case he's saying *how this happen to you brother I'm talkin to you man you don't have to be like this there's places you can get the monkey off your back* and I was thinking *you haven't ever seen a monkey this big* I told him I wasn't a crackhead and he was saying he hates the sanitation engineer shit but it's an honest living and he hates to see a brother so low I shuffled away thinking *you want to go low with me bro I wish* and he's calling to me saying *a man gotta get paid people can help you man* then he got pissed and told me to fuck off I thought *that isn't nice* I thought about ripping his face apart but my leg was hurting so I walked back towards Underneath hearing him yell after me *stupid nigga can't accept no help ain't nothing worse than a stupid nigga* I'm saying *yeah we emancipated brother*

when I got back down here the dark rolled up to greet me and all I could think was *thank God I'm home* I felt my way with my fingers while my eyes cooled I felt my way as the trains whispered to and fro they are snake beasts roaring past my head I can hear them clanking and shuddering and you know if you're not careful they'll oops take you by surprise I can see the people inside the trains like maggots but can they see me I came down hearing the trains singing *welcome back welcome back welcome back welcome back* while I was passing the mural I know it by touch because I found it when I first came down you know there are occasional beams of light and one reflected off the mural when I passed it and suddenly I could see vague images but not enough for a critique

there is beauty down here if you look for it and you know I used to be a critic ALL THE CRITICS LOVE YOU IN NOO YAWK SAY DON'T MASTURBATE I said that Prince he grabs any chance he can to get down and dirty funny little fucker you know maybe I could do an exclusive on the mural artist I can see the headline now PAINTING IN THE DARK the hardest thing would be finding him for a quote he's probably some crack freak weirdo but every time I pass the mural I run my fingers across its ridges and the fine lines there and I feel the confidence of the artist's hands while I'm hop skip jumping over piles of shit and used needles you know the smell doesn't bother me anymore it's the richness of human defecation mixed up with poverty groans and insanity binges but the thing that does drive me crazy is that I never know the time I'm always asking Chaz for the time and she doesn't know unless she's been Topside and what kills me is that we're all brothers down here I've never seen a white boy down here just us every flavour of coffee

I passed the mural and went down the tunnel siding thinking that Chaz would be worried but I hit the room and she wasn't there I knew that because the candles were out I'm looking at them now nearly fifty maybe sixty of them dotted round this room we share I haven't lit them since I woke up Chaz is not here again and it's her who lights the candles I don't want to light them because it might make it easier for the bitch to find me

the bitch is back dancing and laughing so rich and I am terrified I don't mind admitting it this is the first time I have SEEN her she's not hiding in other people anymore I'm finding it hard to sleep eat shit move I lie shaking Chaz has been trying to help but she can't you know me and Chaz live together let me tell you how I met her not long after I got here I was going to get water there's a drip and you put an old pan underneath and sometimes the other people down here steal the shit but that day I couldn't face guarding the pan and it takes nearly an hour to fill up so I left it and came back to the room just chilling then I could hear the screams through the tunnels thinking *damn is that my imagination* I didn't think about Agatha because I thought I had escaped her and I rounded the corner nearly fell on top of them because you know the dark you can hardly walk through it though your eyes get used to it a little bit this girl has got two men on top of her and when I fell over them she starts screaming again like a crazy woman *RAPE RAPE RAPE* and I was like *dang this is not happening* and before I knew myself I lost my temper and beat their asses until they sang please and then I've got this girl and she says she's twenty but I don't believe it I think she's about sixteen and down on her luck looking at me like I'm some hero THAT'S THE WAY UH HUH UH HUH I LIKE IT

women are crazy because next thing I know Chaz starts following me around after she said thanks I guess it's my cute face she came and found me in the room and she started fixing up like she's the maid or something she's telling me that she's got a mattress we could share but I was saying *no girl I just want to sleep* but she is one stubborn woman she says she owes me owes me likes my face my form wants to know me hey that rhymes she used to sit in the room with me when I was trying to get some sleep and finally I asked her what her story was she's pushing her hair out of the way she's a skinny little thing you know I always liked women with meat on their bones and I mean a lot of meat I mean big bouncy breasts and that curvy flap that covers their hot patches I like that but Chaz is slim and I could play her waist like a sax and she tells me about her life old story centuries old she came to NY to hit the big time to explode she said she could dance like a crazy motherfucker and I'm thinking *don't dance* she says things went wrong she started stripping too afraid and ashamed to go home and say *momma I'm a ho now* so she started hitting the pipe and it was exploding her brain making pretty track marks born of heroin fantasies you know I was never one for drugs not even a little Rastafarian sensimillia no way boy that shit kills your ass and Chaz looks at me pretty and I was thinking *damn I should have known this was a junkie* so I said *you get a fix down here* she said no she came down for peace and I could relate to that *haven't sucked the glass dick for a year no needles either* she said

I used to think she was lying but down here's like heaven to her man and I think I believe her now so at night I kiss her drugged out

17

arms and if we were Topside maybe I could love her Chaz knows about Agatha and how the bitch wants me Chaz believes me when I talk about Agatha and I've never been a superstitious man but Chaz calms me down with her oils and incense and she stops me pulling my eyeballs out I told her I saw the bitch the other day and she's just looking at me and saying *where you go the other night Tony* and I'm thinking *how the hell you know I went Topside you weren't here when I left you were gone*

it wasn't hard to find Mikey when I was Topside I followed his career found out he's married to a famous poet ha Mikey always was a creative whore and he's been at Princeton for years I wanted to call him and I didn't want to call him but I guess I always knew I would have to do it that it would be my last option because I came down here with blankets chump change and Mikey's address at Princeton DOCTOR Michael Abraham Tennyson Doctor Mikey got a PhD and shit and I never thought fat boy had it in him no I'm a bitch sure he did I love him I'm glad he's made it because one of us had to so I wrote the letter I told you that I tried to laugh at the big old moon when I went to mail it I wrote to see if my ace boon coon best friend I ever had will do me a favour to see if he'll just tell me the story because there's so much I don't remember just tell me the story of how we came to be pals

4

Agatha looked out into the dawn, thinking of just turned peaches. She'd woken up with a craving for fruit, wanting to be a little girl and let the juice drip onto her blouse. There was a jar of preserved peaches in the kitchen, but she wanted soft fuzz against her lips. She leaned down and lit a cigarette. It would do.

The cigarette smoke sent a small web of tendrils through the laundered clouds above her. She stretched her arms out and rubbed freshness into her skin, her face a dark silhouette against the porch railing. She traced a finger down the rough skin of one cheek and got up tall, her black curls fighting for their rights on the top of her head. She didn't style her hair like the women around her; instead, she bent at the waist and flung the heaviness to the sky, away from her face, and tied it there with a handkerchief. She reminded people of a sailor, binding her craft to shore, the tendons standing out on her hands. At night she sat on what had been her grandfather's bed, pulled the handkerchief off and shook it down. She brushed the thickness to sleep, her pretty, scarred face calm.

This morning time was special to her. She liked watching a new day unfold, birds cursing in the background. It was good to be in the quiet and reassuring to be alive. The night riders had not come. They could come in the day, that was for sure; they could come anytime, but the dark was their hour.

It seemed to her that Negroes always had to be running. If they weren't running across the ground, they were running in their hearts, or waiting to run, waiting for a reason to be running. She'd seen off the last of the hideaways last night and she and Tony were alone once more. A tense ebb replaced the howl in her head.

The howl had begun as it always did: with an arrival. Sarah from down in the Bottom had come up two nights ago, knowing Agatha Salisbury would be on her porch smoking.

'Agatha Mae? You there?' The voice trembled.

Agatha moved into the circle of the kerosene lamp so that the woman could see her. Pappy's house had been wired for electricity before he died - his last gift to her, he said - but she still liked his old lamp.

'I'm here, Sarah. What can I do for you?'

Sarah climbed the steps. She looked like she was trying to squirm under the night.

'We needs ta get out, Agatha. Me 'n Mamma,' she said.

Agatha nodded. It had become familiar.

'You know where you're going?'

Sarah shrugged. Her back was bent. Agatha patted the chair beside her and the young woman sat down.

'Cousin Ennis say we got kin in Pittsburgh. Thas where we aimin' fo'. I been up there sometimes, did some cleanin' work fo' Mr Charlie.'

Agatha nodded again. 'Have you got money?'

Sarah looked at her. 'We don' got much, Agatha. I never know you-' She stopped, embarrassed.

Agatha chuckled. 'Come on, now, girl. You know I'm not asking for me.'

Sarah bowed her head. 'I'm sorry. I shoulda known, yo' grandaddy a preacher man...'

'Doesn't matter what he did, Sarah. This is me, now. I was asking so I know you're going to be alright.'

'We got some. Mamma got some two hunerd dollars, an' she been tryin' ta draw it in small bits, so they don't think nothin'. But they been comin up, comin' up, sayin' they know what Bessie doin' in Alabama, an' we needs ta be tellin' her to stop.'

'You tell Bessie that?'

Sarah smiled slowly. 'Sho'. Mamma them vex, an' she wrote her a little thing, send it on to them chaps in New Orleans, they sen' it on to Bessie, say don' do it, everybody in Acheson County gettin' ready ta

20

be lynched by them peckerwoods. But Bessie don' pay it no mind. Bessie always gettin' ideas ovah herself.'

Agatha saw the pride in the smaller woman's face.

'I guess you all better come when you're ready,' she said. 'I'll tell you what to do.'

She had been uncertain and a little scared when she returned to Edene two years ago, to bury her grandfather. The old man lived to a ripe age and the coloured community came out in full force to see Reverend Salisbury off to meet his Maker. Not a grim word was spoken in the little church on their land. Pappy had been a shining example of Negro dignity. He'd preached the word with a quiet but intense faith. She knew the uppity members of his congregation had wished for a touch more fire and damnation in Reverend Salisbury's sermons, but Pappy Arthur which was what his friends had called him - ignored them. The word, he was fond of saying, could be delivered in a whisper. All who had ears to listen would hear and understand.

Pappy left all his property to Agatha: 102 acres five miles out of Edene. The church he'd built on his land was a large, single auditorium structure with a high ceiling and long, horizontal iron bars overhead to brace the walls. She stood in the middle of the little church the night after his funeral and stared at it. The altar at the rear looked like an apparition, half hidden in the gloom, set on a small platform. There were chairs in front of the platform for the deacons. When she was small, she and the other children in the congregation were threatened with pain worse than death if they dared to sully those chairs or that altar. She walked around, touching the hand-held fans that were set neatly on newly-dusted pews, smelling the sweat of long gone mourners. Eventually, she gathered her courage and sat in the faded chair from which her grandfather had spoken to his flock. Her shoulders moved as she wept. She had nowhere else to go.

The next day she told Reverend Wilson to keep on with the church. Rent free. As long as he kept it up. She wasn't about to embrace the Bible, regardless of those who thought she, such a young, educated woman, would be well suited. She felt no calling. She asked the Reverend to help her sell off most of the land. She didn't want the

21

responsibility of farming. She took what people could afford - small amounts, larger amounts, chickens, home produce. Some people had lived on the land all their lives, as Pappy's former tenants. She was glad to give them their homes.

She had her books and her few items of clothing sent from Brooklyn. The old house didn't feel empty to her. Everybody else thought that Pappy's house was quiet, just her, in five big rooms. She didn't think so. Everything spoke to her. The front door bowed to greet her, chuckling about old times. On the porch her mother's rocking chair sang in a low, reedy voice. It was like a high school reunion. The house embarrassed her with stories she'd forgotten, marvelled at the changes in her, reminded her of the boys she'd liked, brought up old jealousies, dramas, showed her growth and weaknesses that she hadn't noticed. The strangest thing was her graduation to Pappy's room. It still smelled like him; she could almost see him, reading her Bible passages and telling her about the old days until she nodded off to sleep and he carried her to her bed.

Her adolescence had been full of life cycles: the picking of the corn; the intimate, forbidden smell of drying tobacco; dropping a ripened watermelon to the ground so you could bury your face in between the seeds; the two cows calving. They'd been rich by community standards, her grandfather employing three men in the fields. She revisited the kitchen patch at the back of the house and began to care for the fruit and vegetables that were going wild: fat strawberries that stained her apron with juice, plump string beans, gnarled and complacent sweet potatoes, a little bit of sugarcane, handfuls of okra and green peas. She remembered one cow in particular, Pappy had called her Elementary Jones. *Fo' her serious expression an' her beautiful eyes,* he'd said. She remembered chasing their mule - it was a stubborn old thing - and she remembered catching that mule on a fine spring day, just as Jamie had whistled low over the fence. On the first night, after the funeral, she tossed and turned, hearing the bray of the long gone mule and that sorry whistle.

After the first year, she decided to supplement her income with domestic work. She felt her brain rotting between the four walls, felt the need for honest, even dirty work. Reverend Wilson tried to convince her to teach again: after all, she was well qualified after seven years in Northern classrooms, a university lecturer, no less. But she was tired of that life, and even though she didn't admit it to herself, it was unbearable to face any activity that reminded her of Jamie. Jamie with his storm eyes. Him and his terrible mouth: red as her strawberries. She heard that Miss Ezekiel had moved fresh into Edene, and she got up early to reach the woman's place. They agreed hours and a price, and she felt the familiar tug of ambivalence. Work was good. Whites were another matter. And then Amy Green, the local midwife, came to visit.

Agatha had known Amy at high school. Since she'd come back she'd nodded to the woman several times on the street, glad of Amy's encouraging smile, then accepted an invitation to a party at her place. After the party - where Edene men looked at her with unwelcome admiration - Amy came to visit her every evening for a week. They chatted about neighbours and old school friends and it seemed to Agatha that the other woman was waiting for something, a signal, a sentence. On the seventh day, just like the Lord, Amy explained. So much of what they needed was already in place, she said: a network of willing hands and floors to keep the runaways, contacts in Chicago, New York, Washington, even further on; people who know where a newcomer could find work. But there had to be a place for them before they left the South - some of them had already been burned out of homes, or the terror had begun, kicks and gun barrels and mocking laughter.

'You could do a good thing, Agatha,' Amy said. 'You could, if you want to.'

Agatha asked the question she needed to: 'Did Pappy do this with you all?' Amy wrinkled her nose, and she could see the possibility of a lie in the woman's eyes. But Amy had not lied. 'Naw. He never.' Agatha looked at her hands. Amy spoke again. 'But where you think Pappy Arthur collection plate go on Sunday?' That was enough. Pappy had chosen his own way. She would choose hers. Her home was set back in places where mosquitoes held feeding frenzies, where shadows could hide a whole man and his family, where the tangle of trees and

23

undergrowth were friends to Negroes, reaching out camouflaged arms.

Sarah and her mother had been easy. They had relatives, and money, and all she had to do was give them shelter for a while, buy the bus tickets, call their family. All they'd needed was a place of calm, a chance to get from under the terror of waiting and watching. For others, she had to start at the beginning.

She wondered if she was doing enough. Should she be out on the streets or in the cities, sitting at Woolworth counters, ketchup and flour in her hair, being spat on, beaten? She saw herself walking hand in hand with the demonstrators, imagined the citric sting of tear gas. Saw herself on those freedom rides, half of a dark pair in a lonely bus station. Sometimes she thought that what she did do was worse. Amy and the mysterious others she was never told about had the infrastructure in place. But it was she who lived with the runaways' terror. She went months alone, seeing nobody scared enough or brave enough to run. And then they were in her home, their fear turning the walls and ceilings a dull red, solemn discussions of escape threatening to sour the milk.

Agatha didn't count how many there had been. The whites in Acheson County were stirring like a thunderbolt over Negroes talking out and looking to be desegregated. It wasn't so bad in Edene, but she could still feel the frustration, the anger, the hurt. She felt the ones who thought they'd been good to their Negroes, the ones who gave sugar titty and loving to their children. They'd been hurt by all the fussing, the marching, the noise. Civil rights agitation hadn't come to Edene yet, but Edene's children were leaving to find it, trickling out like enquiring tendrils into the belly of Greensboro and Durham. They left families who knew that the postmistress opened their mail, who heard about the circulating lists of trouble makers. Some left, and many of them had come to her. Others begged and ordered their angry children back home. A few returned, to be beaten and warned. Agatha supposed that the ones who returned preferred to take the beating themselves. But many stayed where they were and marched. And their families stole away.

Tony wrote. The light through his window cast a semi-circle of warmth across his bed. Beyond the new-born sunshine, a dresser shivered in a corner. His attention faltered and he put the pencil down. Paper was too precious to waste. He hugged his knees.

He wanted to go out and be with Agatha on the porch, but he wasn't sure. He'd trusted people before. Women who chuckled and squeezed his nose when he and Mamma went to church, greeting their arrival with choral chirps and squeaks. They'd passed him down the pews, a hand to hand to hand dance, patting, laughing, bustling, sitting him on changing knees that were knobbly, plump, sanguine and scarlet, sweating or dry, pink fans abuzz. *Gimme that pretty chile lemme hol' him a while, girl, how you keepin' that Anthony so long look how he grown! Pass him here I said!* Underarm sweat, wide open pores and greasy temples. He was hugged so close he could see nasal hair, big earrings, smell the talced crevices and the cheese behind ears.

When the women were done, Mamma sat him on her lap and stroked the double dimples in his cheeks, jigging up and down to the thank-you-Jesus-Lawd-Amen swell around them. She'd explained the dimples to him: *When you was inside Momma, getting ready to be born, the fairies was so jealous of your pretty face they kick you here an' here 'cause they was tryin' to kick your face in an' thas how you got them dimples.* Her laugh was coarse as sandpaper and too big for her body.

When he was seven, an educated church brother explained that technically, dimples were weaknesses in the skin, mini collapses in his face. This frightened him. He had recurrent daydreams, horrifying scenes in which all his features were suctioned towards the weaknesses. He squeezed his eyes tighter shut, feeling his eyeballs strain. They would, he feared, burst out of their sockets, roll down his cheeks and disappear, one in each tiny void. His teeth would work themselves loose in an awful tug of war that he couldn't stop. Then his entire head would disappear into nothingness with a sickly pop. And it would be the bad fairies' fault for kicking him in the first place.

In his room, he stayed within the confines of the yellow semi-circle, be it lamplight or dawn. Beyond this there was darkness, and he didn't know what waited there. Breathing hard, he forced his eyes open. He *would* go sit on the porch a spell. But he wouldn't talk.

Agatha heard the creak of floorboards as Tony moved around the house behind her. Nine year old Tony. He was due for a birthday soon, and all she could think of getting him was paper. The boy wrote ceaselessly, and she itched to take a look. There might be a clue to his silence in the papers. She chided herself. *Have patience,* she thought. *He will talk when he can.*

Eleanor's telegraph had taken her by surprise. She hadn't spoken to Eleanor, who used to be her closest friend, since she left New York. *Need a favour. Call me.* As she spoke to Eleanor on Reverend Wilson's telephone, she felt the same guilt that had hovered between them as she packed her bags to leave Brooklyn. She hadn't been able to explain before she left. Eleanor wouldn't have understood. She'd heard that in Eleanor's polite voice, and seen it when her friend stepped away from her arms at the bus station. Perhaps that was why she didn't push for more details when Eleanor told her Tony's story. His mother had to go away. Some trouble. The child was being passed from relative to relative and none of them could handle an extra mouth. He needed country air. Summer was coming. That was it. A summer vacation. He was a good child. Well mannered. It wouldn't be for long, Eleanor said.

Wouldn't be long became two months, and eventually Agatha enrolled Tony in school. Bought him underwear, paper, books. The trappings of permanence. She tried Eleanor's number when Tony arrived but it was disconnected. Eleanor hadn't warned her about Tony's refusal to talk. The local doctor said he didn't think the boy was deaf or dumb. He was merely silent.

Now she found that she wanted him to stay on. She wanted to gain his trust. Tony was another life in the five room house, and she wanted to hear him. Her home needed the boy. Pappy had told her that only two could live in the house. Even though his voice was cheerful, she knew that he was talking about her grandmother. The house's history proved him right: first, Pappy and Grandma Alma. Then when malaria

26

took Grandma, Agatha's mother, Anna Mae lived there with Pappy. Then her mother died and it was just her and Pappy. *This house only needs two,* Pappy said. *That's what it likes.* She'd thought about his words when she fantasised about returning to Edene with Jamie. But of course not. They couldn't have been the two in the house.

Tony was special. She felt it in her water. She watched his quick eyes and quick hands. She saw the eagerness with which he handled the books in her place. He liked the ones with pictures that she had left from college. He wanted to battle the large concepts and the complex things. *You're too arrogant,* she thought. *Think your love and your arms and your cooking, the woods and the air will move him, just so? Just because people always talked to you?*

But she wasn't comfortable with secrets. Before this, men had found her an easy ear. At college, boys far too old and hormonal for confidences broke rank and talked to her for hours: about the fish and the dreams that got away, the crank and pull of Brooklyn and the West Side. Even their first grope up a girl's skirt. They brought her their broken lives to heal and she hid her own tears behind their words. She'd thought, no, *expected,* that Tony would run his mouth too. Eventually. But that wasn't fair. Pulling at people wasn't sharing. It was just pulling.

She turned back to the dawn. Jamie had whispered to her on swollen nights, after the loving was done: *May you live to see the dawn, Tat.* He'd hated her name. *Agatha is too old for a pretty woman,* he said. *Tat isn't much better though,* she answered. It was play. She knew the nickname. He'd given it to her years before. Since him, she'd never missed a dawn. She breathed all of them in with gladness.

Tony pushed at the door, hesitant and small in the light. Agatha held out her arms. Taking a breath, he let her hold him. She leaned forward into his warmth and his sleepy eyes and wanted to weep at his silent mouth.

'A smile for you,' she said. She spoke her best English when they were alone. 'Two smiles! A peppermint one, and a lime and honey one. Boy, I've got so many smiles for you.'

He was very still. Agatha held him as she thanked the world for another night.

5

I used to have a life but Agatha took it from me with her incessant need
her indefinable want her passion I used to be a normal man I had a job I
was happy I popped a beer in front of the game on a heatstroked
weekend I was a regular man I was happy with another regular man
yeah you never knew that did you I'm fair I give everyone a piece of me
I'll tell you about him Marcus my baby's name was Marcus and he put
up with my dirty socks if I made him every night Jesus we held hands
in Central Park and I've never been a man to hold hands not even with
the ladies

you know ten years ago I was happy and the bitch was hardly
around at all maybe once or twice a year I would go take a piss and feel
as if someone was looking at me then other times there would be a low
chuckle and I'd think *damn if that don't sound familiar deja vu to the
max* but I tell you it wasn't so important that I needed to be telling
anybody or I would have told Marcus you know I loved him and I still
do but she was waiting for me to steal me away dang there's nothing
like a woman who makes you a promise and she said she'd always be
with me

you may ask why she's played me so long the answer is I don't
know because the bitch isn't getting any younger NO NO SHE'S
DEAD GOT TO GET THAT IN MY HEAD hey that rhymes I think I
amuse her and she likes the chase she enjoys watching me go crazy
wanting her not wanting her her name is Agatha Salisbury her
nickname was Tat and she started coming on strong ten years ago you
see I'd be driving and I'd see her face in the eyes of nameless pedestrians
and soon I was shivering past every single door hoping she wasn't

breathing behind it I'd see her coming towards me on the street her black hair fanned out and erupting in the wind her arms outstretched and smeared with blood and I'd be shaking by the time the person hugged me they'd be like *Tony baby what's wrong* and I'd sink with relief into a sister's greeting and I'd front saying *oh my mind was somewhere else girl I didn't recognise you it's you Anne or Amy or Jane* it got so bad people were raising their eyebrows and I could hear the whispers in Marcus's ear *is Tony OK what's up with him you two fighting again* Marcus would be like *no it's cool he's just tired working you know working on the book* and I could hear them snicker behind their hands *when's he gonna finish the Definitive American Novel* and Marcus having to defend me God bitches bastards all of them

it got so bad I was begging into the empty air all the time *please leave me alone please* I begged ME the best cocksucker this side of Queens ME beg you know I was used to them begging me man always those pretty whores and sweet boys needing my ass whichever way I wanted you know I was the AC/DC king and queen too if you wanted it that way but I was going crazy sitting in my car Marcus's car really begging the bitch to just LEAVE ME ALONE and a sweet young thing passed the car window he stopped and he raised his eyebrows and cocked his head like I was a stand up and he was waiting for the punch line I looked into his face and knew it was a message from the bitch I saw the inevitability of laying down with her she is so sure God I tried to be strong but it was bullshit and I knew my hours were limited

I thought coming Underneath would make it better but I was wrong let me tell you about the time I KNEW I had to check out I think it was a year ago and I got up early Marcus was gone to work because you know girlfriend is a fine fucking ENTERTAINMENT lawyer and I'd told him the night before to leave grocery money and he's snarling in my face and I'm like *what's up with you* he's like *just that this quitting your job to write the best book in the world blues isn't bringing in the rent* I'm saying *you make so much money* he's like *yeah right whatever just that when you're WRITING you have to have the wine and the cheese and the cable and I don't see you complaining about the Versace on your back*

well I was proud you know so proud and I wanted to prove myself so I worked all day and my baby comes in he's happy and apologetic when I showed him four chapters he settled down to read them and I'm singing in the shower while he's yelling to me *we'll go out to celebrate* but when I go back in the living room smelling all sweet and shit he's sitting in a chair picking at his hair hey that rhymes there's my proud manuscript in his hand and he says *Tony what's this baby what IS this a joke* and I look down at my great work that took all day and there it is pages and pages and pages of the same words SHE NEEDS DOORS SHE NEEDS DOORS SHE NEEDS DOORS I thought he was playing me *what the hell you doing with my work* but Marcus was speaking calmly even though his hand on my shoulder was shaking *that was what you gave me baby* and we looked at each other

for a long time before I came down Underneath I didn't know whether I was thinking of suicide yeah it was an option I could have stepped off onto the tracks and caught a train broadside as it were and had splendid moments of consciousness watching limbs fly and blood spray listening to my pelvic bone crack leaving fingers for the Japanese tourists to remember the Big Apple by so I thought of it as suicide for a while the second option seemed a more serious responsibility dodging the train manoeuvring the third rail finding a place in the darkness I didn't know whether there would be space to move or what I would eat where I would piss or whether there would be just inches to stand in whether life would become the physical experience of my back to the wall and the madness of the train speeding past my own personal Purgatory defecating myself and only moving to a new inch when I was up to my knees in shit was that the way it would be and yet I hoped that this would be the place of freedom you see Agatha needs doors she hides behind them she likes challenges there needs to be a door for her to COAX you to open and there are less doors down here Underneath

I spent time outside the subway gathering courage and trying to make a decision paying my dimes again and again or sitting on the platform peering down the sides of the tunnel and while I was doing it I began to notice the ones without homes they were everywhere I watched one man make a bed in Grand Central station and get moved on by the cops every night I watched the way the homeless kept warm

I admired the Grand Central man for his pan-handling skills and listened to him sleep and wondered what silence looked like then you know it one night the guy saw me watching him and his voice was outraged *whatchoo a fuckin fairy man* I smiled and nodded smiled and nodded it was so good to hear his voice without the *help a guy down on his luck I'm a Vet man* whine you know he was so self righteous standing there looking at me in my fly suit him standing there in piss stained rags talking about *yeah you a fuckin queer but don't be lookin at THIS ass bro don't be sleepin an dreamin about THIS ass*

I never saw him again my Grand Central brother but another took his place and there was a Latino girl who rode the IRT night and day in one seat so still that she could have been part of the subway car her clothes so dirty they could have been any colour but it's not illegal to ride all night and there was a pasty faced girl not more than sixteen if she was a day whenever I saw her she applied and re-applied her lipstick swiping it off with her left arm each time until her skin was thick with crimson marks and I think she was a junkie she was fidgeting with her MAC lipstick looking at me like she wanted to eat me up there was another regular who the MTA kept moving on he was strung out stinking so badly that even New Yorkers recoiled from where he sprawled his juicy sweat seeping into their pores as he stank gloriously I thought that if I could only write so vainly so uncompromisingly so grandly with such valour and peace as this man stank I could win a Nobel prize

then a morning came when I knew Marcus was going to put me out again for a while he thought I'd gotten a grip and he was right I had a grip on every lady on the block we hadn't made love for weeks and in between my subway trips I made myself prize trick on 11th Avenue pumping and coming in disinterested females and Marcus could smell them on me and I taunted him with it refusing a tender word refusing touch you know he was walking around with a permanent hard-on which made me laugh and feel guilty at the same time dang if I haven't got enough guilt we met at fourteen he is the love of my life but I never told him so he was stomping around the condo cursing about layabouts and good for nothing BISEXUAL faggots who didn't appreciate a god damned thing so I went for a walk and the bitch was playing in my head

I needed to hide and I found the room Underneath

in the end the consummation of my innocent affair with the subway was simple I tripped over the grating looked down and poured water on the alarm broke the lock looked around let myself in I sat there and waited to see whether the MTA boys were coming it was dark except for the light coming through the grating stretching beams of life across my face a romantic image I thought and the room was perfect so I went back to Marcus's apartment and took two blankets some matches all the food in the house and three hundred dollars I found in my man's drawer and Marcus came home he was near tears *I won't do it again baby stay* he said but I left before he could find the money and the food gone left laughing and laughing and laughing

I waited for months no in truth it was hours you know time rushes and crawls down here I waited for lifetimes each second was a year to see whether Agatha that bitch would come but she didn't I thought I was cool while my brain took a rest I was just fine sitting there in the room and I wrenched the door off its hinges it wasn't hard as I said she needs doors she's got good Southern manners she needs to be INVITED in so I used the door as a bed and I think it was three days four days later when I hooked up with Chaz my passionate Underneath lady and she got me a mattress saying *Tony yo you can't be sleepin on the floor like you some animal man like you got no class man see what I'm sayin* the ground was stinking and I made do with blankets first it was summer I think it was a year ago but I can't be sure you lose time down here I don't know I never know what the time is in the darkness even though Chaz tells me when she comes home and says *homey I'm home* no not really she wouldn't appreciate the irony I told you

I think I'll walk down the tracks to see the mural I've got my matches and my candle in my pocket I'll have a nice day out because I've got to stop thinking about the fact that Mikey's not writing why isn't he writing dang I lost the matches fuck it I have to go back to the room that mural probably has the tired look of the looked at ANYWAY

I round the corner and it's on me with no warning the grey silken train roaring and I'm biting my tongue because the bitch is here she's on top of the train and it's coming towards me hundreds of miles an hour and I'm clinging to the sides of the tunnel and she's running back and forth her hands stretched up for sparks coming off the car she's catching them and brushing them down her thighs like fire grease

I can see her skin and its surface is swirling like water eddies she's not a black woman anymore no and the top of the train is awash with yellow pools she's shrieking with laughter and flooding the stratosphere with her chuckles orange into rust into aubergine into apricot into nude ecru grey lavender lemon ice sun streams blueberry raspberry strawberry peach oh a perfect shade of peach straight back into flames of orange and the train sweeping into the distance and I can see her throwing her head back stroking her own neck screaming God screaming *WHEN I RIP THE SKIN OFF YOUR BACK YOU WON'T BE BLACK EITHER TONY I'LL BREATHE AND YOU'LL BLEED YOU'LL BLEED* and my heart's jacked up to a thousand beats a minute my own throat strangling me God o God Mikey Mikey write me please write me

6

Water cupped his stomach and made him light. He played 'Gator all by himself, paddling from one end of the swimming hole to the next, muttering into the air, ignoring the water's slight chill. In his imagination there were three boys with him: Sam, a large redhead with a million freckles; David, skinny with an attitude and a belching laugh that made the trees rock; Joshua, the oldest and biggest with a suggestion of hair in his armpits and a wild way of grabbing you and ducking you underneath. And him, Mikey, the one that Joshua could never duck, not once. Breathing hard, he squinted. Sam was the 'Gator, across the way, eyes screwed closed, straining to hear them. Mikey swam nearer and trod water behind his opponent. Sam turned his head.

'Gator?' he called. Sam's imaginary voice was squeaky.

'Here!' he yelled in his own voice, diving under the surface. His phantom friend lunged behind him. Mikey swam forward, holding his breath, circling until he could resurface behind the spluttering, frustrated Sam. The other boys, he imagined, would be grinning in admiration. After all, they knew his daring. He wasn't a sissy like David, who clung to Home far too often. Mikey could see them looking at him if he tried hard.

'You ain't never gon' catch Mikey!' he yelled in David's voice. That was deeper.

'I ain't tryin' to catch him, boy!' He played Sam's part, lunging forward. 'I'm comin' fo' you!' Sam's hand brushed David's wet head.

'Home! I'm Home!' David yelled, clinging to the rock designated safe. David was such a girl.

Mikey trod water, mimicking Sam and David back and forth.

35

'You a cheat!'

'Naw! I'm Home!'

'Cheater, cheater!'

He switched to Joshua, steadfastly baritone, trying to make peace. But of course, it was his own voice that calmed the quarrel between ghosts. However clever, old, or handsome his pretend companions, he was The Leader. They called him Mikey, not Michael Abraham and his was The Voice Of Reason. If they didn't like it, well darn it, he'd have them.

He floated, battling in the different voices, and then grew bored. It was too cold to be swimming anyway. He should get out.

'Well. Looky what we got here.'

Mikey rolled over in the water, swallowed some, choked, spluttered.

Tony moved restlessly in the fork of the tree, his legs swinging. He loved climbing trees like this one, with its accommodating branches. When Mikey arrived, he'd decided to keep quiet. He would watch the big white boy. After all, hadn't Mikey watched him? If his head hadn't already been full of problems he would have worried more about the fact that Mikey knew. Mikey had known for three weeks. He'd been scared when the boy had called out from under the house. He waited for Mikey to tell Miss Ezekiel or Agatha that he could talk and when he didn't he was puzzled. Why not tell? He felt as if the white boy had an advantage. Mikey smiled at him sometimes, and it frightened him. He wondered what the boy wanted. He had nothing to give him. Still, Mikey was obviously cracked, hiding under the front porch, swimming around talking to himself. Maybe he shouldn't worry so much. He'd stayed in the tree hoping the other boy would go away. That, or do something that would make them quits. Now he peered down at the three new boys with renewed interest. The biggest one looked like bad news, swaggering up and down the rim of the water hole. The others were smaller, but he reckoned they were twelve or thirteen. He craned his neck. He didn't know much about Michael Tennyson, but he knew he didn't have any friends.

Timothy Crampton grinned. His green eyes were mild, belying the threat of his meaty body. 'What you doin' in our water hole?' he asked.

Mikey flushed, treading water. He'd seen Timothy in school, grabbing at the girls, cutting through the crowd. 'I-I never know...' He hated the thin, weak sound of his voice. The water hole didn't belong to anybody, and The Leader would have told them so. With his Voice Of Reason.

Timothy smiled again. 'Well now, I s'pose they's room for all of us now you say it, boy.'

Mikey sucked his breath in. He didn't want to swim with them, but he wasn't going to contradict Timothy. He tried not to look at the small pile his clothes made on the bank.

Timothy cocked his head at the boy on his right. 'You wanna go swimming, don'tcha Arnie?'

Arnie smiled. An angry pattern of pimples splayed across his forehead. He began to unbutton his shirt.

'Billy, you wanna go swimmin', don'tcha?' said Timothy.

'Sho' do.' Billy was the boy on his left. Tall and dark, he was already bare chested and half way out of his pants, white briefs glimmering in the sunshine.

'Whatcha been playin', fat boy?' Timothy hadn't taken his eyes off Mikey's face, which was rapidly becoming redder.

'N-nothin'...' Mikey watched Billy and Arnie enter the water and disappear up to their waists. They waded towards him. Timothy kept grinning. Mikey thought it made him look hungry. His thighs ached. He'd been treading water for too long. He thought of swimming away, but the idea of clambering out of the Hole nude was even worse than meeting Arnie and Billy in its middle. If only he wasn't fat. If only he was slim and lean and quick and tall, like he was when he was The Leader. He glanced over his shoulder.

'Awww. Now looka here, boys.' Timothy picked up Mikey's clothing. He held the shirt up to his chest. 'Fat boys thinkin' he gon' run. Thas sweet.' He crumpled the shirt in his fist. 'Want yo' shirt, boy? Shit, this thing could fit my pa! Where d'ya get yo' clothes, fat boy?'

Mikey struck out feebly, but they caught him. They were taller than him; their feet still touched bottom. The water reached their marble armpits. Arnie grasped his arm.

'Let's play 'Gator, boy.'

Mikey took a huge swallow of air before they pushed him under. The boy's fists felt like iron clasps as he kicked and struggled to hold his breath. In front of him he could see Billy's ribs moving. Mikey's lungs began to give in. He gulped water. Then, mercifully, he was yanked upwards. Flapping, he belched and spluttered. Water poured from his mouth. Arnie stood behind him, his arms locked around his waist. Billy's face loomed into his, his breath drying the water on Mikey's cheeks. He couldn't speak. His heart galloped.

'Give up yet boy? Talk to me,' said Arnie.

Mikey opened his mouth to speak and Billy's hands pushed down on his shoulders. He could hear their laughter as he went under the green depths again. *This*, his mind whispered, *is the way you drown.*

Tony glared from his hiding place. Maybe they'd be done soon. He couldn't beat all three boys, probably not even one, and Mikey looked past it. He wondered if they'd kill Mikey. They couldn't. No white boy would kill another. There'd be hell to pay. No, they were just being mean. It would pass.

He settled back into the tree. Fleetingly, he remembered Mikey's voice calling out to Miss Ezekiel between snatches of the Song Of Solomon. The passage comforted him. It reminded him of Momma at her best, teaching him from the Bible and singing hymns around the house on a Sunday. The rest of the week had been sinning time. Mikey had saved him. He'd kept his secret. *Maybe he done it 'cause he knowed you wanted him to,* a voice whispered in his head. *Maybe he's nice.* He thought of running for help and then abandoned the option. He didn't want them to see him, and help was too far. He knew what the white boys would do if they caught him. They wouldn't kill Mikey, but no one cared about a coloured boy.

They dragged him to the surface again. Half conscious and beyond fear, he felt them towing him through the water. They were taking him to the bank, voices above him, grunting as the water got shallow. He turned his head and vomited onto his shoulder.

'Stand up, boy.'

He didn't know who spoke. His knees gave way. The steel clasps tightened.

'Shit, I duck you if you don' stand up!'

Chest on fire, Mikey managed to kick out with his legs, feeling mud between his toes. Arnie hooked an arm over his shoulders.

'Grab the other side, Bill,' he said.

'Naw! Nasty shit puked all over hisself!'

'Wash it off, darn it!' That was Timothy. Mikey felt water over his shoulders and in his face. Billy took the other side. Mikey raised his head and looked into Timothy's eyes, breathing shallow, whooping gulps. Timothy's mouth had disappeared into his thin face. Now that oxygen seemed assured, Mikey was afraid again. His white belly hung between them, full as any pregnant woman's.

'I never done nothin-'

Timothy reached out and grabbed a handful of one of his small breasts.

Mikey's screams began to echo through the woods.

Tony couldn't stop squirming. He didn't want to watch, but he couldn't help it. The biggest boy was slapping Mikey luxuriously, as if it were a caress. Slapping his stomach. Back and forth.

Whap.

Mikey screamed. The thin sound disappeared into the trees. His stomach was criss-crossed with red hand prints.

Whap.

Tony squirmed so hard that he nearly lost his balance. He grabbed at a branch. Shaking, he gripped tighter. The leather bag he'd tied to the tree branch swayed.

Snot and tears dripped down Mikey's face. His thick, blonde hair lay cemented across his brow. Timothy laughed. It was a wonderful sound. He gazed at the sore body in front of him.

'Lookit roll, boy!' He slid one finger down a stretch mark that stood out through the imprint of his hands. 'He got marks like my momma!'

Arnie was breathing hard. 'Lemme hit him. C'mon. Lemme try.'

39

'Hold on boy! I'm gonna rock it again!' Timothy raised his arm and let it flow through a large arc. Mikey sagged. Timothy laughed again.

'We got all day fat b-'

Zing.

The rock ricocheted off the back of Timothy's head. Shocked, he grabbed at his skull. They all stared at his fingers. He was bleeding.

'What...!' Timothy bellowed. He glared around. 'Who...'

Zing.

The second rock grazed his temple and shattered to the ground. A third caught Arnie, just below the hip. He let go of Mikey to grab the sore spot. A fourth rock hit the ground, missing its mark.

'Who doin' that? Shit! I'm gonna get you, you little shit!' Timothy screamed as another rock hit Billy in the chest. Billy yelled and began to let go of Mikey.

Zing.

'Hol' on to him, Billy! Don' you fuckin' let go!' Timothy began to run around the clearing, yelling up at the sky. 'Where is you, you fuckin' bastard? Where?'

Zing. Zing. Two rocks missed him by inches.

'He in the tree, Tim!' Arnie yelled. They all squinted upwards. A small form perched there, slingshot poised. Timothy began to advance. Flecks of spittle flew into the breeze as he cursed.

Mikey tried to rise. He was on his knees, one arm still gripped by Billy. Dimly he wondered who was throwing rocks. Whoever it was had a good aim. His stomach burned and smarted. He couldn't breathe properly, or get the image of his own nakedness out of his mind. The older boys stomped around him, yelping each time a stone connected with flesh. He looked up. Timothy and Billy were trying to get closer to the base of the tree, but cowardice and the true aim of the rocks wasn't making it easy. Arnie bled freely from an open wound just short of his eye.

Zing.

Billy yelped and let go of Mikey's arm. Clutching his shoulder, he backed away, taking advantage of the fact that Timothy was occupied. Mikey stumbled forward, stones cutting his knees. Billy started after him but thought better of it. Hesitating, he looked up at the tree.

Obligingly, a rock flew past his head, and, hands held up, he plunged back into the woods, snatching his clothing from the ground.

'Hey!' Arnie was livid. 'Tim, Billy runnin'! Tim!'

Timothy didn't appear to hear. 'I kin see it's some coon, d'ya see? A nigger! Hey little nigger! When I get you down I'm gonna hang you from that tree...'

Arnie began to fling his clothes on. 'I ain't stayin'.'

Crack. Zip.

Timothy howled as a stone stung his elbow. Clutching the pained area, he began to hop around the clearing. Mikey rose to his feet, knees trembling. His hands found the pants Timothy had dropped. Wincing, he pulled them on. He wondered if his saviour was ever going to run out of rocks. Then they'd be in trouble. He edged sideways. If he could get to the tree he might be safe.

Arnie tugged at Timothy. He was dressed. 'Les' go Tim. We kin get him next time!'

Crack. Zip. Zip. Zip. The rocks rained down.

Defeated and furious, Timothy let Arnie pull him away. Suddenly Mikey felt ashamed. He didn't know who was helping him, but he knew he hadn't helped himself. He clenched his hands into fists and began to run towards the tree.

Zip. Zip. Zip. Zip.

Timothy wailed in frustration and rage and turned tail. A stone bounced off Mikey as he ran, but he ignored the pain. Nothing could be worse than the slaps that still burned his belly. Panting, he clung to the tree's base. He watched his tormentors disappearing. *Home, I'm home,* he thought.

'I'll get you, fat boy! I'll get youuuuuuuuuuuuuuu!'

That was Timothy. Mikey shuddered. He knew it was true. He looked up. Tony was slithering down the bark, heading for him. His sure, bare feet hit the ground. Mikey stared.

'They coulda killed you-' he started. 'They coulda-'

'Those boys? Fools.'

Mikey looked over his shoulder towards the dismissive voice. Agatha stood there, puffing slightly. A slingshot swung from her hand.

41

Agatha watched the two boys walking in front of her. They were trailing yards apart, glancing at each other. She wasn't sure whether the friendship was a good idea: the wrath of such as Timothy could have serious consequences for Tony. But still, it was good to see that it might happen. They were both outsiders.

When she'd spotted Tony up in the tree she thought he was making his slingshot ready for a bird. Then she heard the laughter and Mikey's screams. She hadn't been sure she could shimmy up a tree so fast, much less hit anything, even though Jamie had taught her how to handle herself when she was a girl no bigger than these two. They were lucky Tony had two slingshots. He tossed her one when she was in position and they'd worked together to fool the bullies into thinking there was only one of them. Shot and counter shot. She wondered whether she should tell Miss Ezekiel. She doubted that a story of two Negroes whipping three white boys would amuse or please her.

She looked at the boys again. Mikey had stopped to vomit several times on the path - he'd swallowed a lot of water - but now he seemed alright. He offered Tony sweets out of his bag. Tony took the gift shyly.

They reached Miss Ezekiel's gate. Agatha quickened her stride and reached down to touch Mikey's head.

'How are you feeling?' she said.

He looked at her. 'I'm still afraid of them boys.'

She looked down at him and then at Tony. There was a brown smudge on his cheek. She sucked her fingers and wiped it, then rubbed her dirtied hand on the front of his shirt. Giggling, he wrestled it away.

'If you two are going to be friends, you're going to have to use your brains to outsmart them,' she said. 'Remember what I say now: they're fools. Fools. You two are clever as anything.'

Tony and Mikey looked doubtful.

'Kin you teach me to use a niggershooter?' Mikey asked. Images danced in his head. Timothy screaming. Screams created by him. The Voice Of Reason would ride again.

Agatha smiled. 'I taught this New York boy. Don't see why I can't teach you. But you've got to promise you'll never use that word again. Nigger. Niggershooter. It's a bad word.'

Mikey looked thoughtful. 'Bad, huh?'

Agatha nodded. The three of them stood in the cold wind.

7

Agatha is always around she is always waiting preying on me breathing and BEING there fuck it's making me INSANE last night day whatever she was there when I was saying goodbye to Chaz in the tunnels she was so near I could smell her and I flung myself back into our room while Chaz was staring at me I gashed my face when I hit the floor there was blood all over the fucking place but man I'm still staring at Agatha's face through a film of red and I could have fallen in love with the bitch all over again because her beauty is so terrible it's as if heart's desires lie in her eyes and she was mad so mad she reached her arms out to me *tell the story Tony why don't you fucking tell the story you are the storyteller always will be* and she was moving near to Chaz and I couldn't believe she didn't see I'm yelling *move move don't you see her* and I grabbed out for her but I missed because Chaz was across the tunnel before I could say boo she was cowering and I'm thinking *shit she saw her she really did* and then Agatha was gone and I walked over to Chaz and she's trembling and I tried to help her up and she's crying and I realised that she's afraid of ME you know when you know it's bad but you don't know how bad

I wish I could be nice to Chaz but it doesn't seem to matter to her I always collect sidekicks and they could be as fucked up as Chaz or as miserable as Marcus got it doesn't matter it's inevitable that they find me because I work best as a team I am the greatest when someone's cheering me on check it Mikey was a kid with no dignity but he had the sweetest way about him it all comes back in snatches still can't remember why Agatha should haunt me so WHY

I ask Chaz to go to the gas station with the fine brother every day to check and see if Mikey's answered yet and she told me that the gas station guy reached out and touched her arm and he told her that if he had a woman as beautiful as her he would never make her sad *love doesn't hurt bay-bee* I was laughing get *the fuck outta here what are you a Dial An Ad Campaign* then I saw the look on her face stopped and shrugged and she sulked for a while then cuddled up to me

you know what it is I don't hurt any less than anyone else the thing is that I can out-wait anybody because something shuts off while my lovers sulk and rage and all I do is wait until they can't hold it anymore and all the time I might be crying and cursing and hurting inside so bad but I can do anything to out-wait anybody and they have to come and look in my pretty face some more never underestimate the power of two things in this world beauty and style Marcus has style I have beauty and Agatha had them both

so I'm sounding like a crazy fool today but you know there's good news boys and girls there is good news I sit here smelling funky and in my hand is a letter I've been trying to read it you know I turned it around in my hands turned it upside down back and forth I grabbed my dick to dissuade persuade hide distract myself I've been waiting forever for this letter I know it's from him who else knows I'm down here and there's the return address it's his home address I said the man is coming through it's funny but I am afraid to open this because it has my life in it and if he's telling me to go drop on the third rail fuckwit do a Kurt Cobain for all I care do a River Phoenix a Marilyn Monroe because you know honey child did it herself some man pissed her off do a Jimi I think I would which would be one way but I don't want it to be that way

you know I loved Mikey let me tell you why I loved him and it isn't a sex thing this isn't cross my heart hope to die spit in your eye and fry Mikey liked to take care of people even though he couldn't take care of himself and there was something special about this white dude fuck you my African king brother if you don't like it Mikey wanted the whole world to be this godamned great place but he wasn't stupid either or a bleeding heart liberal just innocent Mikey knew all he needed to know when he was a kid I wonder if he got cynical afraid abusive internal depressed suicidal I wonder if he loves his wife if he ever cheated on her

I'm opening it with my thumbnail opening it

I'm still alive the bitch hasn't come for me screaming betrayal I'm still alive and there is no sign of her knocking dang I should have asked Chaz to stay by me only she can keep me calm

yeah OK OK OK OK OK yeah

says he's glad to hear from me that's good asks what I'm up to that's good I can lie and paint it pretty he says it's funny and he's freaked I'm writing because I've been on his mind lying motherfucker he says he knows I'll think it's a lie unless I've changed unless I've become more vulnerable and less defensive he says he's really glad to hear from me and what the hell have I been doing lots of yadda yadda yadda about family hey but it answers questions he's got a daughter hey man you got a daughter *thirteen she is thirteen* he says *she's pretty and bright except for some expensive tooth work* damn the man's a suburbia king I always knew it he says he's married to Zoe Marks and maybe I heard of her or maybe not says he's proud of her *she's a deep strange woman* goddamn the man's calling his wife strange but he says he loves her and they've been married fifteen years he's been with her for twenty two years and he loves her says it's funny that I should write now because I've been on his mind says *why the questioning what's up you writing a book of our lives my lawyer will need to have a word with you ha ha* but I can tell he's not joking *are you writing a book Tony because you are the storyteller* man if you only knew if you only knew

I wonder if Mikey married a bitch I wonder if his wife Zoe Marks is a rock and roll bitch you know once I saw a poster that said she was doing a reading and I thought *she'll be no good* I used to be an arrogant bastard I looked at all the literature in the world and knew I could do better so I went and bought three of Zoe Marks's books and the first one had thirty three poems in all God I was impressed because the girl has so much talent it made me jealous I'd read her poems to Marcus in bed and you know he was always a queen with his eyeballs linked up to faucets so he cried at some of them Zoe has got one there called The Night it makes your skin shiver it reminded me of Agatha so much that

I could have screamed but I kept it down I swallowed the scream there in the bed with my man like I always have done there was one more called Ancient Tongues I think it was or Ancient Mouths all about the nature of love and in it Zoe's talking about a table and a chair the symbolism was a godamned table and chair man and I was horny and blown away by the time I was finished I was totally lost and those were the times when I knew I needed to see Mikey we should have never lost touch I'm sure if we'd stayed together this bitch wouldn't be on my ass I needed to see him but couldn't do it I was thirty three reading to Marcus and I hadn't seen Mikey in twenty years and God knows he might have embraced that peckerwood mentality so I went to see his wife instead

I didn't know Zoe Marks was a black woman I went with some friends not Marcus he wasn't talking to me at the time so I took a girl and a dude and of course I was fucking both of them you know I chose their outfits for the night the girl was called Cassandra Tightrowp I promise you I am not lying that was her name at least so she said Cassandra was one of my kind of girls she was big and intelligent and you could see that sweet pussy imprinted through everything she wore ha like it was calling you I chose her a red bustier two sizes too small and then turned to the guy his name was Chuck yeah Chuck I can't remember his last name we all got out of bed in the middle of the afternoon and showered off the spunk and got dressed Chuck was in a white catsuit believe it girl he was looking fine and we went and no one had the guts to turn us out because I had a rep yeah everybody knew I was outrageous but smart and I know they all wished they were as pretty as me man I used to be prettier than Mohammed Ali hey that rhymes

I used to edit one of New York City's finest magazines OK so it was a no-ad barely scraping past the overheads rag but there was good work in it and hard nosed hacks with good hearts I'm telling you they exist and they weren't afraid of work and I loved it but Agatha took that from me like everything else yeah I wanted to finish that novel but I liked the work too I mean I was the fucking editor but it got so bad that I couldn't make it to a courthouse or even Elton John's latest ha there's a rebel for you without Agatha laughing at me from the faces of backing singers and out of Lionel Richie's spandex and out of anxious reporters and even the computer and I went to the reading to make mischief because I was curious to see who was sleeping with Mikey Tennyson my best friend

Zoe was fine not in the usual kind of way you know I don't go for svelte but her skin man like boiling coffee she wasn't beautiful no just tight and compact her face was plain her hair well Chuck said *girl friend got it going on but she needs to be in that beauty parlour* it was scraped back like Sade's but Sade has got back and Zoe is small I wouldn't want to screw Zoe Marks but godamn she has something special her voice was gorgeous and she read without the book standing and speaking it out from memory you know if I thought that The Night freaked me out on paper well to hear her say the words mmmm I wished Marcus was there because he would have cried and I could have scooped the tears off his cheeks and tasted them I miss him God I miss him

me and Marcus were good together there were good times sitting in Central Park watching the freaks go by every Saturday we went and skated bare chested and showed off you know no one was as good as us we were leaping whirling Marcus dancing and flirting with the girls and the boys going round and round until we got dizzy and they're playing old school rap in the background and they're watching us watching two grown men behaving like they're in the movies Marcus never skated before me it was like he had a bug up his ass before me WHITE LINES DON'T DON'T DO IT BAY-BAY-BAYBEE IT'S LIKE A JUNGLE SOMETIMES IT MAKES ME WONDER HOW I KEEP FROM GOING UNDER ha ha I did go under I did go under Grand Master Flash would have called me a sell out

after we were done skating and driving the crowd wild we'd leave sweaty and pleased with ourselves and Marcus looked so good hanging on to the subway car strap that I'd want him right there and later we'd go to a game or go catch a movie and all the time I stroked his head wanting to tell him how much I loved him but I didn't because it is just another four letter word and it wouldn't have changed my behaviour you know I love you doesn't change anything

on weekends we'd order pizza or he'd take me out to dinner and I'd get dressed in a fly suit for him because he liked it and we'd kiss over the table and drive the diners crazy I could see all the sisters shaking their heads and saying *what a shame what a waste* once we went to dinner and there was a woman across the way in a blue silk trouser suit you should have seen this sister she smoked her cigarette like she was giving head and I was like *wow* trying not to look but looking she had a bald head and huge silver earrings you know she was a big girl the way I like them so I went to the bathroom after she went to the bathroom and checked no one else was there and she was washing her hands and waiting for me and she let me bite her neck and splash cool water over her elegant head she let me kiss handfuls of round flesh I took her top off gently so we wouldn't crush the silk I lifted her breasts in my hands and worshipped them but nothing below the waist I guess I was in the mood for those female restrictions for the teasing gasps and the rest of the evening she gossiped with her girlfriend and laughed every time I licked my fingers I could see she was telling her friend because they were giggling but Marcus didn't know I kept a silver ring she wore on her toe hey that rhymes I don't know why I have to go there I just have to go there because there is nothing like unclothing them for the first time like feeling new naked flesh oh sure there's something comforting about a lover you know but I like the anonymity and it's crazy that Marcus expected me to be faithful crazy crazy I was never going to do it it's not in me and he made himself sick expecting it I was like *go fuck somebody else you'll feel better* but he's making like a female saying he don't want nobody else

one night he did go and get someone else and he came back with fire and sorrow in his eyes he said it bored him and it hurt him and he missed me and he wasn't doing it again *are you happy now Tony* he said *fuck you* he said he wouldn't sleep with me for a week I slept on the couch you know I did

after Zoe read I went up and had the book signed and all the time I was thinking *how did they meet how did they meet* I was trying to look into her face and see Mikey I was trying to imagine how Mikey was in her eyes I looked good searching for the print of his fingers on her shoulder or something that would indicate his presence and I wanted to touch her wanted to send vibes back to Mikey to say *I love you brother*

I miss you I could have said so I don't know why I didn't and she said that I had nice eyes that they made her think of a poem *but of course baby I know that I know I am a muse* except to my own sorry self and as I'm sitting here thinking about all these people I can feel my whole body twist I'm grabbing Chaz's arm because the bitch is singing in the tunnels I can hear her I never heard Agatha sing before it's a child's song

clap hands clap hands 'til Tony comes home
Tony bring milk for baby alone
Baby drink all and give Tony none
clap hands clap hands 'til Tony comes home

yeah it's got a beat and you can dance to it

8

Agatha opened her eyes. She lay quietly, admiring her skin against the sheets. Somewhere in her past she had decided that when she owned her own home, she would sleep in a pure white bed. Nothing stayed secret in white sheets. Transparent sweat made them dull; blood or tears shouted up at you. A white bed was honest. The first thing she did to make Pappy's house hers was lay milk sheets across his bed, replacing the multicoloured blankets. She bought yards of mosquito netting, wound it around the bedhead, attached it to the ceiling, draped it so the final effect was virginal, stark, cocoon-like. Pappy's bed was soft, the way she liked it. When she sank into it she felt clean. Sanctified.

From the left hand side of the bed, through the window, she could see the barbed wire washing line on the Browns' place. The Browns had been neighbours and tenants to Pappy for nearly thirty years. Bea Brown was a chunky, deep-set woman with the colour of mahogany and the constitution of Job. She went about her business with the kind of dignity reserved for very small babies and old women. Her back could have been used as a measuring stick. When Agatha was a little girl Bea Brown had sewn up her dresses and taught her how to plait her hair.

Drowsily, she made a mental note. Surely she had enough money to buy them a real line. She'd seen Bea struggling to take the clothes down without ripping them, cutting herself on the sharp edges.

It was Bea who had first realised how good Agatha was with numbers. Pappy had seen her add, subtract, multiply quickly, but he dismissed it as only part of her intelligence. Now, years later, it was still Bea's favourite gossip at church: how she'd been plaiting

Reverend Salisbury's grandchild's hair and why, you shoulda seen it, not more than six year she was, an' she's tellin' me how many times I plait her hair in a year, if'n I plaited it fo' the next eleven years how many times that'd be, an' it take me ten minutes, so in twenty year I'd a spent how much million billion minutes plaitin' hair, if I add Cissy hair to that, so many mo' million seconds...

Agatha rolled over and turned on the radio. Elvis Presley was mid-croon.

It's now or never come hold me tight...

She rolled her eyes and buried her face in the warm sheets. She still found it hard to listen to love songs. Love songs that had been playing when she came back to Edene with her feelings choking her.

Unheeding, Elvis sang on.

Kiss me my darling be mine tonight...

She rolled off the bed and shrugged a blue housecoat over her shoulders, pulling her hair out of the way. She put one hand to her belly. She'd put on weight since coming back South. Not a lot. Just enough to pull her stomach into a curve and turn her breasts into grapefruits. Maybe a little bigger than grapefruits. Her thighs were still strong. She put her hands to her waist. Not as small as it had been when she was a teenager. She screwed up her mouth. Who wanted to look like a growing child? That was what Jamie told her whenever she'd worried about her looks. She tried to push the thought away. There were more important things to think about.

The last few months had stretched the air to its limit. Reverend Wilson had stepped up last night to discuss the goings on in Alabama. The Reverend was a gossip and a wonderful orator. The way he told it, he may as well have been right there, shoulder to shoulder with Reverend King, wiping his shining brow. The pockets of fat in Reverend Wilson's face creased and straightened as he described the dogs, how they smelled and gnashed their teeth. He outlined Police Commissioner 'Bull' Connor's form in minute detail. If Wilson was to be believed, the big white man had four different arms, because he could throw a tear gas canister, shoot a gun, hold five dogs and still have one arm free to wave his marshals on. Wilson spoke to her like she was one of his congregation. She knew many of them hadn't been able to see the televised demonstrations; she herself had watched it all on the small set in Miss Ezekiel's bedroom. She didn't care about Bull Connor. What she couldn't forget was the children's faces. Quiet first, obedient, stepping out with their parents. Then hidden under grown-up bodies in the rush, as if they'd never been there.

She remained calm as the Reverend danced around her front room. She couldn't be seen to be excited about civil rights and things. Not even with a coloured man. They sat on the porch until the Reverend declared he heard his wife calling him - the same way every time, cupping his hand to his bulbous ear and pointing it in the general direction of his house, three miles west - 'Hear that? That's my wife callin',' - and only then did she permit herself a thrill. It was terrifying, this swell of people, so dignified, then so brutalised. But they were moving. It was Kennedy's time, and she liked him. He reminded her of Elvis, with their twin sulky mouths.

She walked into the front room. It was nearly six o'clock. And here she was, giving up another Sunday. Miss Ezekiel wanted her whole house scrubbing from top to bottom. To get out the summer dirt, she said. Prepare for the September breeze.

Agatha found it harder to leave the house each morning. She'd hoped she could be philosophical about domestic work. Her first job had been cleaning for a white woman. She hadn't needed to; Pappy invested wisely and watched all the dollars and cents. But he'd said it was good for her. Her grandmother had cleaned. Her mother had cleaned. They'd told him all their secrets: how to get blood and food out of sheets and fix the evening meal if there was too much salt, too much sugar. How to bite your lip when the wives called you gal and how to avoid the eyes of their husbands. But it was hard to work in Miss Ezekiel's house. To scrub her toilet and set her table. Agatha had graduated Valedictorian of her class. She had a college education from one of North Carolina's finest Negro colleges. She'd taught maths in New York, beside white teachers. To white students. The Dean asked her to submit a paper for publication. Given time she could have gotten tenure, postgraduate work. She could have got her PhD. She could have been Dr Agatha Salisbury. She was the first girl in her family to finish high school. But she had to go. She needed the extra work. She didn't want to think of the dwindling money in her bank account. She'd spent more money than was wise. And now the roof needed work. So she'd said yes to Miss Ezekiel's Sunday cleaning. What stuck in her throat was the woman's arrogance. Refusal was not expected or acceptable. *You should be used to this,* she thought. *It has always been this way.* But as much as she knew the way it was, she had always fought against it. Even when she was small. She'd agreed to go to work today, but Tony would *not* go. He said he wanted to go down to Amy Green's yard and that was where he was going, even though Miss Ezekiel wanted him to weed her garden. Amy was gentle with him, and Tony seemed to prefer adults anyway. Sometimes she worried that he only had one friend. Mikey. They were so close. She wondered how long it would last.

'Tony?' she called out.

No answer. Of course the boy wouldn't answer. She would have to make sure she was loud enough and then wait a few minutes. She sank down on the green horsehair couch and sniffed at its familiar, musty smell. She raised her voice.

'TONY!' she yelled.

Tony's small face appeared at the bedroom door, a big grin spread across it. These days there were several versions: a wide, crack-yo'-face-in-half one for the good mornings; a smaller, innocuous one that swiped at his dimples when she praised him for his homework; a sleepy, quiet chuckle when she kissed him at night. She treasured those chuckles: to hear the slightest sound from him was wonderful. She wondered how his mother had given this child away. And to Eleanor, who had no patience with vulnerability.

Tony cocked his head enquiringly at her expression.

'Don't worry,' she forced a grin. 'You going to be ready soon?'

Tony nodded, his head bobbing up and down. Agatha walked back into her bedroom to turn off the radio.

The wailing started from the Browns' yard and curved, driving like nails through the quiet grass. Tony's eyes widened. Agatha flung open the front door and ran onto the porch as the shrieking rose higher. It was a sad, frightening sound.

'BEA!' Agatha hoisted her skirts and clambered over the adjoining fence, nearly scratching herself in her haste. The Brown house was a two room hut made out of rough-hewn boards. She felt splinters bite into her bare feet as she banged at the door. The sound of Mrs Brown's grief had not stopped. Agatha called the woman's name again as she pushed the door open.

The bed filled most of the room. Bea spread it with a red cloth in the days so that guests could rest their legs, but now the cloth was ruffled underneath her. She was hugging a radio, one of the box types. It was covered with scratches. She wasn't crying but the deep, high sound coming from her throat was unbearable. Agatha put her arms around the older woman and held her tightly.

'Lord, lord, Miss Bea! Hush now! Hush now!'

Tony stood at the door. Grief was not new to him, nor emotional excess. The church sisters had provided enough of that, flapping like brightly coloured flocks of birds, bending and ducking and writhing, pink crinoline and yellow cheesecloth mixing, slapping hands while tongues twisted, furled, unrolled and flung their bodies into the air. His mother had rolled with the best of them, sisters scooping her from the ground where she lay fainting with the other multicoloured geese, stockings ruffled, undergarments peeping. But he'd never seen this kind of grief. Mrs Brown looked as if God had slipped her bones from their moorings. He watched as Agatha rocked the woman, moaning with her, one of Bea's hands slung across her shoulder.

'Aaaaaaaaaaaaaaaaaaaaaaaaaaaaaaaa...'

The cry was quieter. Agatha rocked, murmuring.

The door behind them burst open, just missing Tony, who stepped back in alarm. Bea's husband, Rupert, stood there panting. To Agatha's surprise, he hardly looked at his wife.

'A terrible thing, Lawd have mercy, a terrible thing!' he said.

Agatha glared at him. 'Man, don't you see your wife here crying?'

Rupert shook his head. 'Sho' she cryin'. Is a day to be cryin', Miss Agatha.'

Agatha beckoned to Tony. 'Tony, you go on and get Mrs Brown some water, you hear?' She shifted her weight to accommodate Bea as

Tony trotted back out of the hut. 'What the hell are you talking about, Rupe? You're hollering and carrying on like it's judgement day and the Lord forgot you on his way to heaven!'

Rupert started to gabble. He shifted from one foot to the other, keeping time with his wife's dejected sound. 'Oh, you ain't heard! You ain't heard! They done kill off them children like they jes' animals, them mens woulda known children gonna be up in that place, they don' care none, they jes' up an' bomb the place...'

Agatha looked bewildered. Tony came back, a cup of water in his hands. She took it from him and began to splash it on Bea's forehead. Bea jumped. Her cry was dying, hiccups and sniffles taking over.

'Speak plainly, man! Who got bombed?' Agatha demanded.

The woman in her arms stirred.

'Four children,' Bea said. Her voice was croaky. 'Four lil' gals in Sunday school.'

Tony examined Agatha's face as they hurried along the road to Edene. He'd never seen her so grim and frightening. He was used to her soft face, and there was nothing soft about her compressed mouth. She squeezed his hand. He tried to ease free and tripped over a stone. Agatha dragged at him.

By the time Agatha finished comforting Bea, the discussion had confused him even more, and now they were late. Miss Ezekiel would be angry. Four little girls had been killed in a church in Alabama. But who killed them, and why would they kill children? He wondered if they were related to the Browns.

'Walk faster, Tony,' snapped Agatha. She pulled at his hand again. Tony tried to keep up with her long stride, skipping double time. Small stones stung his calves. He was scared. Agatha never got mad, except when people were cruel, like the white boys who had tried to drown Mikey. He liked Mikey. Since the water hole incident, nearly a year ago, they often stole off into the woods together. Agatha had taught Mikey to shoot, like she'd promised.

It was difficult to be friends without words, but Mikey seemed happy to fill the silences. Tony marvelled at his openness, talking about Miss Ezekiel and her funny ways, how scared he was of Timothy, how he had to keep ducking him in the big white school. He told Tony a lot about the white school, where they laughed at him and called him names. It sounded like heaven. Mikey spoke about broad hallways, lockers, gym and different classes for different grades. He liked looking at Mikey's books, crisp and shiny-new, wrapped in paper to protect them, mounds of chalk in all colours and newly sharpened pencils. The big white school had an indoor bathroom, where Mikey spent an inordinate amount of time. Tony could understand that. Kids in his one-room school often hid in the outdoor toilet when they were bored, but Reverend Wilson was no fool. He went around and whipped out the offenders.

He liked hearing about Mikey's lessons, worlds he couldn't dream of locked up tight in between the leaves of books in the library. He nodded vigorously whenever Mikey talked about the library. Rows of books as far as the eye could see, and a big black stamp that told you you could have the book for two whole weeks. He knew where he would hide from the Timothys of the world if he went to a school like that.

He was jolted out of his daydream by Agatha's voice. He noticed that her voice changed when she was angry. Became more country, more Southern. He called it The Terrible Voice.

'Darn it, Tony! We're *late* and you're just strolling like you're somebody!' She stopped. 'Didn't you hear me say we're late and we gotta move fast?' Suddenly, she scooped him up into her arms and started to run.

Surprised and afraid, he pushed against her. Her grip was already failing, his sweaty skin slipping as she grunted and tried to hoist him into a more secure position. Surely she couldn't run five miles with him in her arms. He wasn't a baby, he was heavy, and the whole morning was wrong. He could hear her panting. He struggled some more, but she held on tight. Her face twitched, and the marks on her skin stood out. He hadn't noticed that their edges were so raw. He looped his hands over her shoulders and behind her neck, trying to help her, but he still slipped. Agatha muttered under her breath.

'Damn wicked peckerwoods, imagine they killed children.

Children. Just starting their lives. They could have killed men. It's them that's marching. And now I'm late and I swear if this fool woman says 'Boo' to me why I'm likely to take her skinny self and hoist it up some tree and they can hang me up right there beside her why hanging's too good for them...'

Tony stared. She couldn't beat Miss Ezekiel. She'd get into trouble. He would have no-one. Everybody went away.

Agatha slowed to a limp, defeated. She put him down and stared forwards. They walked.

'Ma'am?' It was a tiny whisper. Tony breathed through his nose at the sound of his own voice.

'I swear I'm not taking another day with these shitting white folks they're just terrible have people cowering down like they're fools I'm scrubbing this fool woman's floor with more education than she's got and those children they didn't do anything, *anything*...'

Tony tried again. His heartbeat felt as if it had slowed down.

'Mizz Agatha? Mizz Agatha ma'am?'

'I could have *been* somebody...'

Agatha stopped in the path and looked down at the boy, her eyes filling with incredulity. She knelt in the dirt.

'What- what did you say?'

Part of him wanted to go back on it, now it was done, but he wanted her to stop, be calm, and keep on looking at him with that joy forever. Tony curved the tip of his tongue to the roof of his mouth and spoke his first public sentence since they told him his mother was mad and took her away to The Place Where Crazy People Go.

'Please, Mizz Agatha, ma'am. Don' be scared. Don' cry 'bout the children...'

9

there are two rats in this room with us and I call them Simon and Garfunkel Simon has a long thick tail and a swagger and he isn't afraid of anything man I've seen him do the strut around here like he's the landlord I'll give you one little example once Chaz woke up with him sitting next to her hand watching her sleep like he's her daddy and she was so drugged with Underground not horse not crack I said she's not a junkie anymore but Underground is a new kind of high you know well she was so gone she just said *yo rat* and went straight back off to sleep

Simon eats meat and I've seen him eating our food one day I caught him with some KFC and you could see the furry motherfucker singing to himself *ain't no thing like a chicken wing* but Garfunkel is different he's a coy little rat he minds his business and he's got a hairdo that sticks up straight in the shadows hence the name and Garfunkel hangs behind Simon waiting for him to forage then he takes his share and I swear the Rat Boys have a little love thang going on there you know I think we've got us some homosexual rats which kind of makes me feel like I belong

talking of relationships you know Marcus lived a couple of blocks up the street from me when we were kids and his momma was an attractive woman for an old broad it was cool that she thought I was a good example you know smart at school and she thought her kid couldn't do better than me yeah we were plenty successful but not the way she would have liked it you see the combination of my pretty face and form worked I've always looked like an innocent little kid and the girls weren't scared of me they wanted to look at me and feel me so you know the combination of that and Marcus was all we needed he was the bad one but not on purpose Marcus was born at home with a midwife and he came out on his face so there was some nerve damage and his left eye was all messed up they did some surgery but the best they could do was give him this lopsided look with one eye half open God that eye used to fascinate all the girls there was one child she must have been about sixteen she was an older woman and we thought that was cool well this girl was wet for him she romanticised his face she said that he looked like some kind of pirate with those long eyelashes and that half closed eye she said he looked like he was winking at you all the time

the funny thing was that Marcus was the disinterested one yeah he was holding girls' hands and kissing them carefully but never stealing a feel and it would be me at the movies watching the silver screen knuckle deep in pussy while the girl is panting and looking into my eyes saying *you're so pretty so cute no no I don't want your hand there do it to me Tony God do it to me* Marcus would be in another row still kissing some frustrated fool and he'd get the fast ones because they thought he was a bad dude and they'd be arching their backs trying to look sexy meanwhile Marcus is saying *do you want popcorn or candy* and they're getting angry it was great we were a double punch duo I'd flutter my eyelashes and he'd look cool and that was all it took man the girls ran us ragged

after a while I'm noticing that Marcus is more interested in watching me sock it to some girl than he is looking at his own piece of ass I liked him too and I twitched when he touched me but I didn't know who I was or what to do and we let it pass and he went upstate to college I was the one with a golden scholarship and everybody was so proud but man after two semesters I was bored *they call the first paragraph of a news story an intro* so fucking what puh-leeze when do I get to interview the stars why are we wasting TIME years passed and I messed around like I always have I played the sax I'm telling no lie I played in a couple of bands and spent some time in smoky bars and oily stopovers trying to jog the customers out of boredom I did some time as a cashier and a waiter I split my muscles on construction sites and wiped down dying tables I picked fruit I drove a fuck-off truck and all the time I was tasting everything and everybody and I nearly lost my mind in flesh I lost my virginity at sixteen with a barmaid who was twice my weight and had the mouth of a queen then lost it again two months later riding the Hershey highway I never saw the dude's face then I hooked up with a pal who knew the business and we ran some off-key off the wall fanzines they were totally impractical and too expensive and we were in debt up to our eyebrows but we didn't give a shit by that time I was sweet three-oh thirty years old and I had worked out long before that I liked it every which way but loose

I went to a BBQ in the neighbourhood and Marcus was there and now I knew more so I swam up to him and gave him a chicken leg and a mound of coleslaw and I whispered *damn you so fine boy* in his ear you know he jumped like a bunny rabbit I was like *you are not going to be able to hide these things from me* I was playing it cool and pretending I wasn't shaking with wanting him but shit oh shit his bicep was an ocean of unbruised skin and he was so psyched he spilled a beer down his chest and I wanted to lick him so bad so I took him and he took me for the first time in the neighbourhood with the good smell of BBQ in the background inside somebody's bedroom I can't remember whose and our love affair was on and off from then until the day I came Underneath

he was so faithful looking for rest and contentment and peace he wanted a CONDO and a simple life but I was a party boy and in the first two years I treated him like shit you know he'd be sucking me in the morning as soon as I opened my eyes and I kept peeling him off I was like *so who gives a damn that you love me* oops too late to change now

he got the courage to throw me out after the first year and I was impressed man it was role reversal in a big way so I stayed at people's houses charming their asses into letting me eat them out of house and home and getting the mag off the ground yeah those were the days I was committed and I figured I needed a real job and when I had the time I went around to Marcus to say *come on now lover I know you're joking let me in* and he was cursing me out it was great you know the super nearly asked him to leave and the other tenants were saying all of this homosexual passion was no good for their babies or their cats but I got annoyed after a while because the joke had gone too far and I realised I was losing dignity baby fuck you have got to be crazy ME beg you know I really find that hard to play so I stopped and soon he was sniffing around and I was back in his bed within the year WHAT HAVE YOU DONE FOR ME LATELY OOH-OOH I USED TO BE GRATEFUL FOR THE LITTLE THINGS BUT LITTLE THINGS ARE ALL YOU SEEM TO GIVE that Janet man that girl got it going on except for the nose I'm sure you're not surprised that Marcus threw me out many times after that but by that time I was like *fuck it I'll never beg again* and he knew that so he stopped fucking around even though I never stopped what I was doing because I've always been a slut baby

I wrote Mikey again days and nights ago said that I'm writing a book *semi-autobiographical just want to hear your memories tell me about Agatha good to hear you're well boy I had to write why did YOU never write ha ha* and he answered Chaz brought the letter down for me and her face was stretched tight she wanted to know who was writing and I could see she'd tried to prise it open I asked her what she thought she was doing but I wasn't mad you know it's fair enough well not really who the hell does she think I'm having an affair with down here I mean please I asked her *what the fuck you playing at* and girlfriend had a niggabitchfit she completely lost it says if I don't tell her what's happening she'll push me on the third rail herself I started laughing this little bit of an itty girl couldn't lift my right finger much less anything else she's standing there stamping her feet and all I could do was laugh as she cried it broke my heart I hate seeing her upset but I will show nothing I will show nothing

I opened it with trembling fingers and suddenly I'm in Mikey's world wow he's explaining why I've been on his mind just in case I don't believe him hey this is an interesting story says he met a boy he was one of his students and I'm reading and being all facetious yeah I tell you I was an editor I know big words I'm being all crazy thinking *well Mr Mikey you met a boy huh you looking for young meat I never knew you were one of us* but he didn't mean that of course he said the boy's name was Scott Johnson and Scott reminded him so much of me he was clever with an easy way with words that would blow your mind *like you Tony and the bastards killed him just for money broke into his house and what hurts me the most is that I was only just getting to know the boy and his gift and he died and his stupid ignorant close minded momma all she was thinking of at the funeral was the fact that the boy had some porno magazines under his bed but this boy could have been the next Jean Toomer John Edgar Wideman and he's dead it kills me the injustice I wanted to turn over a new leaf with Scott I know it sounds stupid but I wanted to make his life right and wonderful and full and special because he reminded me of you pretty bright and so full of potential* so why aren't you writing about Agatha all this is nice it's cool I'm fucking James Baldwin but tell me was there ever an Agatha six foot tall scars just so was there

man I sold something I just don't know what can't remember where I compromised I'm getting to where maybe I'll go down the tunnels and look for her ass say *take me* I can feel my brain coming apart slowly stretching I feel every roped nerve I feel the pores in my skin like holes in the road why am I fighting her I can't God save me I can't Mikey I remember you boy I remember your innocence and your peace under the war I hope your woman loves you what did you do brother did you go to a shrink did the love of a good woman save you save you keep the memories whole put them into context you have a child say I never did that I don't said I don't believe in childhood brother don't believe in childhood

10

It was difficult to persuade Agatha to talk about the bombing through her laughter. She picked Tony up and swung him around. She stomped and threw her head back. She covered his face with kisses. She held him so close he thought he would choke. All the time she was laughing, so eventually he laughed with her and they kissed and danced on the gravel with the sun popping oval drips of sweat on their skin. Agatha's hair came loose and fell down her back. Tony helped her tie it up with the yellow rag. Agatha got silly in her excitement.

'Boy, I love you. Say the words out now, Tony. Say anything. Don't you stop now...'

He smiled shyly. The Terrible Voice was gone. 'Whatchoo want me to say?'

She touched his lips.

'Anything. Just sing it out, child. Say the world is fine.'

'The worl' is fine.'

'Yes, baby. Now say- say Miss Ezekiel is a damn fool!'

Tony grinned. 'Thas not good manners. She aim to cuss me...'

'Boy, you're not saying it to her! Say it to *me*. Go on, now! 'Miss-'

'Mizz Ezekiel is a damn fool!'

'Praises! Say it again, Tony!'

'Mizz Ezekiel is a damn fool'

'Again! Louder! Then say anything you want! Exercise that old voice box!'

'MIZZ EZEKIEL A DAMN FOOL! AN'- AN' I LOVE YOU, AGATHA!'

'Yes, baby! And I love you too! Now, do you know the words to

'Ain't Gonna Let Nobody Turn Me Round'?'

'I think so...'

Her face was bright. 'Boy, we're going to sing it all the way to Edene and we're not stopping, you hear?'

They held hands and started to run. They were late, there were three miles to go, and they sang out in between long runners' breaths. It was a morning that Tony forgot too soon. The morning they heard that the 16th Street Baptist Church in Alabama had been bombed, taking the lives of four children like Tony. The morning Tony began to speak again, his fear and joy embracing like first cousins.

Mikey lay in his bed, sweating. It wasn't because it was hot. Even though it was still so hot that the sheets stuck to him. It was because the Soul Snatcher was there.

He didn't know what the Soul Snatcher looked like, because nobody ever knew. But the Soul Snatcher stood on your porch every midnight. And it breathed. He knew it wanted him to get out of bed. His father had told him about the Soul Snatcher. It was more real than Santa Claus, because everyone knew that he was a lie.

He remembered his father lying in bed, talking in between coughs. He wiped his father's brow as he sweated and retched into a bowl. The liquid that came off his lungs was yellow, and sometimes there was blood in it. The little boy carried it to the side of the house and emptied it away. He felt he could bear anything, the no-smell vacuum of the room in which his father lay dying, even the story of the Soul Snatcher. As long as there was no crack in the bowl. As long as he never spilled a drop. He knew that if even a drop splashed on any part of his body he would start running and he would never stop.

'The Soul Snatcher stands outside your door.' His father's eyes didn't leave his during the telling. 'What he is, he's a ha'nt, the worst kind of ha'nt there ever was. When he gets you, he does all the worse things you could think about. He holds you, and he strokes you, and he slowly peels the skin right off your back. You don't realise until he holds his hands right up in your face and you see how red and bloody they are and you look down and see your intestines and your life blood pouring out of you. And when he kills you he puts your skin on and when he's got it on, he can talk just like you, then he goes and torments someone else. The next person he goes to is the person who loves you the most in the world…'

Here his father would stop and peer gravely over the sheets, taking deep breaths.

'That means he would come for me next, Michael, after he killed you, because your Daddy is the person who loves you the most. He would stand at my door, breathing, and I'd feel the hair on my neck rising because I know something behind that door stinks. Imagine it, Michael, you lying in your bed, mosquitoes singing, just setting to sleep, and you hear something breathing behind the door. You don't know what the hell it is, and you call out, you ask 'Who's there?' or 'Whatchoo want?' and he doesn't say anything, he's just breathing there, calm and regular. He hears the fear in your voice and that makes the whole thing worse, because he likes the fear, it makes him strong. And just when you're fit to burst, when the fear has got so bad you want to die, that's when he calls out to you. He calls you, and it's the voice of the one you love the most. The one you miss the most.'

Even though Mikey knew the story, he waited, mouth dry, for the finale. His father coughed and spat.

'It's voice is the voice of the person you'd give your right arm, your heart, your best comic book for, if only you could see them, hold them, love them, be in their company.'

Mikey hadn't known what this emotion felt like until his father had died.

'You run to the door. You don't need to be scared any more. It's the person you love. They're knocking. You yank the door. You're in their arms, Michael, laughing, feeling good, you're not lonely anymore. This is the person you needed. And then the Soul Snatcher takes a deep breath from the warmth of your arms and you're thinking 'What's that smell?'. It's the smell of death. Then he peels you like a plum, rips the skin off your back and you go to Hell screaming.'

Each time he heard the story of the Soul Snatcher, Mikey held his breath for more. There was no more. No retribution. No saviour. No help. Just him, screaming into the pits of Hell, lungs naked, skin gone, with the reverberation of love's voice in his mind. His father told him

65

many stories as he died. But this was the one that stuck in his mind. And at night, Mikey listened for the Soul Snatcher. He tossed and looked out of his bedroom window. He could see it. He heard it breathing. Through the shadows, he saw its face: blunt, red lips and big grey eyes. Yellow froth at the corners of its mouth. His father, smiling gently and calling for him.

'Boy!'

Mikey moved towards his Daddy. He sounded angry, but he was never angry for long. He reached out.

'I said, Michael Abraham, why you sleepin' the day away when you got extra lessons? What goin' on this mornin'? That Agatha she late with that boy, an' you here sleepin'! I declare, y'all think I'm a silly woman!'

Mikey rolled over, the last vestiges of the dream and his father's sick face disappearing. He'd never been awake, and it wasn't night anymore. Miss Ezekiel was standing over him and she was calling herself a silly woman. That meant she was real mad. His belly bounced as he tried to get out of bed.

'Sorry, ma'am. I was havin' a bad dream...' He was still too dozy to remember that sympathy was not his grandmother's strong suit.

'Bad dream? I give you a bad dream! You gonna have to go to lessons without yo' breakfast cause I said this gal she ain't here yet! Two hours late!' Miss Ezekiel pointed an accusatory finger at the book on his bedside table. 'All you be doin' is readin' that trash alla the time, can't even keep them things good, you writin' all over them like you picked money out of yo' pocket! Boy, you think I'm made of money?'

Mikey looked down. He hated the fact that she noticed all the little things he did. It made him nervous. Every time he picked his nose. Didn't brush his hair. Left a crumb on his plate. He sneaked a look at the book. The front page was covered with scrawling numbers. He wondered if he could wipe it off.

They heard the frame door swing back. Miss Ezekiel called out and went into the kitchen. Mikey heard her cursing at Agatha as he poured water into a bowl and sluiced his face down.

'What time you call this, gal? I been waitin' from sun-up and you sleepin' in yo' bed-'

Mikey half-listened, grinning to himself. He could hear Agatha's low, polite voice. That meant she'd interrupted his grandmother. He shook his head in admiration. He wished he could do that, just once. He wondered if Tony had come. Agatha didn't like him coming on extra days. He often thought of telling Tony about the Soul Snatcher. It might stop the dreams.

Tony knocked on the door.

'Hey,' said Mikey, 'I never know you was comin'. You gon' be here later? I gotta tell you somethin' when I come home. A story...'

'We was too late to go over to Amy Green,' said Tony. He grinned as Mikey's mouth fell open. 'So I'm gonna be here. Is yo' story good?'

Mikey stared. 'What- you- what- you talkin'! You talkin'!'

Tony smiled, but he realised that his whole body was tense. This was the real test. Maybe Mikey wouldn't like him talking. Maybe he didn't want to hear anything a nigger had to say.

'I reckoned it was time.' He was comforted by the delight on Mikey's face.

'But- well- I knowed you kin talk, even though alla those times I heard you sayin' out the Bible I was thinkin' I was dreamin, but-'

'MICHAEL ABRAHAM! YOU TAKIN' TOO DARN LONG TA LEAVE THIS HOUSE, BOY!' That was Miss Ezekiel.

Mikey reached for his shirt and shoes. 'I gotta go to stupid extra lessons, but I be back.' He couldn't resist a pause to stare at his friend again. Tony standing and talking. And no Bible stories either.

Tony grinned. 'I kin hear yo' story when you gets back.'

Mikey threw two books into his bag. 'Boy, all I'm comin' back to do is listen to YOU talkin'!' He whispered. 'If you ain't here I meetcha at the tree.'

They went to the big oak down in the Bottom some nights, after the women were in bed. Miss Ezekiel was increasingly disapproving of their friendship, and she gave Tony so many chores on the few days that Agatha let him leave school early, they could hardly do anything. Still, it was fun to wrestle in the moonlight and listen to the owls. Tony made everything fun. And now that he was talking, Mikey couldn't imagine it getting any better.

67

Tony brushed away a huge moth that blundered past his ear. Above them, the moon was a perfect half, like a lemon pie. 'You know Miss Bea says them big ole moths is a soul on it way to Hell, an' when one touch you it mean they tryin' to hold on.'

'Naw...' Mikey's stomach tightened. He didn't want a moth touching him. He wasn't usually afraid at night, but the Soul Snatcher dream had left him with a bad case of the jitters.

'You ever hear 'bout the Brown Mountain lights?' Tony moved a twig out of his way before it scratched his face.

'No,' Mikey said. The Brown Mountain range was over in northern Burke County. 'Why?'

'Well, I tell you...' said Tony. He waved his hands in the air, caught up in his own imagination. 'Lemme jes' listen fo' the voices of the dead...' He lowered his voice and begun to groan theatrically. '*They comin...*'

'Where?' Mikey squeaked. He felt as if Tony's voice was surrounding him. He began to trot.

'They says you kin see 'em on a cloudy night when the moon ain't out. They big balls of light. Some of 'em yellow, some red like blood, an' folks even say they seen 'em blue. Some says they's Injun spirits, dead Injun girls searchin' fo' they husbands. But I hear they rose up in the air when a man name Jim murder his wife Belinda an' they new born baby 'cause he was carryin' on with his other woman, Jenny. Jim don't want Belinda no more, an' one day she was jes' gone. People axin' Jim where his wife be, he say she gone, an' there warn't no baby, but people be searchin' an' found her bonnet an' it was covered with blood. They kept right on lookin' an' they found two human skulls, one a lady, one a baby.'

Mikey had slowed to a crawl. He felt like he was heading straight into the weird lights. He could almost hear the sleeping flowers breathing. The wood seemed to be bending in on them, trees growing feelers.

'You know they says if you raise the skull of a dead man over the head of the man who killed him, why, he can't say nothin' to protect hisself, he don' say nothin' an' thas how you know who done it. So they raise them skulls over Jim head an' he was fightin' an hollerin',

68

took five men to hold him down, but they hold him, an' they raise the skulls, an' his tongue got tied, an' they knowed it was him. Nobody ever knowed what happen to Jim after that, but ever so often, the lights rise over Brown Mountain to show good folks where they found Belinda an' her baby.' Tony looked at Mikey solemnly. 'They raise up themselves like big balls, an' they dance in the wind, an' if you listen...' He paused on the path, one finger raised.

Mikey whipped his head around. 'What? What they say?'

'Listen...' Tony droned, 'They say... Re-meeeember us re-meeeember us... remeeeember how he smash us 'til we was cryin re-meeeember the blood on the bonnet... Mikey... YOOOOUUU re-meeeeeember.'

Mikey tripped, nearly falling. Tony grabbed him. He bent double with giggles.

'Re-meeeeember, don' fall on the path, Mikey... Mikey... re-meeeeember....'

Mikey reached out and grabbed Tony's head in his arm. Shrieking with laughter, they wrestled, trying to trip each other up. Eventually Mikey's weight worked in his favour and he sat on top of Tony. Tony drummed at the earth.

'Lemme up! Boy, I'm gonna kill you when I get up! Git offa me!'

'My, how you manage when you wasn't talkin'?' Mikey bounced up and down on him. 'You gon' beg?'

Tony scrabbled, trying to dig his fingers into his friend's legs. 'Damn if I'm gonna beg! An-' He heaved his chest upwards, but Mikey sat stolidly. '-an' I wasn't talkin' cause you was runnin' yo' mouth all the time!'

Mikey laughed. 'You gonna beg?'

The struggle went on for several long minutes and then Tony stopped moving. Mikey bounced up and down.

'You beggin'?'

No answer.

'Tony? You better beg now!'

Tony lay still. Mikey vaulted upwards as fast as he could. 'Tony! Say somethin'!' He leaned down beside Tony's still face. Maybe he'd squeezed the breath out of him. He reckoned he was heavy enough.

'HAAAAAAAH!' Tony leapt to his feet. 'Boy, you fool! Think you kin kill *me?*'

Mikey dived for him, but Tony was too agile. He stepped out of the way and started to run towards the tree. 'I'm the king! I'm the king! I win again!'

They sat at the tree's base, panting. Mikey pouted.

'You vex?' Tony said.

'Naw.' The pout grew. Tony punched his arm and grinned. 'Min' I leave you here on yo' own, Mikey Tennyson! You gon' tell me yo' story?'

Mikey grinned. This was a story that would scare even Tony, with his precious fast feet.

When he finished the tale, Mikey found that he was shivering. He'd not meant to be so graphic or to take so long in the telling, but there it was, told, and he was nearly as spooked as that morning. He looked at Tony and tried to smile.

'Thas the story of the Soul Snatcher,' he said.

Tony gripped his knees. His usually lively arms looked dead. They were silent for a while. Mikey gazed at the sky. It was so full of stars it looked like someone had spilt honey-coloured salt across a dark kitchen floor. He hugged himself, mimicking his friend. Tony's face had sprung cheekbones. He didn't look real. He looked like a painting. Like he wasn't a real Negro. Didn't they say that coloured could never look nice? Mikey swallowed. Suddenly, more than anything, he wished he was back at his grandmother's house, out of the woods and out from under the salt strewn sky.

'Les' go,' said Tony.

Mikey nodded. He turned his face up as raindrops fell onto his hands.

11

there are some freaks down here man there are psychos worse than me I know because a week after I got here or maybe it was an hour later I don't know but let's say a week I met a man on the tracks who looked like a dirty version of ordinary he wore a pair of sunglasses that made me laugh he said he's been down here five years and the reason he came is because he's a hermaphrodite and no-one understood when he took his clothes off and the pressure got to him I'm like *yeah right you could have gone for celibacy chile why you decide to get filthy to cure the problem* I wanted him to go away so I got nasty on his ass said *show me go on I want to see*

for a boy who says he's got a psychological problem with the thing he had his pants down in next to zero seconds *see see* he's saying *see there's my dick there's the shaft and behind you can slip your fingers inside* now I might be crazy and the darkness it makes you blind but my fingers have experience and I'm feeling and all I can feel is dick and it's small too meantime I'm looking into this dude's face and he's all proud and excited *you see you see the problem I'm under* I'm thinking like *yeah right brother stay black you unbelievably crazy motherfucker talk about wishful thinking* and he grabs his pants up says he's going to dinner now and I never saw him again goddamn thank God I watched him walk away in his shades I WEAR MY SUNGLASSES AT NIGHT OK baby you cool

the metropolitan transport authority police yeah the MTA well we call them the sandwich givers I've never seen one which is funny and great Mr Sunglasses told me he's seen them he says they like giving you bologna but he prefers cheese he says he met one MTA dude and

71

explained his problem and the man bends him over and gives him some right there in his phantom pussy I was laughing *really* I said *yeah* Mr Sunglasses says *yeah that's why I don't like those guys no cheese and they want me like everybody wanted me when I was out of here* as I said before OK then baby OK

Chaz is touching me because she wants some you know she wants a piece of me because yeah we screw she is my little one and suddenly I want to cry because her thick jacket swallows her body and it can be cold down here and I don't want her to take off her shit and freeze her ass but I need her I'm pulling at her oops she's lost her balance she's in my lap and the baseball cap is hiding her curls I'm taking it off slowly and pulling at the waist of her sweats and she's bracing herself against my chest she's so light and harmless I need to be inside her I want to give her pleasure too but I need to be inside her right NOW she's looking down she's saying *baby whatcha doin* I'm pulling at her ankles and spreading them either side of me making her sit on me she's excited and she's running like waterfalls my hands are wet she's talking to me *baby your voice makes me so horny* you know some fine men and women have loved me God knows why I'm bending my knees and there are soft black hairs on her arms

pushing inside her

there are no words for this man God she's a sweet easy fuck and she's laughing as she pumps me we always laugh when we screw I don't know why no I do know why I laugh out loud because it wipes Agatha out of my mind and Chaz is using my stomach as a brace rising falling rising putting her teeth into my shoulder and I'm laughing

I'm holding onto her hips and stopping her I want to be still and silent just me inside her no movement she's grinning and squeezing me and I can hear my own moans and she's saying *this what you want baby* God I think I love her and she won't hold it any more she's rubbing her clit against me demanding she's saying *I gotta come Tony I gotta come let me* I'm watching her lips and her eyes in the candlelight I'm covering her face with kisses as gently as I can she's making those low noises a woman makes when she feels good and I like it when my lovers are selfish so I can give them something she's got me inside her and she's rubbing herself as well when I look down my belly's still flat this is so good watching those hungry fingers I've seen women come in thirty seconds by themselves so why do they need us and Chaz is taking the heel of her hand to her pussy and she's rubbing *oh God* she's losing her mind I've got her hips in my hands Chaz is gritting her teeth against my mouth I'm trying to make the kisses *say I'm sorry sorry sorry* she's going *ah ah ah ahhh ahhhhhhhhhh*

ah ah ahhhhhhh

SO MR TONY IS MAKING LOVE THERE IS NO TIME

her voice burst through my orgasm and I'm pushing Chaz off it's the bitch she's in the beams and she's grinning as big as a bus shaking that hair down and Chaz hits the floor she's yelling *shit Tony I was nearly there* but Agatha is caressing the walls with her long fingers and velvet hair she's smiling at me SHE'S IN THE ROOM she's talking to the walls like they're new *so Mr Tony has time to be MAKING LOVE there is no time* and her fingernails are chalk on the walls I'm sobbing and Chaz is saying *what baby what's wrong* sex used to be the only place I could lose the bitch but she's followed me there too Jesus Christ Mikey you didn't write anything to help me

I've got my hands to my ears saying *bitch shut up shut up* and her voice smells like sin that was the last thing I remembered and then I'm sitting panting I look down and I'm sitting across Chaz's chest sitting on her breasts and crushing them I lift my mouth from her cheek I've bitten her and she's wheezing she's holding her jaw and she's past crying her eyes have filled up her face she's so scared *I'm sorry* I'm saying *I'm sorry* and she's just laying there with her big old eyes I BIT her fuck I BIT her how how I am not that person

she's stuttering *you got me in the corner baby you hit me how could you* she said she was crying and begging but I wouldn't stop and I'm thinking *if I broke her nose we'll have to go Topside and get her fixed up* but it doesn't seem like it and while I'm thinking the silence sits in between us and she crawls over her careful hands full of that sandalwood oil she uses to calm me down I tell you she is as crazy as me can you believe this woman living in this dirt and filth bathing my head in this stuff to chill me out I want to cry I swear to you I want to die hey that rhymes I'm looking at her face and seeing how I fucked it up she's saying *what happened to you baby like you couldn't stop I forgive you* I don't forgive myself

I sit here waiting in this dirt and this crazy shit with this woman with her bruised up face Mikey doesn't love me anymore that's clear and the yellow pools and orange laughter draw nearer what shall I say to keep her away hey I keep on rhyming

I left Chaz I couldn't look at her anymore so I went to see the mural you know I've never seen more than three people at a time Underneath all those fools are down here for what they hope are original reasons none of them have the bitch on their ass they come here because it's cold outside out there the snow is hot on the ground you know the sounds down here are a trip sometimes I go for a walk through the tunnels and look at the beams and the strange lights filtering in there are very few but I stand underneath them and try to soak up some vitamin D from the rays and in the distance I can hear the trains whisper *go and get him go and get him* like a curse

the bitch will take my soul I am convinced of that she will watch me and torture me and then when I am sleeping she will come to me and peel me she will take her time slowly and at first it will feel like a lover's touch I will think it is Chaz she will start at the crown of my head and she will peel the first layer off and it won't hurt it will be like when you have sunburn and she will dig her nails in and go deeper she will sit astride my hips like Chaz and she will bark laughter through the tunnels like a beacon and she will throw handfuls of my flesh into the sulphurous air and she will giggle chuckle smile snigger titter chortle oh yeah I'm a thesaurus and she will not let me die until she prises my soul from my belly holds it up to the darkness will it shine or will it be as black as this place where I live will it be dead already ha ha if it's dead I will have the last laugh and she will go hungry

Mikey I'm pleading with you man tell me what I need to remember

12

Mikey liked the sound of Tony's liberated voice. It echoed through Miss Ezekiel's house and the woods and the backyard, singing, chanting, chattering, noticing. It made everybody except his grandmother smile. Old women remembered their children's first steps; wrinkled brows smoothed; broken-hearted lovers began to flirt again. As for Mikey, he had long decided there was something magical about Tony's voice, and let it go at that. It didn't pay to think about more unpleasant things. Like that night by the tree. It was better to concentrate on friendship, and all the things that Tony saw, which usually turned out to be fun - a bird's nest, or an interestingly coloured stone or hundreds of green and yellow bugs they spent hours batting and moving around a small hill, making armies of them.

Tony tapped on Mikey's window at ten o'clock. Through the glass Mikey could barely make out his face. They'd planned this adventure for two weeks. Mikey had been so swollen with anticipation that Miss Ezekiel prodded his stomach and asked if he was getting any fatter.

He opened the window. Tony smiled.

'Git a move on! They startin'!' he said.

'SSSHHH! I'm comin'!' Mikey put an experimental leg out of the window and paused. He never got this right.

Tony laughed. 'You wanna boost?'

'Sho',' he grinned back.

Tony grabbed the foot and helped. They stood at the sill, breathless with glee.

'You know who they picked?' Mikey asked.

'Yeah.' Tony eyes shone. 'They gots the two we was hopin' fo'.

Red Rooster Dixon an' The Tooley Bomber. Rooster the favourite, but I got my money on The Bomber.'

Mikey sniffed as they trotted through the undergrowth, turning west towards the town centre. 'Where you git money?'

Tony puffed his chest out. 'Ain't jes' you gots money! Agatha gimme a dollar Sunday an' I been savin' it. Course she don't know 'bout the fight. I give it to Luke Brown. He say you gotta keep down low or the white men see you an' ask you what you doin', but he say he think I'm right. Bomber gonna whup 'im in the third round.'

The excitement in Mikey's chest swelled a little more. Every week Tony came to the house with stories: the woman in his congregation who was expecting a baby and nobody knew for sure who the father was; the tale of the thief they'd caught in town and beaten half to death until his Momma begged for him; Tony even knew about Miss Carol, the extra lessons teacher who taught history at Mikey's school and wore her tops too tight and her skirts too short. Since Tony had only ever passed by the white school, Mikey couldn't guess how he knew about Miss Carol's thighs. Whenever Mikey asked him where he got his information Tony would wink solemnly and say that They let him in anywhere, 'They' being the grown-ups. It was just the same with tonight's fight: the appearance of a white boy at a coloured boxing match without his pa was suspect, but Tony knew which grown-up to ask for advice. It was admirable for a boy who hadn't talked but three weeks ago.

'You think I kin bet?' Mikey asked.

'You a'ready put down a bet. Half that dollar fo' you,' said Tony.

'How you know who I wanta bet on?'

'Why? You vex? We kin get back the dollar if we git there fast 'nough.'

'Naw. I think the Bomber gon' do it.' He was happy to go along with Tony. After all, Tony knew about these things, man things, more than he did. 'You wantcha fifty cents back?'

'Whatchoo think I am, boy? The bank? Sho' I want it. But it ain't no problem, 'cause see, you gon' win, an' you gon' win big,'cause The Bomber ain't no favourite. Some machine cut up his foot a year back an' they say he a gimp. But Luke say he ain't have no gimpy left hook

76

in there, an' he been trainin', eatin'. He ready!' Tony punched Mikey's shoulder in glee. 'They be waitin' fo' this re-match fo' a whole year boy, an' we gon' be there! You be makin' five dollars by night's end, an' then you gon' gimme fifty cents, and I'm gon' have me five dollars and fifty cents! Shit, they even says Red Rooster brother mess with the machinery made The Bomber chop his foot, but they ain't got no proof. Nobody never think he was gon' come back from this, but he ready, I'm tellin' you, the boy ready!'

Mikey shook his head. 'How you know all this stuff, Tony? They just walk up an' tell you?'

Tony laughed out loud and inclined his head modestly. Mikey spotted a tall, skinny black man walking towards them. He could see lights winking over the man's shoulder. They were nearly there. He sniffed the air again. Sweat. Male sweat and adrenaline.

'You boys git a move on! They fixin' ta start the fight soon!' said the skinny man.

'Mista Luke?' Tony ducked his head respectfully.

'Whatchoo think?' Luke smiled and patted him on the shoulder. He looked at Mikey. 'This yo' frien'?'

Tony nodded. 'This Michael Tennyson.'

'Pleased ta meetcha, Mista Tennyson.' Luke's face seemed friendly enough, but Mikey saw an eclipse pass over it. Luke had called him Mister. He was used to that, why, all the coloured called him so, but it seemed strange, especially since the man must know he'd sneaked out of Miss Ezekiel's house. He tried to smile. Tony was chattering to Luke about the fight, whether Rooster Dixon was going to come into the ring painted red like he had at the last bout, whether Luke was sure nobody would tell them to leave. Luke answered him, but his eyes stayed on Mikey's face. Mikey shifted. He wasn't used to a black man staring at him with such confidence.

'Now y'all go on over to the ring. If y'all jes' keep low 'till the fight start, ain't nobody gon' say nuthin'. They gonna be too busy. They got some white folks over there.' He looked at Mikey harder. 'If anybody ask you, Mista Tennyson, why, you jes say yo' daddy heah somewhere an' you lookin' fo' 'im.' To Mikey's relief, he turned back to Tony. 'As fo' you, boy, keep yo' head down too. I ain't aimin' fo' Miss Agatha ta cuss me. Her granpappy be rollin' in his grave if he see you heah an' Miss Agatha be vex if she know I had anythin' to do with it. Go on now. I paid fo' y'all.'

The outdoor ring sat lopsidedly in a large fenced-off lot. On three sides rough plank bleachers seated some two hundred spectators. Jokes and insults were high on the air. The apple smell of tobacco smoke swung a charcoal curtain over the clearing. As they crept through the entrance, Mikey saw a group of white men sitting in a section to the right. He looked away, feeling exposed.

A man beckoned to them. 'You boys Luke comp'ny?' When Tony nodded he pulled a ragged piece of tarpaulin aside and pushed them underneath the bleachers to the left, glancing around as he did so. 'Y'all kin see plenty from heah, but don' make no fuss.' Mikey squirmed underneath with Tony. He was glad the space was adequate, but his discomfort increased nevertheless. He wondered if Tony would enjoy the fight more alone. He stared out at the coloured men and boys milling around, eating handfuls of peanuts, peaches, swigging Coca-Cola. To his surprise, there were several coloured women present, laughing in the faces of loud men.

Tony spotted the woman he was looking for. He'd heard her story all week, women touching Agatha's arm, singing and whispering. He nudged Mikey.

'See that gal over there? She the one fixin' to have a baby come March.' Mikey stared at the woman. Her tight dress left nothing to the imagination. Her feet were bare and the hair on her head stood up in spiked bundles. She was very pretty and her lipstick was very red. He saw no evidence of her pregnancy.

'She don' look like she-'

'She don' show yet.' Tony grinned. 'Her name Susie Derkins. Well. They says the bad blood between Red Rooster an' The Bomber all on account of Susie Derkins. Say she givin' somethin' to both of them. But she really love The Bomber - his real name Benjamin Tooley - jes' that Red Rooster got mo' money. When the Bomber get the chop, an' all the talk say it was Red Rooster family do it, she give up Red Rooster cause she never knowed what to think. Then she see she havin' a baby, an' she don't know who the baby daddy. She was gonna keep it quiet, but Benjamin hear she givin' some lovin' to both of 'em. He vex, he nearly fit to beat her, but he never, he hopin' it his chile. An' Luke tell me Red Rooster love ole Susie so bad, he followin' her, beggin', like he gonna die.' He paused, nearly hugging himself in glee. 'Look like them mens was gonna kill each other, so Susie say she gonna be with the man who win this here fight. Luke say he reckon ol' Susie think if they gonna fight, least this way they got people to stop them, make sho' it fair. So it the best fight of the year, an' it got some folks business up in it, so you know it gonna be good! Luke say the referee ready fo' it to be some bloody.'

Mikey peeped out at Susie Derkins. She didn't look like a woman with a problem. Her hand played bold on the thigh of the man in front of her.

'That The Bomber?'

'Naw. I dunno who he be. She better hol' down some, or mo' blood gon' spill tonight!'

The crowd murmured. The mood shifted; all eyes turned to the entrance. Mikey looked with them.

A man stood in between the bleachers, his hands on his hips. He was tall and his fists and feet swelled like ebony spades in the moonlight. They were the only part of him not heavily coated with crimson paint. The man was bare to the waist, his evenly defined, massive red chest heaving. Mikey shrank back. Tony chuckled.

Red Rooster lifted his head. From the far side of the lot another man rose and the crowd sighed. This man was flanked by two others who whispered in his ears. The Bomber was shorter than his opponent, but to Mikey's astonishment he was broader. His naked chest was light, almost yellow. His neat, wavy hair lay close against his skull. His features were alarmingly sweet, as if the ghost of a sister pranced in his face. Full lips peeled back to reveal small white teeth. Snakes of muscle crawled across his arms.

'Lookit Susie...' Tony stared across the lot at the woman. A shorter, darker girl had joined her and put an arm around her shoulders. Susie was no longer calm. She was on tiptoe. Now Mikey saw the subtle thickening at the waist of her green dress. She passed both arms across her belly. Her fingers moved on its surface like a drumbeat as she gazed at The Bomber. He was not looking at her.

Applause began to rise into the sky.

'Go, Bomber! You whup his black ass! Whup his black ass!'

'Red, you know I got money on you nigga!'

A fat black man stepped into the ring as the two fighters moved forward to the centre, staring at each other. The fat man spoke as both men sat on Coca-Cola cases, their seconds fussing around them.

'This heah a fight 'tween Benjamin 'The Bomber' Tooley an' Stephen 'Red Rooster' Dixon. Boys, we gon' have a good clean fight, no head-buttin', bitin' or such like. I'm the referee fo' this fight, an' when I say hol' off, boys, you gonna hol' off!' He stepped out of the ring and walked over to an old wheel rim. He smashed a hammer against it.

'Round One! Come out fightin'!'

The two men shuffled forward, sizing each other up. Mikey inhaled through his nose. He felt as if his heart would break out of his chest. Red Rooster's huge fist whistled towards The Bomber's face but the lighter man feinted skilfully and brought a neat uppercut through the treacherous space. His fist made a dull thwacking sound against Rooster's jaw.

'Uuuuu-uuuh!' Rooster grunted and charged, head down. The Bomber hugged at his back, and they snorted and pushed.

The crowd groaned.

'Go to it, boys! You ain't no sweethearts! Rooster, kill dat nigga!'

'Hit 'im again, Bomber!'

Rooster swung with his right. The Bomber's head ricocheted back then forward. Blood trickled from a cut over his eye. Mikey felt the clearing swell. Despite himself, he raised his voice in the din.

'Go get 'im, Bomber!'

Tony touched him.

'Lookit Susie,' he said.

'I don' wanna...' Mikey stared. Susie Derkins was tearing her dress. Her left breast was barely covered. Her aureole reminded Mikey of an over-ripe plum, slightly puckered, rich coloured. Tears filtered down her cheeks and neck.

'Uuuuuu-huuuuh!' The crowd roared as one. Red Rooster strode around The Bomber, left cut, right cut, swinging from side to side, beating him methodically. Blood trickled from several places on The Bomber's face. He swayed on his feet. Mikey felt sick. The paint on Red Rooster's body pattered off him as he sweated and lunged. Big drops splattered onto the canvas.

Tony jigged excitedly, his eyes going back and forth from Susie to the ring. 'The round nearly gone, the round nearly done! C'mon Bomber, give 'im some! Thas my five dollars!'

The Bomber struggled against the ropes. Pinned, flailing, he tried to protect his face. Mikey saw the fat referee moving forward. He watched The Bomber's knees buckle. Rooster's face was a mass of vengeance. He was smiling. The blows continued. The crowd leapt to its feet. Their howls hurt Mikey's ears. Mercifully, the bell sounded.

Red Rooster backed away from his opponent. He let his friend slew him down with water from a big bottle. The Bomber panted, his pretty eyes bugging out of his head. He looked like a mad man. Sweat and blood obliterated his handsome features. Mikey glanced through the crowd for Susie Derkins. She fought the restraining arms of her friend. He could hear her yelling.

'Lemme GO! Lemme GO!'

Ding. The bell sounded again.

'Round Two!'

The Bomber shuffled forward cautiously, his clean face pressed into another shape. Red Rooster smiled and came for him, smashing one mighty hand against the other. The Bomber danced back and ducked the first blow, wriggled around the second. He hit out like a yellow panther, growling in frustration. The attempt whistled into the wind. Rooster's fist connected again, like clockwork. There was a sickening crunch as his knuckles merged neatly with his rival's ribs. Air gone, The Bomber staggered back. Rooster darted in again, but the referee stood in his way, arms outspread.

When he was a man, Mikey would never again see a fight quite like this one. Perhaps it was because of the stolen night, the ragged tarpaulin, Susie Derkins' bare breast, the first one he'd ever seen. Perhaps it was the way Stephen Dixon smiled every time he hurt Benjamin Tooley. His blows were a dreadful rain of jealousy and victory. Then Mikey heard Susie's voice. It seemed strange that she was able to cut through the noise and the rage, but she did. She had broken free of the crowd and stood, hands on her hips, kissing distance from the ring.

'Benjamin Tooley! You a fool! You ain't no man! You ain't no man I want!'

The Bomber stared blearily at her. The man on top of him grinned, playing the crowd, looping and weaving his clenched hands for laughs as the crowd cheered.

'You ain't no man! This chile ain't yourn! He ain't yo' chile, Benjamin! I knowed but I never tole you! It Rooster boy chile I carryin'! He a man! You heah? He a man!'

Red Rooster danced away from Benjamin, making the hunt last. The Bomber heaved himself off the ropes and shambled forward, but his eyes were on Susie Derkins' face. She lifted up her voice.

'You heah me, Benjamin! This chile ain't fo' you!'

The Bomber plunged forward. Rooster Dixon was surprised by the force of the blow that smashed into his jaw. The crowd howled. Mikey looked around and saw grown men with their heads in their hands and others leaping around in joy. It took only one more blow for Red Rooster Dixon to hit the floor, and he did it with a strange kind of grace. Mikey put his hands over his ears as the crowd's excitement rolled over him. The referee fell to his knees, pounding the floor.

'One-uh! Two-uh! Three! Four-uh! Five!'

Rooster lay still. The Bomber fell back as the count went on. He turned away from the crowd, clutching his midriff. He began to vomit. Mikey watched Susie Derkins' face crease in concern. She moved away from the ring and back towards her friend, pulling her dress around her, as if she had just seen her own breast.

'Six-uh! Seven! Eight! Nine-uh!'

Susie flung her hands up and hugged her girlfriend. The referee was too busy counting, his lips by the fallen man's head, to see The Bomber turn back to the crowd, wiping his chin, staring at Susie Derkins' belly.

The Bomber moved. Susie saw what he meant to do. She began to scramble towards him.

'HE OUT!!!!!!!'

The crowd wailed and cursed and cheered. The Bomber's family bounded up and down. Susie climbed over two men in the swell but she was not fast enough. Perhaps there was nothing she could have done.

The Bomber shoved the referee hard, putting his shoulder into it. With a squawk, the heavy man slid out of the ring and into the dusty crowd.

The Bomber kicked Rooster in the face. His feet were bare, but the force was deadly nevertheless. Red Rooster lay unconscious as the bridge of his nose broke. His lips disappeared in a froth of swollen flesh and born-again bruises. Then Benjamin Tooley, whose heart was broken and who had never loved any other woman save Susie Derkins, knelt on Red Rooster's chest and began to strangle him. Susie reached her man before the referee could recover, before anybody could react, and then the ring became a sea of struggling men, her dress jewel green at its centre. Tony found out later that Susie's attempts to remove The Bomber actually delayed matters. She was hitting him so hard that the men had to pry her loose before they could take Benjamin's fingers from where they were embedded in his rival's neck. Susie was screaming the truth: that she had only said it to make Benjamin angry. *Only so's you could beat him, Benjamin!* It was too late. Benjamin Tooley was disqualified and charged with attempted murder. Ten year old Michael Tennyson swore that he would never forget the sadness in Susie Derkins' eyes as the semi-conscious Red Rooster held her small hand. But he did.

Tony dreamed all night about the Soul Snatcher and woke up with his own screams in his ears.

13

latest letter from Mikey is all about His Great Parents the lovely middle class parents that Mikey got he says his adopted mother reminded him of Agatha so it was the second time in his life that he felt loved his NEW mom tucked him in at night and his NEW dad was cool he played ball with him and talked girls with him and they sat at a table and ate meals together and took holidays in Florida and once the weight came off he was a perfect son the one they always dreamed of maybe I could have gone right if I got nice middle class parents

Mikey says *OK I'll answer the question since you can't get the soul snatcher out of your mind but I don't want to be doing this because it's old business and maybe it should stay dead I stopped feeling like shit a long time ago but you're asking me so I will tell you what I remember I remember climbing under the house and listening to you recite the Song of Solomon* but that wasn't good enough I was searching the letter for him to tell me about Agatha I mean was there ever any Agatha brother was there ever any fine six foot tall if she was a mile tits that'd make you stand up and smile Agatha who loved us but he's telling me how ashamed he was that he couldn't get from under the house *but those were old days Tony you better need this it's old stuff you wouldn't recognise your old friend because the fat days are ancient history and we would have torn up Princeton together if you were there with me I had more women than I could handle but I was always going to be a one woman man I guess it was in my genes from the start but if you want me to OK I will do you remember that you were picking pecans*

fuck the dude must have cleaned up good because you know acne was born raised made out had cappuccino and died in his face poor bastard

you know Marcus's momma always admired the woman who fostered me she said *Miss Benedict the cleanest woman in this neighbourhood* like that was the best thing one woman could say about another ha clean she might have been but she was a sick bitch Marcus's momma didn't know how clean she was her name was Carla Benedict and she was a fucking compulsive I mean she never abused me it's not the same old story YOU CARE BUT YOU DON'T LOVE ME I KNOW IT BUT IT STILL HURTS TO HEAR THE TRUTH you might think I'm a crazy man singing while I'm talking but down here you need to be able to find a way to party

Carla was crazy and the task every day was to see how many times young Anthony could brush his teeth and wash his hands wash the hair on his head strand by strand you think I'm joking I had to set the forks at square angles and pull the bed covers tight just so and one wrinkle meant her fixing me with a look that cramped my stomach baby that look made me puke like crazy Carla said that my slippers had to be right there when I flung my feet out of bed and she woke up each morning to watch me do it

Carla had her own child a skinny little thing called Yvette she didn't treat her kid any better than me but what I'd like to know is why they don't tie their tubes I mean why do they let sickos like this breed and then give them more I mean is it some kind of joke and that was my life I can't say it has scarred me you know that better men than me would be jitterbugging around a funny farm by now ha not me I'm just Underneath I hear Yvette is doing the ho stroll but she makes sure they wipe up after themselves Yvette is a godamned dominatrix I'm not surprised are you

I joke but I'm so scared the other day night who knows who cares Chaz came in and touched me and I shat myself as I live and breathe you think I'm proud of that I let loose a load as we stood there Chaz disgusts me I mean how can the girl be near me I beat her and she's up in my face looking to wipe my ass and talking of ass wiping I just thought you see I'm a feminist too what if she gets pregnant Christ I don't want to think about that no no I'm going to ask her what she's

85

doing to take care of herself

Carla had a boyfriend his name was Ronnie DeSouza he was a big man with power in his arms and legs there were hillocks of muscle standing out in his purple black fat and the muscles played catch as catch can with the curls on his chest and he was a giant to us when he stood by Carla her arm couldn't reach around his waist and her head came up to his navel Ronnie was in the army so he wasn't around a lot every time he came home on leave Carla made me scrub the toilet with a toothbrush not mine no that would have been abuse I tell you no one abused me and each time he came I thought *is he Carla's baby-daddy is Yvette his kid* I had to wonder because there wasn't any daddy talk in that house and Yvette never called him daddy you know he was Mr Ronnie sir to us

Carla went crazy when Ronnie got leave she'd never say he was coming but we'd know because the craziness went double time the day before she'd give me this little itty bitty rag to wash down the steps however many times I did it she'd still be yelling instructions out of the window above my head with kids passing and laughing then she'd set me to every square on the kitchen floor while Yvette went through clipping the stray threads in the carpet Yvette got some hot blue dye and covered the patches that showed through and once Carla screamed for a whole hour because her child got the wrong shade I tell you the woman was bug eyed and staring you'd think the girl had committed a fucking felony so we'd clean and clean and clean and clean clean till we was mean that rhymes that rhymes I wish I'd dragged Carla down here with me because her eyes would have rolled up in her head and she would have died when she clapped eyes on this shit pit did I ever tell you about the smell BUFFALO GIRLS GOIN ROUND THE OUTSIDE ROUND THE OUTSIDE ROUND THE OUTSIDE DOSIE-DOH YO PARDNER what kinda stupid ass song is that anyway

Ronnie was a godamn rock he was made of metal there was nothing Carla could do to spook him man she'd fuss over him as soon as he walked through the door fawning and smiling *say hello to Mr Ronnie children* and we'd be standing there with enough grease in our heads to fry some serious chicken and he'd be like *hello son hello girl child how're you* and we'd chorus *fine sir and how are you* and then he'd dismiss our asses with one flick of his little finger then Carla would sit him down at the table and the feasting would begin the man's control was amazing Carla be sitting there watching him eat and we were all filled up from before because Mr Ronnie didn't eat with children at least Carla had the decency to feed us first he'd sit there and I'd watch him cutting his fried pork into squares spearing each one into his mouth never letting the meat touch his lips breaking off the bread Carla and him deserved each other not a crumb would fall and I've never seen that again in my life someone eating with no crumbs Carla made our lives hell but she wanted to please him so bad it was funny I was better behaved when he came maybe it was because he took her focus away from us maybe because he was a man's man

I see Agatha as sure as I can see Mr Ronnie cutting his meat and it didn't matter what Carla did Ronnie kept that same expression his eyes still his mouth a fat line and a noble nose to look down on her and once he was supposed to send a cheque but he didn't send anything for the whole of four months if Carla hadn't been a neat freak rather slit her wrists than spend a dime freak we would have been in serious shit she worked at a factory fitting blue yellow and white plastic tops on little bottles and the heat fried her hair in the middle there was a big patch that looked like dry grass so before Mr Ronnie arrived she'd pour grease all over it

Carla would get tired on night shift she did doubles she told us if you didn't catch the glass bottles as they came down the conveyer they were liable to smash and you know it one day she went to sleep and the bottles are crashing tinkle tinkle tinkle tinkle around her and she didn't hear a godamned thing the bastards nearly aced her ass for sixteen little glass bottles

Mr Ronnie came late one summer he hadn't written or called or nothing and Carla's head was all picky and when he came through the door she was on him *you bastard you bastard how am I supposed to feed these kids when you not acting like a man* she's clawing at his face but the man was rock he was steel he was NOT playing that shit he picked her and her claws off him like she was a tick and crushed her into the sofa in one supple move Carla's crying *how could you do this* and every time she paused for breath the man is like *are you finished* like she was nothing like she could have her opinion but he stood alone like a rock then Carla really lost it she goes into the kitchen and smashes a big old coconut cake she baked right out of her savings all vanilla icing on her clean kitchen floor and Yvette nearly died of shock I was pretty freaked too but Mr Ronnie was cool he was still sitting on the sofa his hands resting lightly on his knees and he's saying to us *are you going to school how is school children need school* he's not moving while Carla is up in the kitchen smashing everything even when she starts yelling *I'm gonna cut myself look I have a knife I will* all he does is look up straight into her face then he looks through the window all calm and shit *please do* he says like she's asking if she can help herself to a simple glass of wine *please do please do* just like that and I'm like wow that's way harsh

I spent a lot of my time in petty crime God I was such a cliché I was like hundreds of other poor kids I was shoplifting and bag snatching nothing spectacular I was just bored but I never robbed an old lady no the thrill was getting the dinero from men who should have known better I tell you about beauty and style I looked young for my age and when I first got to Carla Benedict honey chile never had any money so I'd sit on the corner and turn on the tears and I told the passing ladies and gentlemen *I lost my money and Momma's gonna kill me* and they'd be diving in their purses and pockets like you wouldn't know and it worked until some fool went and told Carla because you know in the neighbourhood nobody ever kept their mouths shut everybody just up in your business and at school they said I was talented but had no discipline I wanted to be a journalist ha screw political uprising girl I wanted to be up there with the stars I wanted to interview all of them and turn their guts upside down on a beautiful page

I never wanted to be a bad man but I guess I became one using women and men using their words of love like they were cheap lies you know anyone who ever loved me was heading for a fall because there is something in the offer that I can't stomach WHEN I GET THAT FEELING I WANT SEXUAL HEALING SEXUAL HEALING BABY MAKES YOU FEEL SO FINE you ever notice that Marvin Gaye was one ugly dude women say they loved him yeah right like that's a gift anyone can say they love you anyone anyfuckingone

14

'MIKEY!'

'Yes, ma'am?'

'Boy, looka heah, don' be callin' out to me like you grown! Come an' look in my face!'

Mikey walked into the kitchen where Miss Ezekiel stood waiting. Behind her, Agatha washed dishes. He saw from the stiffening of Agatha's shoulders that she disapproved of his grandmother's tone. Miss Ezekiel's yells always made him jump. Until he moved to Edene, Mikey thought that every lady spoke in a high, breathless voice, their lips twitching. This was how they spoke to his father as Peter Tennyson moved through the town, lowering his head politely.

Miss Ezekiel smoothed her white gloves. She was dressed up for her Saturday visit to Mrs Jenkins' place.

'When I come back in here I want to know you done every scrap of yo' homework, boy,' she said.

'I done it-'

'Did I tell you talk? How you gon' be back-talkin' me in front of niggers?' Mikey saw Agatha's back twitch.

'But I done-'

'Boy, I don' want to hear any of yo' stupid excuses. Jes' you make sure it done. I ain't got no time to be chasin' after you.' She resumed her fiddling, adjusted her hat, smacked her lips. It was a self-satisfied sound. 'You ain't gonna turn out like yo' good fo' nothin' momma if I got anythin' to do with it.'

Mikey stared at her.

'You know that yo' momma never got a lick of learnin' in her life. I try with her, but she wasn't listenin' to nobody, she always knowed her *own* mind.' Miss Ezekiel snorted. 'Thas why she never come to nothin'.'

He felt rage bubble up in his throat. She was talking about his mother like all the other people, the ones who'd never had the courage to gossip in front of his daddy. Miss Ezekiel wouldn't have said so if his daddy was there.

'Mizz Ezekiel ma'am, I was tryin' to tell you that I already done-'

'Michael Abraham. I am *tryin'* to make sure you don't turn out nothin' like yo' momma. An' you should jes' praise the Lord an' thank me that I never lef' you after yo Daddy dead.' She sighed. 'I knew I'd have to struggle with you. Them white trash ways jes' bred in the bone.'

He couldn't stop himself.

'She *your* daughter. If *she* trash, you-'

Miss Ezekiel's eyes popped open. She looked as if someone had forced her to swallow something nasty. She stepped towards him. Mikey stepped back, his bravado dying.

'*What you say to me?*'

'N-n-nothin'.' He tried to swallow. 'I never mean-'

'Boy, you think you a man? You think you kin sass me in my own house?' She seized his shoulders. 'I sen' you into God's heaven befo' you sass me! You know what I do fo' you? If you *ever* know what I done fo' you-!'

He bit down on his tongue as she began to shake him, slowly at first, then faster.

'*I put you out in the street befo' you sass me!*' His teeth chattered. Tears threatened. His daddy had never done more than cuff him over the head.

'I never- I never- I never-'

'YOU SHUT YO' MOUTH!' Miss Ezekiel shoved him into a chair, rattling the kitchen table. She loomed over him.

'Say yo' eight times,' she snapped.

He stared at her, not understanding. Agatha stopped washing the dishes. She turned to face her employer.

'Miss Ezekiel, the boy said he done his work already. Why-'

'*Am I talkin' to you?*'

Agatha shook her head. 'No ma'am.'

Miss Ezekiel turned back to Mikey. *'Say yo' eight times!'*

Mikey tried to clear his head. He knew his eight times table but his chest hurt. 'Eight time one make eight. Eight time two make sixteen. Eight time three make twenty four. Eight time four make thirty two...'

Miss Ezekiel turned away and spoke over her shoulder. She smoothed her gloves as if nothing had happened. 'I want this chile to say his eight times till I come back.'

'Eight time five make forty. Eight time six make forty eight.' Mikey swallowed. She never came back from Mrs Jenkins' until sun-down, and it was only one o'clock. His voice faltered at the thought. 'Eight time *seven* make forty eight...'

'What?' Miss Ezekiel snapped. 'Eight time seven make what?'

'Forty...' He'd repeated himself. He couldn't believe it. He opened his mouth but she quieted him with a glare. 'You gon' see how you stupid. Jes' like a nigger.' She looked at Agatha. 'Gal, what eight times seven make?'

Agatha's face was stone.

'Gal, you too stupid to answer me?'

'Fifty six,' Agatha said. 'Eight times seven is fifty six. Nine times nine is eighty one. Forty five times nine is four hundred and five. Eighty five times sixty three is five thousand, three hundred and fifty five. Seventy one times fifty two is three thousand, six hundred and ninety two.' She stopped. It was an old game she and Pappy played from as early as she could remember.

They stared at her. Miss Ezekiel pulled at her collar. She looked as if she was going to have a seizure.

Mikey started again, quickly. 'Eight time seven make fifty six...'

Miss Ezekiel swallowed spittle. She tried not to gawk at her maid. 'You know yo' eight times?' she said.

'Yes. Ma'am.'

'Eight time eight make sixty three...' said Mikey.

'When I come back I want you to tell me this boy ain't *stopped* his eight times. An' you have him aroun' you so's you kin hear him say it out.'

'Yes ma'am.'

'Eight time ten make eighty...' said Mikey. He wanted to laugh.

Miss Ezekiel fanned herself and struggled with her dignity. 'Very well. I gotta give him some of the Lord's ways, jes' in case he turn out like his no-good Momma. Lord bless her soul.' She picked up her handbag and walked out of the kitchen, firing a look at Mikey over her shoulder.

He started again. 'Eight time one make eight...'

Agatha walked out of the kitchen. Still chanting, Mikey rose and watched her go onto the porch. Minutes passed. He could see her craning her neck, watching Miss Ezekiel.

'Eight time two make sixteen...' he said.

'Mikey, stop.'

He looked up at Agatha. Her face was so kind. He wanted to know how she did that with the numbers. But he couldn't stop. Somehow Miss Ezekiel would know. Maybe she was right. Maybe he was a bad boy, and it was bred in the bone. After all, Miss Ezekiel had brought his momma into the world. His lips trembled.

'Eight time three make twenty four...'

Agatha placed her hand over his mouth. She did it gently, and it seemed to Mikey that she looked at him as if she knew everything. Like she knew all his life, like they were old friends. Like she knew more than even Tony knew. He stopped speaking and breathed in. Her hand smelled like soap and cinnamon.

'Tell me about your momma,' she said.

His daddy had been good to him. Patient. Firm when he needed to be. There were days that Mikey had to beg him to stop cracking jokes, because all the laughter made his belly burn and his head dizzy. He thought that his daddy was perfect, most of the time, except for his unruly, thick hair and his tendency to spit when he spoke. Mikey still remembered the agonies of standing with the local pastor, watching globs of spittle settle into the earth around them. Finally, when the minister couldn't bear it a second longer, he'd leaned closer and whispered importantly: 'Cleanliness is next to Godliness, my son.' His father stared back. 'The Lord sends a little message every time I spit, boy. He says I'm *alive*.' The pastor reeled back, stunned, and his daddy turned on his heel. He bent down and whispered to Mikey: 'You alive, boy?' Mikey cupped his hand over his mouth, trying to stuff down the laughter. 'I'm alive, daddy!' He never understood the refrain. His daddy said the same defiant thing each time he did something the town disapproved of, but his eyes were sad.

They went to the movie house on his eighth birthday. They saw *The Mummy*. Afterwards, when the credits rolled and the last piece of muted music crept through the building, he waited patiently as his daddy talked to Mr and Mrs Ferguson. Polly Ferguson bobbed next to her parents, every fibre of her seventeen-year-old self pointed in his father's direction.

Mikey stood to one side, staring at a poster of the Mummy. He closed his eyes and remembered Boris Karloff's delicate, wrinkled face and sinuous movements. The Mummy was even older than his father. His daddy had grey hair. His daddy was nearly fifty. Well, forty-five, really.

'Hey.'

He remembered her mouth. It was the first thing he saw when he opened his eyes. Cherry Smithson had a big, red mouth and she chewed gum. He could see it sticking to her teeth and peeling away as her jaw moved. She was the lady who collected money for the movie tickets. He knew that she got to see all the movies that showed at the theatre, and more than once he'd envied her. It seemed a perfect job, watching movies and taking money.

Cherry Smithson's eyes darted back and forth from him to his father, who was walking towards the exit with the Fergusons, arm in arm with Polly. He was still speaking to Mr Ferguson. His father glanced back and raised a hand to indicate that he should wait.

Cherry Smithson smiled. 'Your daddy ain't gonna be long. What's your name?'

'Michael Abraham Tennyson, ma'am.' He put on his politest voice. He wanted Cherry to like him. Maybe she could let him see free movies. Movies were a treat. Which meant that they were reserved for birthdays and extra special behaviour.

Cherry smiled again. She patted. him on the head. 'My, Michael

Abraham Tennyson. Ain't you a well-mannered boy! You a big boy, too! How old is you?'

'Eight years old, ma'am. Today my birthday.' He paused. Perhaps she would think he was hinting. But Cherry was too busy staring at his father's thighs. She shook her head and turned back to Mikey.

'My, that's nice,' she said. 'You wanta see somethin' special?'

Mikey nodded. 'Yes please, ma'am.'

She took his hand. 'Come on, then.'

He paused. 'My daddy said I should wait for him.'

Cherry shrugged. 'Won't be long. It's a big surprise.' Her voice was coaxing. 'I know your daddy. He wouldn't mind.'

Mikey thought hard. Movie secrets beckoned to him. Maybe she could give him a Mummy poster. They walked towards the bowels of the theatre. Cherry Smithson was still smiling, but her grip on his fingers was tight. The hall past the viewing theatre smelled of dust and the shadows of the chairs seemed to huddle together. Mikey sneezed.

Cherry pushed open a tan door. They stepped inside the room. Mikey looked around, disappointed. It was a normal room, with little more than a desk, two chairs and some empty cups. The dry air smelt of coffee and cigarettes. Cherry opened a desk drawer and began to search through papers.

'I got a special surprise for a birthday boy right here.'

Mikey stood at the door. The heat stuck to his back and the air was too still. He cast an eye around the dead room and then looked back at Cherry's busy hands. She didn't look nice anymore. She looked mad. Uneasily, he wondered whether she was alright. Maybe she wasn't supposed to be in here.

'Here you go, Michael Abraham Tennyson.' Cherry waved something. 'You like pictures? I gotta special picture.'

He hesitated.

'We kin go back to your daddy soon, boy. Jes' looka here fo' one minute.'

He looked into her face. It had gone pretty again. He wondered whether she was going to show him the Secret of Movies. The way that they made the pictures move on the screen. He crossed the room as she pulled out a chair for him.

Cherry laid the photograph she had found on top of the desk, face down. She took a pack of cigarettes from her skirts and lit one, blowing smoke into Mikey's face. He felt nervous again. He'd seen the big NO SMOKING PLEASE signs. They made his father mad.

'You know how yo' daddy came to this town?'

He wondered what that had to do with a photograph.

'Ain't nobody in this town know where he come from. Was almost nine years ago. He jes' up an' come one day, when it was cold. He didn't have no more but the clothes on his back an' he never have no family here.' Cherry blew out another cloud of smoke and narrowed her eyes. She was still chewing her gum. 'I was nineteen, and the first I heard was my momma talkin' 'bout the stranger that jes' come. I wanted to see him, 'cause I heard her tellin' my aunt Polly that the stranger had thick, black hair with a natural wave an' the kinda muscles that showed he warn't no stranger to hard work. Thas the way she say it, sound like a fairy tale.'

Mikey was too intrigued to say anything.

Cherry told him that Mr Daley, the local chemist, claimed he was the first to meet his daddy. He came parading into the shop, Mr Daley said, as bright as you could please, and asked where an honest man could find a day's labour. He bought cigarettes at the five and dime and strode around the main street for an hour until Mr Daley called him back and said there could be some work on his house and that there was always call for a man with good hands, if that was what he was. By the time the stranger found board through Mr Daley's wife the news was on the lips of every unmarried woman in town. Mrs Daley was quick to tell her sewing circle that the stranger had paid for his accommodation from a big roll of notes, biggest that she had ever seen. She reckoned he was a thieving, shiftless, good for nothing tramp. He'd probably slept in the street before he stole somebody's money. Mrs Daley said it was sinful the way wives craned their necks that first Sunday, trying to catch a smile.

'You know where yo' daddy come from?' Cherry asked.

Mikey shook his head. His eyes went back to the photo. Cherry turned it over.

It was an old photograph, and it had obviously been bent and folded

95

several times. The woman in it was full-length, standing next to a large wooden building. The light blue dress she wore had puffed, dotted sleeves that stopped above her elbow. Mikey counted seven dark buttons down the short skirt, trying to understand the picture's meaning. The woman's hand was on her hip. Her long blonde curls fell invitingly over her left shoulder. She wore a wide brimmed hat, twisted to one side. She was laughing into the camera, and pulling her skirt way up past her right thigh. Her bare leg filled the page, vaudeville style. She was the prettiest woman Mikey had ever seen.

'She a movie star?' He was sure that she must be. Normal people were not that pretty. Not even Cherry Smithson, who was looking down at him with grim satisfaction and a red bow in her dark hair.

'Naw. She ain't no movie star.' Cherry looked annoyed. 'Her name was Allison. She fucked anyone who ever asked fo' it.'

Mikey's mouth dropped open. He had only ever heard such bad words when Abe Talbot, the local drunk, roared his way through the town centre. Abe made ladies cover their ears before he started in cussing. Maybe Cherry was a bad lady. He shut his mouth. Maybe she was a monster. A monster like the Mummy. Maybe she wasn't Cherry Smithson at all.

'She was a slut and a tramp and when we was fourteen she use to go round the back of the school an' play with the boys' things until they was happy and her hands were dripping with their nasty stuff. When she was sixteen she'd go parking with Chester Bates an' be sittin' in the front of his automobile, bouncin' up an' down on him, with all the boys cheering her on, like a slut, an' my boyfriend, why, he couldn't stop askin' me why I don't put out like Allison. Why, she'd fucked every man in town befo' yo' daddy got here an' we never could believe he'd go set up house with such a little tramp.'

Mikey stood up and backed away from her. He couldn't understand what she was saying to him. He only knew that these were the worst words anybody could use. He couldn't comprehend why a grown-up, especially a lady, would want to speak like this. She was plainly crazy, or even a monster, but he couldn't sass her. His daddy would be mad if he was rude to a lady.

'Miss Smithson, could you please take me back to my daddy?'

Cherry Smithson laughed. The sound was nearly as frightening as the words coming out of her mouth. She dipped back into the drawer and took out a pencil. She wrote something across the photograph and pushed it into Mikey's hand.

'You be sure to keep this picture of yo' Momma, y'hear?'

Agatha smiled at the little boy. She clenched her fists. 'That must have been a hard thing to hear,' she said.

Mikey wrinkled his brow and shrugged.

'I dunno,' he said. He was silent for a while.

Agatha rubbed his back. 'You want to stop talking?' she asked.

'No,' he said.

Cherry made him find his own way back to the foyer. By the time he got there, breathless and near tears, clutching the picture in one sweat-soaked hand, his father was looking for him. The lump in Mikey's throat was so bad that he could only thrust the picture towards him, hoping that it would explain everything.

His father looked down at the picture and the word written there. Cherry had scrawled 'SLUT' across Allison Ezekiel's face. He couldn't remember the expression on his father's face, it was too long ago to remember, but he knew how he had felt about it. He'd been terrified.

His father had told him that his mother died while she was in hospital having him. But it wasn't true. After Cherry Smithson gave him the picture and his father stood in the foyer, ripping it to shreds and stamping on its remains, it seemed that everyone had a story to tell. Somehow Cherry Smithson's evil had opened a flood-gate of old tales about Allison Ezekiel, especially after Cherry passed it around that Mikey's pa had his child up in ignorance, not even recognising his own momma.

Mikey heard them at school, on the road, at the soda shop. He grew tired of hearing about his mother's sexual exploits. How she worked her way through every man who wasn't a God fearing Christian, and even some of them, too. How she disgraced the schoolteacher when she got caught in his wife's bed. The time Allison Ezekiel mooned the local Church Women's group when they tried to take her to the bosom of the Lord.

They said the only thing she didn't do was give some to the niggers, and even then, no-one was sure. How it was a shame that a good, God fearing woman such as Miss Charity Ezekiel should have such a daughter to bring up by herself, her husband dead and gone, no man to take a firm hand. How when his daddy stepped into town and worked hard and long, everyone was vying for that wife spot and the town was in an uproar when he chose the local whore. They said that his daddy was bewitched. They closed the church doors to him when he stepped out with Allison. They said he wanted to save her from herself. Even Miss Ezekiel had warned him, gone up to his house and damned her own daughter, saying she was no good. And coming down the hill she was heard to mutter that it was God's way, and thank the Lord that gal was out of her house.

Mikey learnt the birds and the bees fast, but not in the usual way that kids do, in whispers behind school-boy hands. Everyone hoped his momma would calm down after she gave birth. When the labour came on her, unmarried and swollen, she'd gone to the hospital to have Mikey, and they'd only let her in because his daddy shouted at the doctor. She was very calm, they said, standing there, waters already broken, curving her spine every time another contraction rippled through her. When his father left her side for a change of shirt, and to gaze at his new-born son, Allison had gotten right up off the bed, as calm as anything, and walked out never to be seen again. It was typical, they said. What could you expect of a girl like that but to cut and run?

His daddy was silent for the rest of the night. Mikey sat in the back yard looking up at the stars trying to think about the Mummy. It was better than thinking about the woman in the picture. His daddy had told him his momma was very pretty and very nice. He waited for his father to tell him more of the same, to come into the yard and put an arm around his shoulders. His father had not come, but his smoking became heavier. A year later he was dead. Miss Ezekiel said that they found him stiff and cold, Mikey curled up beside him. They found one paper, asking that Mikey be given for safe-keeping to Miss Ezekiel, who came to the house and informed the little boy that they were leaving town for Edene.

Dying, he thought, wasn't like in the movies. In the movies the person got to say their last words in a clear whisper and they got to say everything they wanted to, and you knew they were dead when the big music came in. His father had taken his time. When his daddy couldn't get out of bed, he assured his son that everything would be fine. It was just a summer cold and he had to be strong, now, and help his pa. Mikey went to the grocery store every week. They ran up an account, but it was fine with the owner. Everyone knew his father was good folks, and every man had his hard times. As days passed, Mikey sat on the edge of the bed and begged his father to let him get the doctor. There were no friends to support his plea. His father didn't have friends. He'd worked hard. He'd never trusted anyone in the town except Allison Ezekiel.

Mikey sat in the big chair by the bed and fell asleep in it to the rhythm of his father's coughs. He fought sleep for as long as he could, listening to the sick man rave and mutter. Near the end, there were no more stories. His father's eyes rolled into shiny whites. No more stories: just names, bits of conversation that made no sense, insane litanies of doom and fear that slipped down his chin along with a thin, unceasing froth. Mikey wiped his chin and listened. His father's lungs were two bags of slime. He could hear it moving a mile an hour, sluggish and thick. And when his father finally fell silent, he watched his chest rise, counting until the next breath came, one-two-three, hoping that he wouldn't get to ten. If he got to ten without the next breath, his father would be dead. He counted and hoped that his father was right, that everything was alright, that it was just a summer cold.

Agatha fought down tears as Mikey sucked the ice she gave him.

15

Mikey is a head case it's like pulling teeth like I'm getting little white crumbs from his pen even though I've been writing and asking insisting freaking out dang there was a time when all I had to do was look expectant and the ass kissers would be like *how high can we jump for you Mr Pellar sir* and now I can't even get one white boy to tell me what I need to know I'm like *humour me talk to me like I'm a two year old tell me what she looked like* YOU ABANDONED ME LOVE DON'T LIVE HERE ANYMORE always hated that song and finally

she was a tall woman she was slender and curvy she had a beautiful body and she tied her hair up on her head she was bi-racial a beautiful woman but she had the strangest deformity on her face exactly half of her face was covered with a birth mark but it wasn't a port wine stain it was the same colour as her skin it was more about textural differences than colour differences it was like someone traced a pattern on her face it was appealing and certainly it didn't stop the men from wanting her do you remember Luke Brown who wanted her no I don't remember any godamned Luke Brown who the hell was that

he says Zoe found a photo of him at fourteen his adopted momma gave it to her and she came down on his ass *never knew you were so big why didn't you tell me* she put the photo in his face and he says part of him was shocked and repulsed not that he forgot how fat he was no the Academy Award for Forgetting in a Supporting Role goes to Tony Pellar just that he refused to know or to think about who he used to be

Zoe said his adopted daddy told her that when he first came to them fresh with a Southern voice as broad as the world they made him do sit ups hundreds of them they made him eat salads and they checked the bed for candy and invoiced him for his allowance to make sure he didn't spend it on food he had to show a receipt for every comic book every ball game every record he said he shrugged when he was reminded and his wife was just standing there saying *that's why you do it don't you see that you store them that pile of paper you always bring home those receipts for gas and chips and Coke* and he realised that very night he had written himself a receipt for the tips of the day and until now he never made the connection and Zoe's on his back about what else did he leave out how could he have this life experience and not tell her dang why women got to know every time you ever farted or sneezed I can't imagine Mikey not fat he says he's still big but it's mostly muscle *not bad for forthy three huh Tony so it would be good to see you buddy we could have lunch*

I never had a daddy God knows who he was all I know is his last name and that is such strange shit I mean check it suppose you're going about your business and empty your balls one night and oops there it is start of a kid but you never know about it and the woman or women never tell you but there are these kids walking around with maybe your nose or your mouth or the essence of you inside them and then what I want to know is since I'm such a slut what if one day I meet some young thing very fine and I screw her or him because there is something so incredible so familiar so great about their eyes or their spirit and it's my kid but I never know it's my godamn child because the woman never told me see what I'm saying I don't know and the kid don't know and what if I never find out or suppose you screw your father I mean does something happen in your karma hey that rhymes does something happen in the universe because of that incestuous moment even if you don't know even if it's not your fault or do you really know deep down somewhere in your Y chromosome that actually this flesh underneath you or on top of you is OF you I mean do you know somewhere in your subconscious somehow and do you feel permanent guilt forever more they say incest is best but I'm not so crazy down here that I don't think that's sick I suppose I have an Oedipal complex in reverse I'm scared I'm going to end up in the sack with my father some day and I'm telling you I wish I'd killed my you know I wish I'd killed my momma death is a common denominator in my life so many people have died it depresses the fuck out of me Mikey wrote and told me about the water hole and I haven't thought about that in ages like everything else I suppose and he reminded me how we called slingshots niggershooters and he's saying *do you remember how Agatha told me not to say nigger I didn't understand at the time but I heard how important it was to her in her voice so I stopped I knew what name calling meant even though I didn't understand can never get the racism* he told me that when he was in the water hole he would pretend he had friends I guess I figured that out I remember me on top of the tree hey that rhymes but first I thought he was crazy swimming around talking to himself

now tell me do you believe that the majority of the world is evil or what and do you believe people are born evil because that little kid that used to plague me and Mikey Timothy yeah that was the sonofabitch's name well he was a trip but do you suppose he was born cruel I wonder what it feels like to drown ha Mikey knows I wonder how I will die there are so many ways to choose from there's old age rotting down here with the rats calling out the masses to feast or there's the third rail or injection or poison how about a gun or will Chaz stab me or the MTA could find us and take us to a shelter and some crazy could get it into his head to off me but of course I think it will be Agatha who does the deed in the end ha ha

you know I'm sitting here chewing half an apple Chaz got for me Topside thinking of all the people I turned the charm on I got the scoop from Teddy Pendergrass pre wheelchair and Lionel Richie in the good old days before he was kicking ladies' asses and Bill Cosby there was a moralist even Aretha that girl sang for me man and Africa Bambaata and the exclusive yeah Michael Jackson pre op they were all talking to me and my girls and boys we were the Undergrounders before I got here our mag was a cult rag like you've never seen

Chaz doesn't believe me she laughed when I told her Cosby had a runny nose and Michael used to have a fine Afrocentric one but it's not bad for a university drop out huh I wonder if Mikey ever read our magazine I know Mr Ronnie would have been proud of me and Chaz was like *yo baby if you was kickin it with the stars how come I never heard of you* I patted her ass *probably because you weren't born yet Miss Twenty Three Year Old But Every Man Underneath Can See You're Sixteen Max And That's Why They Want A Piece* she was giggling and I held her for a while it seems like just the other day when we were laughing and now she isn't around so much but the bite mark on her cheek is nearly gone and that's something

Mikey said *now that you're writing a book Tony well Agatha can really rest in peace do you have a publisher I'm sure it's a great book I never said anything to anybody about Agatha isn't that wild I just wanted to lose myself in the new life forget about the old one I never did forget but I didn't tell I feel guilty but I'm glad someone kept the promise I guess it must have been worse for you*

I don't know what he's talking about what the hell is he talking about shit shit shit what is he talking about but if I tell him I forgot the man will know I'm crazy and ask questions what is he talking about

I never did keep my promises doesn't everyone know that I made Marcus so many promises that I would clean up get my act together love him like he should be loved I think Marcus started to hate himself because of me that I'm sorry for but I never told him you know he was a good confident kid and his eye never bothered him actually I think it made him feel special he was such a well adjusted kid and when he finally came out it was with total ease he surrounded himself with good friends and even his momma was cool about it after she cried that Never Gonna Have Grandkids Cry but they all hated me in the end they begged him to leave me I think if he hadn't met up with my poison he could have had a good life but I stripped him materially first brought in hardly any dinero stripped him mentally then emotionally OK yeah I could see the layers of his positivity peeling away because he changed and I saw it but I didn't know what to do perhaps it was because he felt he couldn't really move me or affect me because he would do things to try and piss me off and I was impassive even though inside I was bleeding and I think it all destroyed him slowly but he kept trying he kept thinking he could love me into loving him the way he needed even though I never kept promises you know there was no one for me to come out to and all the rest of the brothers would say I was lucky yeah that's me sitting on the sexual fence and LUCKY with it

103

I'm walking thinking and there she is oh my God there she is Agatha the bitch OH SHIT she's under the beams in the tunnel near the mural holding her hands up to the light and I can't take my eyes away what does she have in her hands God what is it looks like a piece of the door that I used to lie my head on why is she knocking on it rap rap rap rappity rap she's breathing and changing oh my God it's Mikey look at the sores on his face my God you still have that sweet lopsided smile brother no no he's gone and it's her again now it's the Mikey thing what's he saying *come play with me have a swim Tony* dear God he's spewing water *come play with me I want you to tell me a story* OK I'm coming I want to play I want to be a kid again even with the terror and the South I miss you Mikey I'm coming

where

where's he gone

GODAMNIT he was there where's he GONE

16

Tony's torn shirt lay in her lap. Agatha turned the fabric, her needle darting in and out. The boy was only twelve, but he was soaring into the heavens; she wished that she could march right out and buy him something new. Not any cheap things either.

She stitched and counted down. She'd calculated how many stitches would finish the ball of black thread. The swift movement of numbers in her head would have comforted her if she'd paid attention to them, but she didn't. It was like breathing. *How many leaves on that tree, Agatha? How many shakes gonna make all them leaves fall off Agatha? How many peas in the bowl? Guess how much pieces of dirt in the yard, Agatha.* If she'd thought back, she could have remembered hundreds of questions like the ones her school friends had asked her in the yard. She didn't. She tried to live now. With Tony, adolescence biting at his heels and his groin. Last week Bea Brown had taken it upon herself to say that it was a shame and disgrace, you have this boy coming on three years, his people never done nothing to help you, but she'd stopped her. She knew folks who had it worse.

She pretended that Tony was her son. It was a gentle realisation. She'd let the knowledge of wanting him bounce quietly off her consciousness and then spin away. If she went further into the feeling she would have to face her loneliness, and how much she wanted a child. How sorely she wanted touch, and tenderness and closeness. And even worse, how she'd decided that it was never going to come to her. Fighting the well of feelings would give them a name, so instead, she floated above the depth of them, loving Tony.

The changes in him were amazing. He was still a quiet, thoughtful boy, still hidden between the growing piles of paper in his bedroom, but he no longer walked around the house as if it were paved with broken glass. He joked with her and worked obediently in Miss Ezekiel's yard, earning his keep. He was top of his year at school, only sometimes she had to pull him back to his work when he was bored.

Every spare moment saw him in a corner, scrawling. She marvelled at his concentration. His creativity seemed to come in spasms, long interludes when he stopped writing, screwed up his face and got lost in his imagination. Then, as if something spoke in his ear he wrote again, furiously, flinging each covered page beside him. More than once she passed his room long after bed time and poked her head in when she saw the thin light under the door. The sorrys emptied from his mouth as he shoved papers under the sheet and promised to close his eyes. She recognised the passion: she'd seen it in her more talented students. A hunger. An urgency for self-expression. She felt foolish when he and Mikey sat on the porch, leafing through paper together. Foolish because she was jealous. Tony showed Mikey his writing. She'd seen Mikey lying on his tummy in the sunshine, reading luxuriously.

Tony was a hard boy to know. As soon as he gave up one layer of himself, he created another, more impenetrable than the last. It pained her that after so long, he still refused to talk about the past. She asked him questions that he answered with stubborn monosyllables.

'You remember your momma?'

'Yessum.'

'You ever know your daddy?'

'No ma'am.'

'Have you got brothers and sisters?'

He ducked his head. 'No, ma'am.'

'You can tell me anything you want…'

'Yessum.'

She saw him pluck up his courage. Held her breath.

'Agatha, you sendin' me away?'

'No, Tony. No.'

She didn't tell him there was no place for him to go. He didn't seem interested in the past, as long as he was not returned there. When she mentioned Eleanor he looked uneasy. So she reached for him, not knowing that she colluded in his game of denial. He twisted out of her arms. Like most boys of his age, he didn't want to be held. Except for Mikey, who hugged her every morning before school, when Miss Ezekiel wasn't looking. She wished she'd been able to hold Tony as a baby. She wished she'd been there for both their births.

'Miss Agatha?'

She looked up and through the front door. Bea's nephew, Luke, stood on the porch, twisting his cap. When he hung around Bea's house on a Sunday, she saw Bea looking at her with that you'd sho' make-a-good-in-law sparkle in her eyes. It amused and irritated her. She bit down a smile. Stood up and smoothed the front of her skirt. Watched him look at her hair.

'Hey, Luke. What brings you here?'

Luke twisted the cap some more. He was almost too skinny, but his eyes were big, like a cat's, and the dark pupils seemed to fill them night and day.

'Well I jes' thought I'd pass by an' ask you if you need some help 'round the yard. I was down with Aunt Bea an' she said y'know, what with the boy bein' young maybe he ain't ready to be doin' the heavy chores.'

She put her hand on her hip. Luke Brown was a good looking man. But she didn't want him working on her roof. And she couldn't stand the lies.

'Luke, you know there's no heavy work to be doing 'round here. I sold off the land when I came.' She put her head on one side. 'Why don't you tell me why you really come 'round?'

Luke swallowed. Lowered his eyes. She permitted herself a feeling of triumph. All the women wanted Luke. He had a fiery, confident way about him that made them play with their hair and imagine his hands on them in the evenings. Right now he looked as if someone had pushed that fire into his belly and told it to sit obediently.

'Well, now you say it...'

'Or maybe you haven't come why I think you've come. Maybe you've come to tell me how you've been taking my boys up in the woods to see all those men beat each other's brains out.'

'Boxin' a fine sport fo' a man. Ain't nuthin wrong with-' Luke stopped, confused. 'How you know I-'

107

Agatha smiled thinly. Such games. For what? 'What goes on in this town that I don't know, Luke? My grandaddy has folks everywhere who tell me what goes on to affect me and anybody I love.'

Luke frowned. 'I see that you done make up yo' min' bout who I is. If you think I'm a man without no character you jes' said so. I'm sho' sorry to trouble you.'

She looked at his retreating back and was surprised at her own disappointment. The fire had come back into his whole body, just as sharply as her impatience had taken her. Something about it impressed her. Maybe she'd been unfair. The truth was that she'd laughed when she heard about the boxing matches. Boys would be boys and she supposed boxing matches were part of it.

She went back to the shirt. She counted stitches and thought about all the men who'd stood on Pappy's porch. A woman needed a good man, and she had plenty to choose from. They came around less the longer she stayed in Edene, and that wasn't the way it should be. A woman her age should have been married by now. Thirty one this year. That was no young girl. She supposed the men who smiled with her as she passed around town thought she'd got high faluting ideas since she went off to college.

She put the shirt away and decided to take a stroll down to see Susie. They'd become friends last year, after people started gossiping about Susie's first pregnancy. She'd seen the young girl in town and stopped to say hello, surrounded by folks cutting their eyes past them. Susie was Mrs Susie Dixon now, and nearly off her head, what with having to nurse Red Rooster. That was a man who didn't waste time. Rooster had Susie in front of Reverend Wilson quicker than anything after the fight even though he'd had to be helped down the aisle by his best man. His steps were a broken waltz. Agatha watched dark circles snap in Susie's face as she said her I do's. She had her baby six months later, a little boy she called Daniel and Rooster had her expecting again, the boy not even a year old.

That was where a blood promise got you. Pappy told her no-one should ever ask a body to make a blood promise, neither should you make one to anyone else. Blood promises came out of fire, wild emotion, jealousy. They were gasped out in the middle of a fight, when a man had his hands around your heart, squeezing, or spoken very softly in your ear as the sheets exploded beneath you. People would murder over a blood promise, and Pappy should know. Especially if there was any clue that the promise would not be kept. Agatha forced a smile. Luke Brown was a good man. An honest man with Bea's morals. She thought that he was taller than her, and she liked that. But she didn't want to make him any blood promise. The light in his eye was too bright.

'Miss Ezekiel sayin' why I still spendin' time with you.' Mikey leaned his head against the tree stump and sucked in the Sunday afternoon. He waited for Tony to say something. Tony continued to pare at the branch in his hand, yellow-brown chips littering the earth in front of him.

'You hear me?' Mikey said. He wanted Tony to say that he didn't care what that darn miserable woman said.

'Yeah, I hear you,' said Tony. Splinters flew up into his face and stuck. People thought he was Mikey's errand boy when they ran down Edene's main street. He knew Mikey didn't notice.

Mikey grimaced. 'What you say 'bout it?'

'I ain't said nothin',' said Tony. At school the others asked him what he was doing with that fat old white boy. He didn't answer because he didn't know what to say.

Mikey was puzzled. Tony had an opinion on everything. 'I mean, what you think 'bout what she say?'

Tony flung the branch, which was now a stump, into the bushes and picked up a second. 'You gonna stop, you gonna stop,' he said.

Mikey shrugged. 'I ain't said that. You my friend.'

'Well,' said Tony. He waited.

'Don't matter that you coloured,' offered Mikey. He didn't like it when Tony was silent. It made him wonder whether Tony would shut up one day and he'd never be able to get him talking again. 'Tony, kin I ask you somethin'?'

'Sho'.' Tony let the tense air out of his lungs.

Mikey rolled over on to his back. He lay there, wheezing. 'Why you stop speakin' alla that time?'

Tony concentrated on cutting a new branch. The blunt knife slipped in his hand and peeled a tendril of skin from his thumb. He sucked the flesh. Agatha had asked him that question. He didn't want to try and explain.

'I guess I was shy,' he lied.

'That was some shy!' said Mikey.

'Yup,' said Tony.

'But- but where you learn the Bible?'

'You wanna go over to Agatha's?' said Tony. Memories were crowding his head, and to his alarm, he could feel sly tears at the back of his throat.

'Sho.' Mikey struggled to his feet and surveyed his chest, which was rising and falling rapidly. 'I need to lose some a this here weight.'

Tony clapped his back. 'When you get older it all come off an' the girls be on you. C'mon!'

They turned west.

Agatha walked up the dirt tracked road, scuffing her feet into the sod. Days like this reminded her of childhood. Sunday afternoon, after church. She saw worshippers flocking back from Pappy's church - she still thought of it as Pappy's - and waved. If she went slowly, there would be time for Susie to get home, wash up and start supper. She sniffed at the parcel in her hand. The still-warm cornbread would help Susie's meal. She wondered how the woman's pregnancy was progressing. She was round as a pumpkin, all belly and legs.

'Agatha-Mae! Agatha-Mae!' She heard Bea Brown's voice and turned. The larger woman was puffing in her direction, her daughter Cissy on her heels. Agatha stopped and waited for them to catch up. Bea was resplendent in her Sunday finery, her crimson hat only slightly frayed at the edges. Agatha thought that it looked like a Christmas cake.

'Bea, you're aiming to kill yourself, running around in this hot afternoon.' Agatha spoke as the women drew alongside her.

Bea was too winded to reply but Cissy piped up, excitement running down her cheeks through perspiration. 'Miss Susie fixin' to have that baby right now, Miss Agatha. Early. Amy Green done gone up an' Mamma an' me come to see...'

110

'Cissy, stop talkin' and lemme rest on yo' shoulder.' Bea put a large hand on her daughter's arm and leaned in. Cissy rocked. 'Agatha, you run on befo' us. I hear that baby comin' right now. We be there soon.'

Agatha moved swiftly but it was still only a jog. The baby was early, but Amy was young and strong and what she lacked in experience she made up in courage. Her mother was a midwife before her and she knew what she was doing. Last year Mrs Allen's backways-set baby had come edging and squalling into the world just fine after two days of labour and it was all because Amy massaged Mrs Allen's forehead and thighs tirelessly until the end. As she took the corner at a clip, Agatha almost stopped in surprise.

Luke Brown's head was so close to the white man's that they may as well have been kissing. Agatha slowed to a walk. She'd seen this man before. She'd seen him hawk spit to reshape his fine red moustache, leaving bubbles of saliva to sit on the hair until they burst.

She nodded her head as she stepped to pass them. Luke Brown looked like someone had put guilty and afraid in a bowl and whipped them up into froth.

'Hey gal!' The white man scratched his cheek. 'Where you goin' in such a hurry?'

She stopped. Put on her good nigger voice. 'I's jus' goin' down in the Bottom to see Mrs Dixon, sah. She fixin' to have her baby.'

The white man grimaced. 'That little gal married an' swellin' fo' Rooster again? She a pretty little thing befo' she get knocked up.'

Agatha nodded. The way that he talked about Susie put her teeth on edge. He was the kind of man who spent his youth mounting cows, expecting to graduate to coloured women. Susie was the most elegant pregnant woman in Edene, and the set of this man's tongue, darting out of his mouth, soiled her. Susie's skin shone red-brown and her neck was polished. No wonder she had men fighting over her. Her legs had been known to stir a preacher man to eulogy.

The man smiled and Agatha tried to remember his name.

'You tell Susie I said howdy, an' I'm hopin' she look just as fine when that baby pop out.'

'Yessuh.' She moved past the men, cutting her eyes at Luke. She

111

didn't like to think of him looking at this man, much less talking intimately with him. Luke looked down.

'Tell her Clancy Miller say so, hear, gal?' said the white man.

Agatha bit her lip. Yes, she knew of Clancy Miller. How could she have forgotten? He was that no-good sonofabitch who had gone away for a year after he was implicated in the rape of five Negro girls. Not one of them older than eight. Not a titty between them. She shot another look at Luke, and this time it was savage. She thought that Luke better have no choice talking to this man. Why, Clancy Miller better have called him off the path and commanded Luke to come up in his face.

'Yessuh,' she said. She began to run again, lifting her skirts. She decided that she didn't care that the men were watching her bare legs.

Red Rooster's house was very quiet. Agatha was surprised at the bare porch. Community births were just that: people milling back and forth, round about each other, chugging beer, Coca-Cola, lemonade, waiting, gossiping, swapping stories of their own labour pains. Sometimes pregnant women came too. They were the quietest, listening to the yells, being pinched and teased and hearing predictions of their time. Mrs Allen's husband - he of the backways-born child - had sprung a temper during his wife's labour and told everyone to come offa his stoop and mind their business, how he wasn't fixing for every woman in Acheson to count the hairs between his woman's legs. The women laughed and ignored him. It was tradition for the men to fret and yell and sometimes even cry.

Agatha stepped into the tiny house. It smelled like shit and liquor. The shack had two rooms, like Bea's: the front room and the kitchen, where the couple slept with Daniel. The kitchen was the warmest place, with the wood stove. Amy would take Susie in there.

'Amy?' she called.

'Pappy little gran'chile.'

The sun had run away from the shack, so she hadn't seen Red Rooster. He sat in an old cane-bottomed chair in the corner of the room. He was naked to the waist, his legs covered with a sheet that had lost its virginity aeons ago. He was not drunk, but she could see that this was not for want of trying. Dust crouched on his arms. Daniel lay asleep on his chest. Agatha steadied herself. It wasn't as if she hadn't seen a living dead man before. They were all over town, some drinking, some gambling. All lost.

'Afternoon Rooster. I heard your wife's time has come so I ran down to see if she needed any help. Bea Brown and Cissy are right behind me and the others are coming on too.'

She was conscious of his size. She wondered how the chair bore him. His once toned belly hinted at fat. Two missing teeth made him look old. She felt a jerk of compassion. Behind him, she heard low, harsh breathing. Susie's voice sounded like a cracked hymn.

'Pappy lil' gran chile...' Rooster said again.

'Rooster, how can you be sitting drunk with that baby when your wife is getting ready to give you another one?'

Rooster widened his eyes. 'How you come in my house sassin' me? Gal, you crazy?' The words were angry, but his voice was blurred and impotent. Daniel moved restlessly. Agatha fought down an urge to snatch the boy.

'Everybody knows I speak my mind, Rooster. But I never meant to make you mad.' She called out. 'Susie? Amy, you in there with her?'

'Agatha-Mae?' It was Amy's voice. The low moaning kept on. It seemed to fill the house, twisting its way under the smell. There was something magical about Susie's labour-call.

'Amy in there,' said Rooster, as if he hadn't heard her voice. His movements were languid, like grass in the wind. He chuckled. 'Amy in there with my wife an' my chile gettin' ready to born.' He thumped his chest. Daniel stirred again. 'My chile!' He looked down at the baby on his lap. To Agatha's horror, he pinched the boy, twisting the flesh on his plump arm. Daniel woke up with a wail.

She moved forward. 'Gimme that boy!'

'You know she go see him at the jail?' he said.

'You're hurting him! Give me-'

'Naw. Wait.' His eyes were pleading. 'You know she go see him at the jailhouse, like I'm a fool? An' when she come back I wanta lay my hands on her so bad, Agatha. But I never. Shoulda beat this chile right outta her belly.'

'Rooster, you've got to give me that baby.' Daniel was sniffling and twisting. Behind them Susie's voice filled with blood and effort. Agatha wanted to stand there and let it run over her.

Rooster shook his head. He moved Daniel roughly, holding him in the crook of his arm. Daniel hiccuped and smiled weakly.

'Naw. She a whore.' He stopped, tasting the word. 'Now then, I said it. Swore I never would say it. My wife a whore.' He looked surprised. 'An' now you see all sake of her, I gave up my good house, livin' right here like a dog. Pappy lil' gran-chile. Susie a whore. I'm lovin' a whore. But then ain't no miracle she don' want me none.' He struck the side of his leg and the sheet quivered. 'Bomber make sure of that.'

The sound of Susie's crying filled the room, as if the whimpers had burst into flame. Daniel began to wail again.

'Bear down, gal!' It was Amy, calling over the sound. 'Bear down jes' some mo' an' we bringin' this chile!'

Agatha leaned forward, and grabbed Daniel. To her surprise, Rooster did nothing. He closed his eyes as his wife's voice filled the space.

Agatha kissed the little boy's head and pushed at the kitchen door. Her fingers came away dirty. She was just in time to see Susie's baby crown between her legs. She couldn't take her eyes away. Dimly, she felt a touch on her shoulder as the child slithered out of Susie's body, as Amy lifted it carefully and laid it on Susie's chest. She could see the tears down Susie's face, and wondered if her own cheeks were wet. The pressure on her shoulder intensified. Angrily, she turned to face it.

'Rooster, come see this child and stop pounding on me!'

Luke Brown stood in front of her, beaming. 'What she have? Boy?' he asked.

'Is a girl! Big baby girl!' called Susie.

Agatha was surprised at the strength in her voice. Despite herself, she let Luke hug her. She felt a flame at the base of her spine as their hips met. He was at least four inches taller than her.

17

what else did Mikey say *do you remember the nuts do you still like pecans actually did you ever put one of those juicy pecans to your lips or were you too afraid of Miss Ezekiel did you think she would tell you you were a thief* yeah Mikey man I remember I stole the nuts in handfuls and stuffed them in my shirt I figured that she had so many I could have some too

haven't thought about the South for a long time haven't been back since I came to New York because I think I'm really a New York boy as soon as I got back here I ate deep and long of the Big Apple and all it had to offer it's not like it wasn't racist here too but here they eroticise you and I've had no problem peddling my flesh everybody remembers that about me

Mikey reminded me how he saved me and how I saved him from under the house if he says so YES I can picture the houses now I can see them both Agatha's and Mizz Ezekiel's that bitch grandmother of his and big chunky couches and ice cream machines because you know Ben & Jerry have nothing on Southern home made ice cream and what I remember is Mikey eating more of that ice cream than I've ever seen one person eat then or since

I know what I do remember I remember that I've been afraid all my life how many of us black folk been living with fear like it's food I don't think I knew what it was like to calm down until I came back North I lived with the image of the hanged in my mind we all did I never saw anyone lynched but I lived with the possibility of that all the time I heard all the stories of that boy I can't remember his name they said he whistled at a white woman and they found him and drowned him they weighted him down in the nearest river and another time some woman yelled rape and there had been six brothers in the vicinity and you know the whole town went looking for them and they found four the other two ran and ran and the WHOLE I say the entire town men women and children hung those four high then split them open like they were worse than dogs and they tied their bodies to the backs of cars and dragged them back and forth

you know what lies at the heart of a Southern town excrement that's what layers of shit on top of hatred and fear and rage that's one thing that Mikey couldn't understand he could only look at me shaking in my shoes with wide grey eyes and try to see what I saw

I was afraid of monsters under the bed and I was afraid of the man who sold groceries and the big white school principal and Miss Ezekiel and I was angry all the time but I remember the beauty of it as well occasional cotton fields because we weren't a cotton state like Mississippi big fat bundles of it golden brown tobacco and fine church sisters rocking in their seats there was one lady who used to dance at the gin joint she would rub a rag between her thighs now she was no church sister and give it to the men to kiss afterwards her breasts overflowing from her purple dress how have I come to fear Agatha yeah though I walk through the valley of the shadow of death I shall fear no evil thy rod and thy staff shall comfort me

when I got here I thought my friendship with Mikey would continue I mean hey till death do us part right he's agreeing says his real daddy told him *there is a year in the life of every boy child that binds the rest of their days it's called your fate year if two boys go through their fate year together someone is guaranteed to come out hurting they are bound together in some indefinable way until the day they die* it's bullshit of course but hey it's a theory everybody got a theory I suppose even stupid ass Peter Tennyson dropping his ass dead in front of his kid deserves a theory Mikey's going on telling me how he had to bathe him wash him feed him stubborn bastard wouldn't call a doctor then it's back to this fate year crap *there's too much going on in your fate year you see you aren't in control* who the hell is *you struggle but the fates darn away at your life picking the wool for the yarn spinning the wool and finally crunch down come the old scissors*

116

and you've had it but when you share your fate year with another boy the fates work the wool of your lives in tandem they cross and re-cross their spinning patterns and there is a bigger chance of disaster the wool gets tangled the cutting has to come sooner than you expected I suppose we shared a fate year you and I imagine my daddy getting philosophical on me Greek mythology for God's sake yeah yeah I learnt about the Three Fates too TELL ME WHAT YOU MEAN THERE HAVE BEEN SO MANY YEARS

if you have eyes to see you can spot us down here rolling and making love in the darkness spitting and shitting and whining like it's Christmas wonder what Maya Angelou would think of THAT there is another couple down here and the guy likes to sleep on top of the girl he says it's to protect her from the rats I don't know it looks to me sometimes like she's dead because I've never seen her move and he shifts her body and her arms adjusts her like she's a bed and there are times when it is so cold down here my lips stick to our three cracked cups and all I can do to fend off the shivers is to sing Chaz covers me with her winter oil and we burn and look at each other in the candlelight she is still so kind I sleep most of the time I try not to daydream or hurt her I hear the trains plotting and scheming saying that there won't be another year that I stay alive you know the trains scare Chaz but they don't scare me baby because the bitch has all my terror sown up

there's one guy down here they call him the Creeping Man and they say he's been down here forever he never sleeps and he never stops walking because his honey killed herself slipping onto the third rail and he's determined that it's not going to happen to him he never sleeps the Creeping Man and the whites of his eyes have disappeared into black so no one on the trains can see him they say he's an evil man that he's all eaten up with rage guilt bitter bitterness sour in the mouth they say that once he found a young boy the boy was boiling water and the Creeping Man held his hands in the water until the boy passed out he did it for laughs then he held the boy by the wrists and he pulled the skin off like an overboiled chicken and left him there moaning and fluttering after he took a bone for a souvenir

it's happened again and this time I knew I was doing it I woke up and Chaz was going through my shit and it looked like she was just about to take one of my letters and read it so I grabbed her leg and I pulled her down and I bust her in the face I nearly lost myself in the feel of her flesh there was something sweet in this experience a losing of self like there was no morality like NO ONE could tell me what to do like violence was pure and I was indulging in the best of that purity and I'm hitting her thinking *there is no one to stop me I can do ANYTHING I like* but I only hit her three times because she begged me not to and I told her that I wouldn't do it again and then I lay down and thought about this new secret and I guess I am an animal now and I understand why the Creeping Man did it no big psychological theory the Creeping Man is mad and he could yeah you know he boiled that boy's hands because he could do it and the whole town killed those boys because they could do it

18

Tony sucked his pencil. This was the part of writing he liked most: when the pencil flew across the paper as if it had nothing to do with him, when voices seemed to drop into his brain like visitors. He imagined the words clambering down out of his head, swimming along his arm and shoving themselves onto the page.

His current hero was trapped in a big house, surrounded by ghosts threatening to fly through the cracks in the walls. His hero had found a big mysterious vat of green gloop that turned out to be Ghost Poison and he was using it to fill in the cracks as fast as he could. The problem was that the vengeful ghosts had swallowed three of his fingers and the pain was making it hard to work. Behind him, Princess Winona cried and yelled how she could see the ha'ants coming. Princess Winona was the prettiest girl in the Universe. She looked remarkably like Winona Welty, who sat two rows behind him at school. His hero stopped pasting the wall long enough to kiss her. Princess Winona smiled at him and stopped crying.

'Hsssst!'

Tony looked up. The woman had appeared so quickly and unexpectedly that he'd not heard her.

'Good evenin', ma'am,' he said.

'Miss Agatha inside?' she asked.

Tony looked at the heavy bag on her back. He could tell from the way she looked around her that she was one of the strangers. He knew what to do. He beckoned the woman onto the porch and outed the lamp. She looked at him gratefully.

He hurried towards the kitchen. Agatha stood at the table, making biscuits. He loved her biscuits. They were as big as a man's hand.

'A lady here to see you,' he said.

Agatha blinked. She began to wipe flour off her hands. 'Bring her inside, quick.'

Tony pattered back to the porch and looked at the woman. 'She say come,' he said. He realised that his heart was beating too fast.

He left the women in the kitchen. Agatha didn't like him up in her face when strangers arrived. They slipped into the house at night, without warning. He often awoke to an unknown face at breakfast, or someone darting past him to get to the tin bath. They never stayed longer than four days, and he'd forgotten most of their faces. He did remember three women, all with babies under the age of one, like triplets, with faces the colour of broken hearts. The babies were peculiarly silent. And an old man and his wife, who patted him on the head and scalded him with their eyes.

The strangers never went outside. They buried themselves in Agatha's bedroom as if they were rabbits. They spoke in whispers and their breaths stank with fear. Agatha walked around the world as if she was trying not to break her toes. She burned herself on Miss Ezekiel's iron and washed the clothes too hard. When the strangers left, he could tell that they were gone from Edene forever. Like ghosts.

Agatha put a plate of food in front of the woman in her bedroom and shut the door. It had been a long time since someone had come to her for help. The woman's name was Corinne. Her eyes were thin disks, set far on each side of her nose. She wanted to go to Chicago. The night riders had come out to her place three days ago. They had her brother's unconscious body with them. It was a familiar story, and Agatha didn't flinch as she listened. No, what bothered her were the woman's next words, casual in their finality.

'Everybody in trouble know they kin come heah.'

Everybody know. Who knew? The wrong people? She avoided the college students giving out their leaflets in town. She never listened to the radio news when she had visitors. She was more nigger than anyone else when she spoke to white folks, burning as she ducked and scraped. Except for Miss Ezekiel. Miss Ezekiel was one of the reasons she'd started to think about going back to New York.

She feared for Tony. She wondered if he talked to Mikey about these people who walked through the house. In the beginning, she told him they were friends, but the lie was stupid now that he was older. She saw how nervous Corinne's arrival made him. She could get a job in New York. Even teaching high school, although she was sure her old college would have her back. She could push Jamie to the side, if it meant that Tony was safe.

'Tony, come in here and eat something.' She heard him groan.

'Don't make those noises at me! You hear what I said?'

'Yes, ma'am.' His face was a half-sulk. He wasn't used to her snapping.

'What are you doing?' she asked.

'Nothin'.' He only groaned when she interrupted his writing, and he thought she knew that.

'Boy, don't tell me nothing. I asked you a question.' He looked puzzled.

'Jes' writin'.'

'Looks to me like that writing is more important than your school-work.' She followed him into the kitchen and began to slop food on a plate, banging the spoon. Tony put his papers on the table. 'You have done your schoolwork?'

'Yes, ma'am.' He glanced longingly at the paper.

Agatha made her mouth small and round when the strangers came. She sat down and pushed the plate towards him. He began to eat, sulkily. She stared at him, as if she had never seen him before.

'Tony, let me read some of what you're writing.'

He looked at her, alarmed, then shook his head.

Agatha folded her arms. 'You know I used to be a teacher. At college. I've got more sense than any of those teachers you have at high school.'

Tony kept spooning the food.

'I'll tell you if they're good. I'm sure they're good. I'd never let anybody else see them,' said Agatha. She was aware that she was wheedling.

Tony opened his mouth. 'But you teach math,' he said.

'That doesn't matter. I'm still a good reader.'

121

Tony thought of the strangers and the way they ducked and sidled through the house and the woman who had just come. He never got to know anything. Agatha treated him like a baby. The woman would be in the house however long, and Agatha would just keep quiet, like he was blind.

'I make you a deal,' he said, hesitantly.

Agatha leaned back in her chair. She nodded for him to continue.

'You tell me- tell me where them people in here goin' to, why they comin' here-' He saw her eyebrows dip down her forehead, but he kept on, '-an' I give you a story to read.'

Agatha stood up and walked away from the table. She leaned against the wall, thinking about it. Bea said she spoiled Tony, but perhaps it was time that he knew. She'd rehearsed an explanation many times inside herself. Maybe she'd been foolish not to tell him.

She sat down again. 'Deal,' she said. 'I never told you because I reckoned the less you know... but you're growing up and maybe I should say something...' She trailed off. 'You're not supposed to tell anybody about this, Tony. I could get into some mess if people knew. And I'm only telling you the things you need to know.' She paused, looking hard into his face. 'These folks in the house, they're leaving the South altogether, and I help them to get away.'

'Why they leavin'?'

Agatha sighed. She had a curious expression on her face, one that he didn't understand. 'You know how they killed those little girls at that church? Well, there are some Negro folks who are angry about that, who think that we're not being treated right, we aren't deserving of the way that white people are treating us. Some people have been marching on the streets all over the country, trying to show them that we're not going to stand for this foolishness, we're human too.'

'But the little girls wasn't marchin'.' Tony said.

'They don't care.' Agatha bit her lip. She reached for his hands and held onto his fingers tightly. 'The people who come through here, they're running up North 'cause their children are marching and the white people 'round here are finding out about it and they don't like it.'

'What they do to 'em?'

122

'They're giving them a hard time, threatening them, telling them to tell their children to come on home.' She swallowed. 'Sometimes they hurt them bad. Like the girls.'

Tony turned the information around in his head.

'Why you like Mikey?' he said.

Agatha looked surprised. 'What do you mean?'

Tony tried to find the words. 'White folks be treatin' niggas-'

Agatha put a finger to her lips. 'Don't say that. Say Negroes.'

Tony tested the word on his tongue. 'Negroes,' he said carefully, 'If white people be treatin' us bad, why you like Mikey? You always huggin' on him.'

Agatha shook her head. 'Mikey is just a little boy. He's trying not to think like these peckerwoods. And he's got his own problems. But you've got to understand that he can't be coming up here like he does. He can't know all of this. He might say it to the wrong person.'

'Yes ma'am.'

'Promise?'

'Hope to die...'

'Spit in yo' eye!' they chorused together.

She grinned. 'So you gonna give up your story?'

He smiled back. 'Yes, ma'am.' He pushed the papers across the table to her.

That night, reading his story, she laughed to herself. Tony's prose erupted from the page into her bed. She drank in the clarity, the richness, the raw sophistication of the words. She wept over the bits that moved her. Dreamed him a great author. Woke up with stanzas stuck to her thigh.

In high school, the merciless drip-drip of teasing from Mikey's schoolmates had settled into the kind of disgusted silence only reserved for the lowest of the low. As breasts grew and sinews stretched into the beginnings of maturity he was cast down among the other pariahs, those too worthless for the time it took to pull a prank. The ninth grader who smelled as if something had died in his mouth. The smattering of girls deemed too unattractive, or too shy to join in with any clique. Even Timothy Crampton did no more than growl at him in the hallways. Mikey regarded Timothy's cessation of bullying with alarm: if even Timothy would not deign to torture him, all his school days loomed large with rejection.

He wondered whether they would have eventually overlooked his size if early adolescence had not gifted him with a prize crop of acne, weeping whiteheads that he tried not to pop in the mirror. Whatever the case, life had been the same dreary exchange of nothingness as his fellow students looked through him and towards their futures. At least it was quiet, until today, in the library.

The library was the one place he could avoid all the popular people; they preferred to hang out in town, swapping sodas and jokes, twisting to jukebox sounds. The library was his sanctuary, until Timothy walked in, sliding on Betty Harvey's heels. Mikey froze, but Timothy was too busy looking down the front of Betty's ruffled blouse to notice him. The ends of her straight blonde hair touched the roundness that filled out the back of her skirt. To Mikey's horror, she settled into the seat in front of him. He ducked down, hidden by the partition between the two desks.

'So you not gonna date me?' Timothy said. His green eyes were sullen. Betty tossed her hair. Mikey could hear the thud of her books on the table-top.

'I never said that,' she said.

'So what I got to do to get with you?' Timothy leaned towards the girl, but she swatted him.

'You gettin' too fresh for me, Timothy Crampton.'

'I'll do anything to go with you, Betty. Jes' tell me an' I do it. Anything you want. My daddy got a new automobile! You should see it! We could go for a drive. I could take it out...'

Mikey writhed at the sound of Timothy's voice. The second-biggest boy in the school, begging. He wished he was anywhere else. He wished stupid-ass Timothy Crampton hadn't been kept back two grades.

'You think I want to be seen with some common thief, boy?' Betty's voice was scornful. 'You crazy!'

'So... what you want me to do?'

'Nothing,' she said.

Defeated, the big boy turned to leave, but Betty Harvey wasn't done.

'My, how you give up easy! Huh!' The seat squeaked as she turned.

Mikey knew Betty, and he could imagine the expression on her face. That saccharine I-just-done-shame-you-but-if-you-try-harder-you-might-get-me-just-might flutter of her eyelashes.

Timothy reigned himself in. 'I ain't giving up.' He lowered his voice to a whisper. Mikey held his breath. 'What I gotta do to get you? You so pretty...'

She tossed her hair again. 'My momma said that I'm not to date any boy who ain't *sophisticated*. You gotta be *original*, boy. You gotta say something I never heard before.'

Thas two words he ain't never heard in his life, thought Mikey. He wondered whether Betty knew what they meant. He felt her rising and walking away from the bench. He let himself breathe. So, Timothy Crampton wanted to date Betty Harvey. He chuckled. It was exactly the wrong thing to do.

'Whatchoo laughin' at, fat boy? You laughin' at me?'

The older girls sat on the western side of the room, the boys on the east. Both sides were murmur-filled, three of the boys squabbling over some miscellaneous male prize, the girls giggling and nudging each other as Tony returned to his seat. He hated reciting. It didn't help that the girlish giggles reached fever pitch each time he trudged to the front; this new excitement seemed to have coincided with his thirteenth birthday. Agatha took him to the movies and then for an ice cream soda. He insisted Mikey come along, ignoring the discomfort in Agatha's face each time Mikey gave her a soda-sticky kiss. Mikey sat with them in the coloured restaurant, but fifteen minutes hadn't passed before Agatha signalled it was time to leave. At home, she cut them both great hunks of home-made cake and seemed happier to return Mikey's affection.

Tony turned thirteen on Saturday. By Monday, it seemed, a great missive was passed down from On High and each of his footsteps were greeted with a chorus of female hilarity. Four days ago Bethanne Collins had darted over to him in the yard, a gaggle of girls behind her pretending not to watch, and told him they'd voted him cutest boy in the school. Tony didn't know what to say. The words sounded good, but her tone spoke of feminine secrets, and he couldn't decide whether the whole thing was a big joke.

Even Agatha seemed in on the gag: the baby-kisses between them had stopped. He didn't mind. He felt older than Mikey. His friend's neediness seemed childish. Agatha kept up a stream of jokes with their neighbours, usually in his ear-shot.

'Look at this boy, how he's growing tall and good looking.'

'You right, Agatha. Careful now, he be bringin' home a girl soon enough.'

'That's fine, Bea, as long as he treats them right.'

'Well now, girl, you raise him too good fo' him to be raisin' hell.'

The idea of a girlfriend sounded strangely pleasing to Tony. He hated reciting on an average day, but on the days that Winona Welty was present, which was most of the time, his stomach did flip-flops. Her big, dark eyes and her smooth hair pleased him.

He pretended to drop a pencil and leaned down to retrieve it, glancing over his shoulder. He caught Winona looking at him. She smiled, hiding her mouth behind her hand, and nudged Bethanne Collins. They both giggled. Tony stuck his tongue out, picked up the pencil and turned back to the front. Seconds later, he couldn't resist another glance. There she was again, ducking her head and laughing, always laughing. She flashed her eyes at him and looked away, like she didn't care.

He tried not to feel too hurt. After all, if he was the cutest boy, there was no doubt in his mind that Winona was the cutest girl. The fact seemed meaningful. She walked older than the rest, except for Bethanne, whose curves kept pace. Each time Winona was called on to recite, there was a sway to her hips, in her jeans two years too tight, that made all the boys whistle under their breath. Crow whistled too loud the last time, and they had to endure a twenty-minute lecture on the wages of lust from their indignant teacher. Tony wondered whether he could muster the courage it took to request a seat on the girls' side. Before the great Thirteenth Year had come upon him, such a move would have been cried down as sissy. But he thought that now they were older, the boys might look upon him with reluctant admiration. The cutest boy in the class in a sea of girls. He shrugged to himself.

After school, he watched Winona run down the hill away from him then trudged the three miles to Miss Ezekiel's house, where he'd promised Agatha he would prune the garden. He found Mikey in the middle of a panic attack. He listened to the tale, sighing inwardly and putting thoughts of Winona aside. He couldn't think of anything else Mikey could have done in the circumstances, but the whole thing was stupid. Timothy had been all ready to beat him down, he'd had a fistful of Mikey's shirt and the skin underneath, ready to frog-march him out behind the school. They both knew what would have happened then. But he still couldn't believe what Mikey had promised. He chopped at Miss Ezekiel's neat bushes, thinking.

'You tell Timothy Crampton that you gonna get Betty Harvey fo' him?'

Mikey's face was utterly miserable. 'Yeah.'

Tony threw down a branch. 'Now I know you stupid. You ever *talk* to Betty Harvey?'

'Naw.' Mikey sighed.

'An' he believe you?'

'I dunno. Maybe he can't think of nothin' else. I said I got a secret way to do it, somethin' that gotta work. He askin' me how come he ain't never seen me with no girl. I said I don' do it for me, but I done it fo' some other boys, an' I ain't tellin' who, 'cause they gon' be mad.'

Tony was still astonished. 'An' he *believe* you?'

Mikey frowned. He thought he'd two-stepped his way out of the fray with style. At least Tony could give him that. He'd been so convincing that he'd half believed he did have the power to transfix Betty Harvey. 'At least I stop him killin' me!'

'Yeah, right *now*. But he gonna really kill you when he find out you can't do shit!'

'You don' have to be getting on like you crazy!'

Tony shut up. He hated that word. It made him feel like hitting

127

out, and fighting Mikey wasn't going to help any. Enmity between them would just mean that there would be no one except Miss Ezekiel to mourn at Mikey's funeral after Timothy killed him.

If Mikey had been coloured, he could have asked Crow and them boys to help him beat on Timothy so he never said boo to anybody - least of all Mikey - again. He wasn't popular, but he knew that the other boys respected him. He tried not to think about all the things he could have done for Mikey if he was coloured. Or if he, Tony was white. Both impossible. Sure, he'd heard that two little girls had desegregated the big high school up in Bates County. He heard they were having a hard time, and their families were proud of them. But that kind of thing would take time to filter down to Edene. And he was sure he wouldn't be respected in a white school. Or cute.

He thumped Mikey on the back. 'There's only one thing we kin do. Maybe you kin get Betty fo' that fool an' I kin get Winona to stop laughin' at me.' The Winona story was an old one.

'What?' Mikey looked hopeful.

'I'm gonna write some letters,' said Tony. 'Letters that make those gals cry.'

19

well you know it finally happened the MTA found our ass while I was wandering off in the tunnels because I do that more now Mikey's letters are making me stronger and Chaz was Topside or somewhere else God knows where she hangs out sometimes and I came back and the door of the room was boarded across I stood there swearing and sweating so afraid that was my HOME those MOTHERFUCKERS so I'm reading Mikey's letter in a different place we are deeper now yes Chaz and me we came further into these tunnels and we left Simon and Garfunkel behind it was Chaz who found another room it's not as big as before it's like a big cupboard and we've got to do without the ice box and the mattresses they probably took all that away and now it's really pitch black and I can see that the black has layers and shades and a devil in each one

Chaz has been crying for her stuff and she's just started again and I can't stop her crying she looks like she's sprung a leak EYES WITHOUT A FACE GOT NO HUMAN RACE EYES WITHOUT A FACE FACE FACE I'm hugging her and trying to keep her warm but she misses her oils and she's saying *Jesus Christ what am I gonna do when you freak Tony what am I gonna do when you freak ain't no place to run in this two by four ain't no oil to put on your head you gonna kill me Jesus Christ you'll kill me* I am afraid for her so we're making a deal we should have thought of it before she has some money yeah she saved fifty dollars I never knew and she's going Topside to buy some rope and every time she is here she'll tie me up it won't be so bad

we've been here three nights now and it stinks even worse than

129

usual the ropes fuck me up there are weals on my hands and legs and Chaz is crying again she's feeling guilty and I'm going nuts *woman what the hell you want why don't you leave then what the fuck is the alternative what I say what is the alternative why you here with me anyway why don't you fuck off I can't help you none can't help myself LEAVE*

it seems like she hasn't stopped crying since we got here so we're making another deal she'll stay away more and give the rope burns a chance to heal then bring me a meal to make up for the absence hey that rhymes but when she sleeps here I'll be tied like a hog just in case everything becomes a nightmare

I never told you about my Momma I told you about Carla Benedict and her daughter and Mr Ronnie so let me tell you about my momma while blood trickles trickles trickles down my hands where I pull at the ropes that Chaz built we use them all the time because I am OUT of control I am roaring my brain hurts it pounds with the memories I never forgot my Momma she was a gem the real one not Carla not Agatha what a wonderful selection I've had in life I remember her face I can see it like it was yesterday

I thought she was beautiful until the world told me she wasn't she was light skinned she had brown chalk hair and her face and her hair were nearly the same colour her skin was always peeling and she'd rub margarine into her cheeks but no dice ladies and gentlemen flecks of her skin still fell marked her journey as she walked and her lips were mismatched the top one belonged on another woman it hung over the bottom one which was a thin line her forehead bulged and her eyes were small like black nickels her eyebrows were one inch lines hanging out in her face like they were waiting to apologise she had nearly no eyelashes and her hair was seaweed on a rock but I was her child and I thought my momma was beautiful

I was a boy not a man so I didn't see how twisted her body was didn't see she had no butt and a big pouched belly hanging off as a punishment for pregnancy so all I remember is her holding me and the roughness of her elbows and knees and she'd tell me how pretty I was *momma loves you honey* I know that momma I know that

never underestimate the potential destructiveness of a person who wishes they had style and beauty you know they will sell their soul to the devil as quick as it takes to say gimme a firm butt an attitude strut big brown eyes strong thighs mouth to weep for dick to speak for breasts or waist or lies that tantalise

the woman had me do everything except vogue in front of her *baby walk up there in that suit I got you let momma see how fine you is ain't nobody prettier than my baby* in the bath there was only one little bit of soap but she'd wash me three and four times *momma gotta make sure her baby stays pretty so when we go in that church nobody can say I don't take care of you* she watched me and I felt her gaze like a laser her eyes never left me she sat with me in the bed and stroked my face and arms she told me I had soft skin *Momma's baby gonna rule the world with his pretty face* she whispered it like a prayer *you gonna be famous you gonna get rich with your pretty self*

I never knew she was ugly until I was old enough to hear the gossips in the church *where that mule face Tonia Morgan get that pretty chile from* there was one lady in there always asking my momma whether I really came out of her belly or she just found me on the street and my mother would shrug her shoulders and when we went home I asked her *momma you never found me on no street did you and* she's stripping me down putting me in more clothes you know she spent all the little money she had on clothes for me and I'm trying to get her attention *momma you didn't find me did you* she's saying *stand still we gonna make sure this shirt look good on you sure you come from momma honey don't you worry* but another day I'd be in the room and she'd look down at me and say *Lord Lord you so beautiful where Momma get you from* and I'd ask her again *Momma you sure I'm yours* and that time she looked at me like she didn't see me it got to the point where I couldn't ask her anymore because when I asked she'd cry or she'd throw up in the bathroom I guess I got that shit from her oh aren't we drama queens darling

I have a theory yes I think I was hers but I think she couldn't believe that I came from her she just couldn't connect the dots I think my father was probably three ways fine because I sure don't look like her you wouldn't believe it seeing me down here but man I used to tear shit up there'd be times when Marcus be lifting me away from the mirror because I did like to look at myself mmm hmm and my baby he knew how to dress me for success it's true I was high maintenance

you know I went to see her ten years ago yeah my momma in the nut house I always knew where she was at and I got permission even though it took some time to prove who I was but I did it Marcus didn't know and she was the way I remembered her just much older that same naked misshapen face with no eyebrows and hardly any eyelashes the girl needed a makeover and I'm talking plastic surgery level and the white coats they let me sit a while beside her and she was talking but all she could say was that she was sure that my Momma was proud of me *such a handsome young man such a good looking God fearing young man who you say you is again* I'm holding her hand and saying *Momma you don't remember but I'm your son I'm Anthony* she looked at me *never had no kids* I'm like *Momma you don't remember me it's your son Anthony* I tried to think of something I could share with her that would make her remember but they were all bad memories and she's repeating herself *such a handsome young man* got all flirtatious and shit she's telling me *now young man you shoulda seen me when I was a young girl you woulda wanted the sweat on my brow* and she lifted her skirts just a little bit on her thighs God this sixty plus woman and all that made me think of was her in bars begging men to come home so I left and Marcus looked at me all night we went dancing and I could see my mother's face in the strobe lights that big lip stretching over that little lip and I was chuckling because dang if you don't laugh you've got to cry and Marcus smiled at me *what's so funny nothing* I said *oh nothing* Mikey's stopped writing again it's been a long fucking time and what shall I say to keep the bitch away

my Momma didn't like men but she had them just the same it's not like she did anything in front of me but on the nights the church sisters kept me I could hear the gossip *that girl gone to the bars again* and once a sister brought me home early she pushed the door and she's calling *Tonia where you at* I walked forward and Momma was in the kitchen and there's a man sitting at our table with a beer cracked in front of him and Momma's on the ground and she's stroking the end of his pants leg like she was afraid to touch his flesh the church sister came up behind me and we're waiting for Momma to say *hey* to look up to say anything but she didn't her fingers were fiddling shyly and the man was looking at the top of her head I could see my Momma's underwear she wasn't sitting good her dress was all hiked up and then she said something *tell me that you love me tell me that you love me tell me that you love me* and we stood there and I remember feeling itchy and she's talking like we weren't there so the church sister calls her name again but neither of them looked up so in a little while the church sister took me into the bedroom and we sat me on one side and she on the other listening to Momma's voice in the other room flat dead *tell me that you love me*

there have been people who loved me SOME people did I know they did there was one girl I made her pregnant five times and she had five abortions then my funny bone kicked in when she wouldn't leave me alone because this girl was going down to my man's work talking about how she KNOW I love her and I'm going to be with her and marry her and Marcus is like *get this woman off my case bad enough you sleeping with her she's threatening my job* so I took to sending her Mother's Day cards ha one a day then I ordered her flowers lilacs orchids white rosebuds and the card said CONGRATULATIONS ON YOUR BABIES until she gave up on me I'll never forget the sister I saw her on the road months later and she looked at me like I was the Devil himself then she sent her brother around to beat me up and guess what he was a brother in the spirit so I fucked him too no-one is ever going to get one over on me in this world because you're the weak or you're the strong and ONLY THE STRONG SURVIVE

Chaz came home ha ha if you want to call it that and I said *listen baby no more sex there is an official sex ban because you know babies we don't want to be making babies down here where the sun don't shine but the shit sure does* and she looked at me so sorrowful *you don't love me anymore baby* I just said *we got to be real* and she looked at me all melting and I said *fuck it* and we screwed for hours I made her scream but there was pleasure this time and I prayed that the MTA don't find our asses and give us sandwiches I never said I was perfect right never said so

20

Night snatched its shift as the boys walked up the hill, shoving each other playfully. They'd spent the afternoon composing letters to Winona and Betty. Tony decided on the words, and Mikey copied them down. Tony decided Mikey wrote like a slim person: his script was slanting and graceful. They decided to show the letters to Agatha. She was a girl and she would know what girls liked.

Tony pushed open the gate that led onto Agatha's property and looked up at the dark house. He stopped suddenly. Mikey bumped into him. Tony stepped back and trod heavily on his friend's foot. Mikey yelped and began to hop around on one leg, half-laughing. Tony stared at the house. Agatha only kept it dark when the strangers were there, and he'd forgotten about Corinne.

'What?' Mikey asked. He rubbed his foot.

Tony searched for an excuse. None occurred. 'Mikey- I- I think you should go on home.'

Mikey looked surprised.

'You said we was gonna find out what Agatha think of the plan.'

'Yeah, but I forget she say she goin' over to see Missus Dixon after she leave Mizz Ezekiel.'

Mikey shrugged. 'Don' matter none. Mizz Ezekiel gone to her prayer meetin'. She not comin' back till late. I won't stay...' He looked into Tony's face. 'You a lie!'

Tony swallowed. 'What- what you mean?'

Mikey began to laugh.

'You lyin'! I seen Luke Brown lookin' at her like he hungry. He in there, I reckon.'

Tony managed to look suitably embarrassed. 'You know Agatha

don' like people up in her business.'

Mikey turned away. 'Thas OK. I don' want her mad. She gon' marry him?'

Tony kept grinning. 'I dunno. I see you tomorrow.'

He watched Mikey leave, sighing with relief. He took the porch steps two at a time. The house looked deserted. Maybe Agatha *was* out. He hoped Corinne would stay in her room. He opened the screen door and yelled.

'Agatha, ma'am?'

'Boy, you hush !' The whisper was glacial.

Agatha moved forward and blocked the door with her body. The light from the match in her hand streaked violet smudges across her face. Tony opened his mouth and then shut it with a snap. He felt a plunge of alarm. Agatha grabbed his arm and pulled him towards her.

'Agatha, what-' Her fingers dug into his arm. What could have made her so angry? Had she seen Mikey?

'Don't you say a word!' Agatha stopped. She raised her head towards the darkness, listening.

'Tony?' It was Mikey's voice.

Disbelieving, he turned towards his friend. Mikey stood at the bottom of the steps.

'Hey, Agatha. I never know you was here. Tony, you never gimme the y'know the letter.'

Horrified, Tony looked down at the letters in his hand. He looked up at Agatha. Her face was thunderous.

'I'm sorry. I tried to get him to go on home-'

'Shut up!' Agatha snapped. She glared at Mikey. He stared back, shocked.

'Mikey, go on home now.'

'I'm sorry, I-'

She interrupted. 'Come another time, is all I'm saying.' She tried to smile, but it didn't reach her eyes. 'Go on now, Tony will see you tomorrow.'

As quickly as he could, Tony darted forward and passed the note for Timothy to Mikey. Mikey trotted into the yard and through the gate, glancing behind him at the black house. Tony squirmed. Agatha had hold of him again and her nails were still cutting into him.

'I never mean- I jes' ask him to come- I forgot-'

'Hush!' she snapped. The match had long gone out and he could barely see her. 'Come on in here!' Then, as if she had changed her mind: 'Why you bringing white folks in here like we're living in paradise? You stupid? I told you last night about all this! Boy, I could take my hand to you!'

Tony hung his head. She'd never hit him.

'Is jes' Mikey. We was comin' to tell you-'

'You're forgetting that you and Miss Ezekiel kin not the same! I told you! Shit! I need you to help me. Shut your mouth, and don't tell *anybody* what you see in here.' She glared at him again. 'Especially not Mikey!'

He nodded.

'I mean it, Tony! You're old enough to know!' She pulled him into the front room.

Tony heard Corinne before he saw her. She sat on the couch, her head down. She was weeping. Candlelight glinted off her wet face. Underneath her sobs he heard something else that made his stomach curdle. It sounded as if someone was swilling syrup in their throat.

Tony put a hand over his mouth and stared harder.

Beside Corinne, a dark figure twisted on the couch. It seemed to be at an impossible angle, hanging off from the waist down. Its back was arched. Tony could not guess an age or see a face. He moved closer.

The liquid rattle went on as the thing writhed.

'What- what- who-?' Tony stuttered.

'*Never mind.*' Agatha turned him to face her. 'Listen to me. I need you to run as fast as you can. Go over to Miss Amy's house. If any other folks are in there, don't let them see that you're scared. Tell Amy I need her. Tell her now, and bring her things quiet. You hear? She'll know what you mean. Tell her I said now, and quiet.'

Tony turned to go, but a voice stopped him. It was the thing's voice, and it came from the depths of the couch. It was an unspeakable, tearing sound, as if its teeth had become razor blades. He looked back. The thing was trying to get off the couch. It was looking straight at him.

Corinne cried out.

'Don' sen' the chile nowheres,' the thing said. Tony stared. It was a man, a huge man. The man's head touched the ceiling. He coughed, shaking Corinne with the effort. Her sobs had become hysterical.

'*Tony, get going!*' Agatha hissed.

He turned again, but the man's voice was relentless. 'NO!' Gore sprayed from his lips and splattered onto the floor. Tony realised that he was gargling on blood. He wanted to obey Agatha, but he couldn't move.

'Kill me,' the man said. He collapsed backwards and lay trembling, an awful convulsion of limbs. The words came from his lips in streams. '*Kill me kill me kill me too late kill me kill me.*'

'TONY-!' Agatha stopped.

The man was silent. Tony watched Agatha's shoulders sag. Corinne sank forward, her forehead disappearing into obscurity. Tony began to shake. The man couldn't be dead. Strangers didn't do that. They came and they left.

'Tony,' Agatha said. 'Go over to Rupert Brown next door. Tell him to come.' Her voice was soft again, like he was used to. 'Tell him I said now.' She lifted one hand to her face and he saw for the first time that her hands were blood-streaked, the hands she had touched him with. 'Tell him I said quiet.'

After Tony ran for Mr Brown, Agatha told him to go to bed. The boy obeyed, relieved to not have to stay in the front room. She told him to use a candle instead of turning on lights, and he undressed, still shaking. The bed was hot. He tossed, trying to get the dreadful rattle out of his mind.

He wondered whether dying people knew that they were dying, whether they really understood that in some seconds or moments they would not be there anymore. He listened to the sounds in the house, Agatha and Mr Brown muttering, the back door swinging open. What were they going to do with the dead man? Who did he belong to, and how had he got so hurt? What was Corinne going to do? He tried to distract himself by thinking about the letters. He remembered Mikey's: *Dear Betty, Your hair is gold like a king's ransom. Make me rich. I would like to take you some place and make you laugh. Signed, Timothy Crampton.* He liked his note for Winona the most, but now dating her seemed stupid and unimportant. *Dear Winona, Your skin smells like rain when it falls in the morning. Your eyes are as clear as poems. Let me whisper some to you. Signed, Tony Pellar.*

Agatha sat at the kitchen table, her face in her hands. Her eyes burned. They felt red, and strong coffee didn't help. It was nearly midnight. Rupert Brown had come across and taken the body away. She was surprised at his strength. He wrapped the dead man in old sheets and sacks and hoisted him over his shoulder. She didn't want to think about what Rupert would do with the remains. She knew she should be speaking to the girl, Corinne, who was in her bedroom. Or to Tony, in his bedroom. But she couldn't move. The evening had been a travesty from the beginning.

The man had arrived at her door shuddering, as if he had a fall cold, or malaria, but when she got his coat off, she realised it was much more serious. His chest was soaked with blood. It poured over her hands and the front of her dress, as if the coat had held it in. She wanted to vomit. She wondered how he'd managed to reach her. He mumbled Corinne's name as she tried to treat his wounds.

She knelt at his side, trying to think. She could get Amy. She was the only one with medical knowledge. But the stranger would not let her go. He clung to her skirts when she tried to move, liquid pumping from his chest. He rambled from subject to subject, talking about his daddy, who had been a doctor upstate, how he believed, believed, believed. She wouldn't be able to get to Amy in time. Her dress, hands, neck, were all soaked in his blood, and it would be too late if she stopped to wash. Her head ached.

It was only then that she recognised him. He was one of the CORE students. She'd seen him before, outside the Woolworth's in town, talking. She'd pretended disinterest when he thrust a paper into her hand, with its black letters at the top: The Congress of Racial Equality. She let it flutter from her fingers. They were brave kids, coming to

Acheson County, and especially Edene, Klan country, so small and insignificant. She watched him out of the corner of her eye as he laughingly berated another woman who refused his message. These students didn't understand. Edene was small, and if people were going to hear their message, they were going to hear it at night, not in broad daylight, in the middle of town, in a sea of tight white faces.

She'd never seen anyone die. Pappy passed on peacefully, in his bed, with neighbours around him. She hadn't been able to come home in time. She wished that she'd been there. Thinking of Pappy and their relationship made her think of Tony. He would be scared, and she had to tell him what was going on. But Corinne must come first. She stood up and walked towards her bedroom.

She found the woman crouched on the floor. She seemed half asleep.

'How do you know him?' Agatha asked.

Corinne looked up defiantly.

'I asked you a question. You gonna answer me?'

'His name Paul Brady. He one of the CORE folks,' Corinne said. Then, as if it were an after thought: 'He my man.'

Agatha sat down on the bed. 'You never told me you were mixed up with those people when you came! Shit! You told me you wanted to get to Chicago!'

'I do!' Corinne snapped. 'Paul get some fool idea say he an' some other chaps gonna burn down the courthouse tonight. I never want none of it, so I come here. Figure I could find a way to leave.'

'So nothing happened to your brother,' said Agatha. She took Corinne's silence as confirmation. 'Why did Paul come here?'

Corinne sucked her teeth. 'Cause I tole him if he change his mind, he could meet me here befo' I leave.' She looked old. 'I guess somethin' go wrong.'

'I don't understand. Those people could have helped you. Why did you come to me? Shit, if those peckerwoods find out they're gonna think-'

Corinne interrupted her. 'Think what? That you fightin'? Trouble is, you not fightin' enough, you playin' saviour. You either in this or you ain't. Can't have it two ways.'

139

Agatha stared at her, fear tight in her stomach. 'Get out of my house,' she said.

Tony put the letter aside. His arms itched. Agatha was going to chew him out for bringing Mikey. She might even send him away. When he arrived four years ago, he came home each day expecting to see his bags packed and his papers in a neat pile. Only time had quieted his fear. He couldn't understand why Agatha kept him. They weren't related, and she wasn't some rich woman, working as she did for Miss Ezekiel. He tried to help as much as he could, following behind her, learning how to tend the garden, keeping himself away if she was busy, trying to learn Miss Ezekiel's foibles and chores as fast as possible. Agatha never complained. Everyone else had a stream of complaints. Cousin Eleanor was the worst. She hadn't stopped muttering for the whole time he stayed there, the edges of her mouth turned down, shouting in his face when he refused to talk. Her husband was sour and quick with his hands. When he hit Tony it was the back of his hand across the mouth, as if he would beat the words out. They were so nice to everyone else, but when they were alone at home, Eleanor's husband said the word all the time: *Crazy boy, you not talking again this morning, crazy boy? Crazy, just like your Ma.*

So he worked hard at being a good boy for Agatha, wary each time she moved unexpectedly, suspicious of her hugs and pats. He couldn't understand why anyone would be so good, for no reward. Eventually he pushed the fear to the back of his mind, but it visited him whenever the strangers came. They scared Agatha, so he was afraid too. One day he would do something wrong and that would be the last straw. And now the time had come.

He jumped at the tap on the door.

'Tony? You sleeping?'

Agatha walked into the room, her skirt full around her body. Tony saw that the violet marks on her face and her dress were streaks of dried blood. Her chest was drenched with it. She followed his eyes.

'I want to talk to you...' She lifted the fabric away from her chest. 'Look at me. Wait. I'm going to clean myself. Don't sleep yet.'

He snuggled under the sheets, wondering how she could think of sleep. She came back clean, except for a single smudge on her upper arm. He tried not to look at it. She sat down on the bed. Her neck and her back were stiff.

'Looks like I can't treat you like you a man,' she said.

He twisted the sheet, ashamed.

'Tony. A man died here tonight. Somebody beat him until he was nearly dead. Can you understand? You think everything is fine, with your little white friend and your writing. Boy, you know people out there dying? You can't live in your head anymore, Tony. That's a luxury. This here's the South. Negroes been dying here for hundreds of years.' She leaned forward and grabbed his chin, forcing him to look at her. 'Boy, I'm not playing. What I'm doing here means I could be dead. You think these white folks are playing? You think my grandaddy yard and the little money I've got in the bank and my education mean anything? You understand that they could come in here right now and kill me and kill you and then go to church on Sunday and feel happy, like they'd done the Lord's work?'

Tony began to cry. He couldn't help it. He heard her words. But all he could think about was going back to New York. She was sending him back, that was for sure. He would run away first. He couldn't go back. The memories would crowd into his head. He would have to remember everything.

'Please, Agatha, I know you mad, but please don' sen' me away.'

'Boy, you never even told me what you're afraid of up there. You've never given me any reason *not* to send you.' She knew she was being unfair. There was nowhere to send him. But she had to put the fear of God in him. It could mean his life.

Tony's mouth worked. He wanted to tell her. But if he did, she would send him away for sure. She wouldn't want no crazy boy in her house. No boy with a crazy mother.

She let go of his chin. 'I have to think about this.'

He crept under the covers.

Mikey looked up into Coach David's face. He didn't like him, and that wasn't just because he was the Coach. The man held him in contempt. He hated giving Coach David the note every Monday. Miss Ezekiel wrote him a new one each Monday morning. They all instructed the Coach to excuse Michael Tennyson from gym, on account of His Condition. Mikey never knew what Condition she referred to. The Coach never asked. But each time he handed the man the paper his heart sank. Coach David did the same thing every time: he stared at the outstretched hand as if it contained some kind of very nasty bug, or a snake, waiting to uncoil from between Mikey's fingers. Then his eyes swept over Mikey, as if he'd realised that the bug in question was standing before him on two legs. He gestured to a seat on the far side of the courtyard, as he was doing now.

'Go sit down,' he said.

Mikey trudged towards the seat. Gym was inside this week, the other boys tossing a basketball around, yelling and elbowing. Coach David always made him stay to watch. He wondered why. Everybody else with a note was sent off to home room. But Coach David sat him on a small, hard chair to watch the boys sweat and cheer and curse. Occasionally, he saw the Coach staring at him from the excitement, as if he hated him. The chair seemed deliberately small, his backside overflowing on each side.

Timothy Crampton burst through the entrance to the court. He dragged a string bag, bulging with basketballs.

'I got 'em, Coach!' he yelled.

Mikey cringed. He'd given Timothy the love letter as soon as he got to school. The other boy was faintly derisive. He looked at the floor, trying to sink himself into its depths. He'd promised fast results, but maybe it wouldn't work. Then Timothy Crampton would take him back to the water hole and really drown him.

'Fat boy, you done good!' Timothy was passing him by, the basketballs streaming from their net like dented, orange aliens. He winked. 'She said yes. I owe you one.'

Open-mouthed, Mikey stared after him. He felt a heavy hand on his shoulder and turned. It was the Coach, smiling.

'Michael, I want to talk to you.'

This was it. Mikey waited for the lecture. He watched Timothy Crampton with his broad, athletic shoulders and his confident lope.

'I know you don't like sports.'

Mikey ducked his head, but the Coach was having none of that.

'Raise yo' head an' look at me, boy!'

Mikey looked up, hating the man.

'You gettin' your momma to send me these notes-'

'It not my momma, Coach, it's-'

'I don't give a good godamn if it's the Lord above, boy!' Coach David shook the latest note under his nose. 'You know how many of these things I got? Why, I could drown in them! That ain't dealin' with the problem, boy! You fat an' you unfit an' you lazy. But I know why. You just need a little confidence.' He puffed out his chest. 'You need somethin' to make you feel like a man. I'm gonna leave these boys to their ball game, an' we gonna do somethin' about it. We gonna make it so you go home an' tell your *momma* you *want* to be playin' sports!'

Mikey decided not to correct him.

21

woke up this morning and the world was bright because there was another letter and I could lose myself in the memories Mikey told me about the big fight and I could see Susie Derkins and Red Rooster and the Bomber I could see us kidding each other on the road I'm here in the cupboard and I can remember sunshine and the way it hits you in the mornings

I am as fine as I can be and I am punching through the dark as the memories take me over they are engulfing me and enthralling me I remember my strength I remember who I was and who I was going to be and I'm so cool even with the trains whining I'm feeling sunshine on my thighs I'm full of precious thoughts MEMORIES DON'T LEAVE LIKE PEOPLE DO THEY ALWAYS STAY WITH YOU mine didn't and it's like opening a jewellery box something special from a sweetheart as I think as I REMEMBER

the water hole and its cool depths good for us not for strangers the squirrels and the house where I sat and wrote stories and Bea Brown telling me I'm a fine young man these memories are coming in undulating hums like someone turning the sound up and down

but the bitch is here again and I can hear the whimpers starting in my throat she is angrier than ever and her screams are bouncing off the walls they are falling at my feet and in my lap her screams are splashes of orange phlegm and the whole of her face is crawling with scars intertwined with scars and she's screaming through blood *YOU WILL HEAR ME YOU WILL HEAR ME*

through the gloom I see him that little boy I found so long ago he is right in front of me and I'm crawling forward and touching him I'm passing my hand over his lips and feeling warm breath on my palm and the sunshine in my mind is burning me *he's alive* but even as the joy fills me I'm looking for the bitch *what is she up to I know this is a trick* and sure enough she is there bending over him too

I'm scrambling across the room and I can hear my voice in my ears like I've lost it gabbling *no no no please don't hurt him* she isn't following me she's leaning across the little boy and breathing and she's looking up at me and her voice is quiet but I can see the danger in her eyes and she's whispering *you think he has a momma Tony you think he has a momma* and she's lifting the sleeping child she's standing up she's over me with the boy above her head and her arms are locked straight she's going to throw him at me *NO*

the sunshine is gone Agatha is gone and my hands are over my head please give me a sign a clue I don't know what you want me to do Marcus baby come and get me help me fight with me he won't come because all that is left is the pain I showed him

when Marcus was angry he'd stomp around the house cursing about good for nothing PEOPLE who thought he was their SUGAR DADDY well he never had any problems he was such a brilliant young thing he's been working with that firm of his since he was twenty one they begged him to join I've seen Marcus up in the courtroom doing his thing and yes he is good he is good you know a couple of his cases have been in the news and he's on the TV being an articulate brother yeah he was cool about being a gay brother but wasn't like he was going to YELL about me the MAN he's been with half his life no and they paid for him to do his Master's and buy a condo the man got stocks and shares all over the place OK I never wanted to be a drain on him but he was so tight with the dollars and it wasn't like I didn't hold him at night yeah even that night he was asked to the Emmys because he did that little legal eagle deal with some Hollywood actress I'm not saying who and this articulate brother MY MAN took his best girlfriend because he couldn't be seen as a fag and his company knew he was gay because he went to enough meetings where they asked him to keep a lid on it and they were happy to have such a fine Negro then Black then African-American brother up in the place *as long as you don't bring the dick sucking blues up front into the spotlight* and every time I tried to show

145

him they were nothing more than racist homophobic bastards he'd tell me I just let the isms and phobias hold me down he said *life is what you make it sweetheart* I said *yeah life is fine for you lining their pockets with your brain cells* and his hands became occasional weapons I can hear him cursing at me I remember the time we fought and all I did was laugh until he smashed a vase over my head yes there were bruises I haven't told you about but it was my fault I laughed at him until he had no choice but to beat me

you know that I'm forty three years old and the first time I lived alone was here Underneath before Chaz came even when I went to college I had a roommate I dropped out and went home to Carla Benedict and there she was her and Mr Ronnie fat and complacent at each other's sides Ronnie still not dropping crumbs Carla still staring in his face like he's God's gift and he was coming off with *boy look how your mother struggle to give you a good education and all you are is a no good drop out* well I couldn't take that shit as if SHE up and gave me the scholarship and I would have punched Mr Ronnie in the face if I'd stayed so I left and I made a living fuck them I was ENOUGH then I hooked up with Marcus and he had dollars the boy did sure have the dough I told you about the pages when I wrote the same words over again and Marcus looked terrified and I sat on the living room floor my knees up tight and together and I'm saying *I can make you understand Marcus* and he comes to his knees and takes me in his arms you know that was the last time we made love and he didn't let me do anything he was blowing his sherry breath all over my body and I swear he touched every hair but I couldn't come for him

I'm crying again and there are too many tears I'm smashing my hands and feet against anything hard and I'm trying to understand I will understand as long as she doesn't hurt that little kid

got another letter and it looks like we're all fucked Mikey's wife is getting ready to do the divorce rap she says he won't talk and she's tired of trying to know him and getting only golden emptiness in return and he sent me a photo of him and his daughter WHAT A MAN WHAT A MAN WHAT A MIGHTY GOOD MAN SAY IT AGAIN the photo strips away the sodden picture of him in my mind because the boy grew good and I sit here touching his face it's not about sex godamnit NO it's not you should see him he has a blonde beard now and a skinny moustache he wears a jacket and jeans and his face is a moon it's round and good and his daughter is beautiful do you know that awkward I dunno what the fuck is happening to my body but it feels good anyway song well his daughter her name is Leigh well she got that song bad all up in her Daisy Dukes with her long brown legs and her short curly hair and God I looked and looked and there I found it baby his innocence his hopes his dreams all up in the kid's eyes

I'm so tired and all I can do is keep turning the pages and reading he says he and Zoe had the king of bust-ups he says Zoe was bawling and he nearly bawled too thank God his kid was out of the house she was gone to stay with Mrs Adopted Grandmother from Heaven and Mikey let Zoe read the letters he's been writing to me *I had to do it was the only way* and Zoe's saying *ohmigod your daddy died in front of you and now there's this man you haven't spoken to him for years and you hated yourself oh Mike* she calls him Mike he said he can't have anyone call him Mikey *reminds me of you and everything that happened you know what I'm saying* Jesus Christ my friend no I don't I'm seeing so much but I know there's more

pride is killing me softly because how can I ask Mikey for more I think that asking him to write to me is the first favour I ever asked of anybody what is wrong with me I am closed tight like a Chinese puzzle you get for Christmas you know the one that you fear opening because you'll never get it closed again and suppose I open the puzzle that is me and remember EVERYTHING what if I touch the puzzle and unwrap it from its bright green Christmas paper and mess around with it what if I start to open the wooden layers and find my soul screaming at me what happens then

my Momma cried all the time and sometimes there would be whole days when all she did was sit and stare at the wall rocking to and fro telling me the devil was struggling out of the wall she'd tell me that the devil was trying to get out and mark my face and she'd be damned if she was going to let him come through *those same fairies who was jealous of your pretty face they coming too* they told her that if she kept one eye on the devil he wouldn't be able to get through *you go on and get some bread for yourself out of the kitchen there* Momma got

147

some serious business watching the devil so he don't hurt you that was after she lost her job at the Bar Bee Q restaurant in Queens and the church brethren took up collection for her and the rest was from the men who didn't love her

I would sit and watch her rocking and beg her to let me see the fairies too I was just a little boy and I thought maybe I could beat them up or they could have the dimples back if they'd just leave her alone and I know this is bullshit I know that she was crazy seeing spirits and shit but then I wonder because I see Agatha as clear as day ladies and gentlemen be careful what you wish for because it might come true I begged my mother to let me into her world so I could help her I wanted to see those spirits and that devil and tell them to leave my mother be and now I do see them laughing out at me from Agatha's face I wanted to kill the spirits if I could have just understood what my mother was going through maybe I could have saved her from the WAR HUH GOOD GOD Y'ALL WHAT IS IT GOOD FOR ABSOLUTELY NOTHING SAY IT AGAIN

22

Mikey stared at Coach David. The man was red in the face, lolling on a low, ugly couch. It was only 11am, but the lipsticked girl standing between them wore an organdie evening frock. The dress had been made for a woman one size smaller. Seams strained, a garish shade of purple. The girl's dull blonde hair looped into her face.

'Michael meet Rosie,' said Coach.

Rosie raised her purple skirt. Mikey stared. Her pubic hair was black.

Tony sat on the floor of the classroom. The teacher was late, as usual. Around him boys and girls teased, flirted, threw things at each other. He may as well have been somewhere else. The noise seemed to move towards him and thud against an invisible wall. He felt a suggestion of its effect. Nothing else.

He'd woken up on Sunday morning to find Corinne gone. He stayed in his bedroom, afraid to look into Agatha's face. He tried to write. Nothing came. He was dry. Then Sunday was Monday and he stood over Agatha's bed, wrinkling his nose, trying to pluck up the courage to wake her. She saved him from the effort, one slender arm rising from the brilliant sheets to wave him away.

'Pass by Miss Ezekiel and tell her I'm sick,' she said.

He didn't remind her that trouble would follow. He reckoned she knew that. He looked at her. She was hardly visible among pillows and layers, half-asleep in a bed of whipped cream.

'Tony Pellar!'

He looked up. Winona stood in front of him, her hands on her hips. Somewhere in his overcast mind, he remembered her letter, sitting by his bed.

'What?' he said. His tongue filled his whole mouth, sliding against his teeth.

She sighed. Despite everything he felt something flutter in his chest. She was so lovely. Sitting below her, he watched the graceful curve of her body wrestle with womanhood and win, sloping upwards, legs bursting into hips, twisting and pinching at her waist, swelling into breast, carving her chin. She was matte black, her blouse like cherries, a bubblegum band in her newly-cut hair.

'You gonna make me say it again?' she said.

'What?' he said. He wondered whether he knew any other words.

'If you don't wanta take me to the movies thas all you gotta say.'

She turned, as if to leave, but her right heel stayed on the ground near his knee. He strugged to his feet and forced his tongue to the roof of his mouth.

'You wanta see a movie with me?' he asked.

Winona Welty smiled.

After she heard the front door slam behind Tony, Agatha dragged herself out of bed. *You haven't slept since Saturday,* she reminded herself. *Lying in bed, obsessing. You have to sleep sometime. Sleep or get yourself moving.* She stood on tiptoe in the front room and looked down at the couch. She'd scrubbed the bloodstains all Sunday, and with every motion of her hands she felt surer. She would take the boy and get out of Edene. She'd walk those city streets again, zig-zagging her way through the air that used to belong to Jamie. She'd look at the buildings he looked at. Anything to get away from the smell of Paul Brady's blood. She could still smell it on her, behind her ears, at her collar bones. Had she swallowed some? The smell reminded her of Miss Nancy, one of Bea Brown's friends. Miss Nancy had worked as a factory drudge for twenty five years, tearing out turkey innards. No soap would ever make Miss Nancy smell anything but raw.

She walked into the kitchen and poured herself a glass of lemonade. She gulped it down, holding the glass with both hands, like a child. It was raining, water pattering down onto her windowsill. She pulled the window shut and poured another glass. She drank greedily. She felt as if she could drink a river.

She picked up the heavy jug and carried it into her bedroom, one arm crossed over her stomach. In bed, she hugged the jug as if it were a lover. She looked at the mosquito netting. Millions of stitches. She put a hand up to her face. Everything was hundreds of pieces twined into other pieces.

She dipped her fingers into the jug, raised her arm, and let drips of lemonade trickle onto the netting. The liquid sat there in pale yellow bubbles. She scooped and trickled again. The lemonade looked like urine against the white. She sniffed.

'Agatha? You in there?'

Shocked, she saw that she sat in a puddle of liquid.

'Agatha?'

She closed her eyes. It was Luke Brown's voice.

The prostitute hunched her back and moved her hips up and down. Mikey tried to enter her for the third time. It was no good. His fading erection lay against his thigh.

Rosie put her hand down and took hold of him. Her fingers felt soft, like rolls of sweet dough. Her grip was as erotic as a wet fish. She pulled, making irritated noises in her throat. She thumped his shoulder.

'Boy, get offa me! You heavy!'

He rolled over to the other side of the bed, ashamed. Under his cheek the sheets smelled like old tin and bad marriage.

Rosie lit a cigarette. Blew spent smoke into the air. In profile, her face was not unkind. He realised that she was younger than he thought. No more than seventeen, he guessed.

'You gonna tell me why yo' daddy bring you if you ain't ready for a fuck?' she asked.

He blushed and tried not to look at her vagina. Under the hair it was neat and slightly wet, one lip bigger than the other.

'He not my daddy.' The thought made him feel even more ashamed.

'They usually is.' She waved the cigarette. 'What? You don' like girls?'

Mikey pulled his pants up to his waist. 'I'm sorry...' he said. He glanced between her legs again. He didn't know that was what girls looked like down there.

'The way you lookin' at my pussy I'm thinkin' you like girls.'

He tried to explain. 'I never know we was comin'. He my Coach. I never want-'

Rosie yawned. 'Oh. I was wonderin' how that man have so much boy chile. He come here all the time with 'em. They usually pretty good.' She patted him. Clumsy reassurance. 'I mean they do it quick, so I don' hafta wait too long.' She pulled at her nipples. They were tiny and flat. 'You a nice little boy. If you don' wanta do nuthin' we kin just set here a while. He pay fo' a hour. Or if you kin think of somethin' that get you goin'?'

Mikey screwed up his face. There was something impressive about the way she lay there, naked, as if it was normal. She was prettier than he'd thought, too. Only the lipstick was wrong. It distracted the eye from the boldness of her breasts and the pleasant, oval shape of her face.

As if bidden, Rosie reached up and wiped her mouth. Mikey took a deep breath.

'If you kiss me...' he said timidly.

'I don' kiss nobody,' she said.

'Oh,' he said.

She leaned away from him and pushed the cigarette butt into the floor. He wondered if she lived in this room, by herself. He watched her stamp on the still smouldering cigarette with her bare foot, as if it was nothing. Her harp ribs were frail and clear through her skin. Poetry.

'Kin I touch yo' back?' he said.

'My back?' She shifted closer to him. He reached out and rubbed his fingers over the soft black down on her body. He rubbed the back of her neck and pushed the hair off her blank face. It fell down her back, glowing.

As the film rolled into motion, Tony discovered something new about Winona Welty. She was more than beautiful and clever. She was what Bea Brown would call a fast girl. The movie was not five minutes underway when he felt her very hot, very wet tongue in his ear.

Shocked, he glanced around him. They were in the coloured seats, and he'd seen people they knew when they came in. Couples embraced in the dimness. No-one seemed to care.

Summoning courage, he put an arm around her shoulders and turned to face her. As his first kiss began, he wanted to choke on the spasm of desire that passed through him. She smelled like peppermint, and something else he couldn't recognise and decided was girl. Their tongues slipped and rolled around each other, her saliva making his mouth wet. She poked her tongue into his mouth. Hesitantly, he returned the gesture. Winona sucked his tongue so hard that he felt as if the root would rip away. He panted. She giggled against his face. He brought his arms up, gathering her sumptuous warmth towards him. His erection felt like his tongue - as if it would fill the world.

Winona put her hands down. He felt his heart stop as the tips of her fingers whispered through the space between them. She loosened the red arm rest. It clattered to the floor under the crescendo of onscreen music and his puzzled stare.

'Well, we is in the kissin' section.' She giggled again. 'Everybody know they comes off!'

He started to speak, but she kissed him.

'You kiss good,' she said.

They sank into each other's mouths. Tony kissed her cheeks, her hairline and her neck. He sucked at the fragrant flesh above her shoulder blade, electrically conscious of his own hardness and the closeness of her breasts, only a deep breath and a little courage away. She made the decision for him, pulling his hand to her right breast. He almost sobbed as his hand closed around the willing softness. He didn't know what to compare it to: it seemed independently alive under his palm. He squeezed. Winona moaned in her throat. His penis twitched and began to leak fluid. He hoped he could get rid of the stains before he got home. He kissed Winona's mouth again, more confident this time, and harder as he brought his other hand up and settled it on her left breast. She did not stop him, her eyes closed tight. He kneaded her chest fiercely, half-kneeling, rubbing his groin into the broad expanse of her thigh. He wouldn't think about Agatha. She didn't care where he was.

'Ah-ah-' said Winona.

He stopped. 'I hurt you?'

She opened her eyes and snuggled nearer. 'Naw.'

He knew she was lying. He slowed and gentled his hands, delighted when she arched her back, a little sigh seeping through her lips. Boldly, he brought his thumbs up to her nipples, experimenting, acting on instinct. They felt long and hard beneath the fabric, and he decided that he would die if he could not feel their nakedness. He undid the top three buttons of her blouse and drove his hands in between the gap. Her chest felt hot and her nipples were as sharp and hungry as he'd hoped. He lifted one breast free of the fabric and flicked his tongue across it.

Winona pushed him away.

His head came up, the taste of her still burning across his mouth.

'What?' he said.

She tucked herself back into her top. He watched her nipples vanish.

'You reach second base. You gotta hold on a little bit now,' she said.

She turned back to the movie, cuddling into his armpit. She kissed his cheek, and he wondered at her ability to turn the desire on and off. What had she done with it all? He throbbed, his head light and his loins heavy. He shifted in his seat and tried to concentrate on the film.

'You wanna go steady?' he whispered in her ear.

Winona grinned. 'Thas what we doin', ain't it?'

Luke stole a glance at Agatha. She was in a strange mood, and he wondered whether he was the cause. He could tell that she wanted to be alone, but he hung on stubbornly. Part of him was fascinated with this new incarnation of Agatha Salisbury. The mischievous insults were gone. Maybe she was too tired to think of back-talk. There were bags under her eyes that he'd never seen there before. He watched her leap up each time he drained his glass, enquiring whether he was comfortable, whether the rain was getting him, like she could change it. All these things, but she hadn't taken his damp coat, as if she was willing him to leave. The porch set them back from the wet, but the toes of his shoes were damp. She talked too fast, and her mouth was too dry.

'You should see Susie's baby. She called her Pearl. She said she wanted to call her Agatha, but that man of hers kicked up an almighty fuss, so she didn't press him. That Rooster wants me to come over and tell him something, like he does anything but snore and chat foolishness when she needs help...'

Luke put down his glass, the ice tinkling against the sides. He would have preferred coffee on a day like this, but it didn't seem right to ask.

'Rooster talk too much now he don't fight,' he offered.

Agatha nodded her head. 'When I see that man he's going to get most of a piece of my mind. Now he has poor Susie out at the Miller's place working. All the girls I know say they'd rather starve than work for Clancy Miller.' She blinked rapidly, as if she had just registered her own words. 'That man is one sick fool...' Her voice trailed off.

'Mmmm,' said Luke. He didn't like mention of Clancy Miller. He knew that every woman in Edene was vexed with him, working for the man. But Clancy paid well for a good carpenter, and he didn't see why he should discuss his livelihood with any woman who was less than his wife.

Agatha looked at his glass. 'You see I'm chatting on about Susie and you're thirsty! I'll get some more for you.' Her skirt swung against his legs as she moved towards the house.

'Agatha... I never...' Luke sighed. She was gone. Each time she got up she brushed against him. It was driving him mad. Her dress was impregnated with a unique scent, and he wanted to bury his mouth into her wrist every time she set the glass down.

He looked around the porch. More than once, he'd admired how nice she kept the place. The paint was less than a year old. There were blue mats on the floor and a clean cloth on the porch table. The rocking chair looked too small for a grown woman, but not quite a child's. Vaguely, he remembered his aunt telling him that Agatha's mother had been a small woman. No more than five feet tall.

Agatha reappeared juggling lemons, a sugar bag and a jug full of water. He rose to help her.

155

'Have to make you some more,' she said, cheerfully. She caught a lemon before it rolled off the table, and sliced through it. He wished that he could calm her. He was intrigued and repelled by her jerky movements.

'How come you can cuss the man most people in Edene 'fraid of, and you can't set still with me fo' five minutes? You look like I'm gonna eat you up, girl.'

She pressed her lips together, let her breath out in a small puff. Forced a laugh. 'I've never heard such a stupid thing!' She stood up again and crossed her arms. Luke pushed scented fabric away from his leg and looked at her.

'Boy, if you're going to sit here on my place you better straighten up! Just because your auntie lives over there doesn't mean I won't get vex on you!'

Luke burst into laughter. 'So, you either cussin' or you chattin' foolishness! Woman, when the last time you let a man sweet you?' Delightedly, he noticed her mouth twitch at his audacity. She wanted to smile. For him. He wanted her to.

'Not for a long time. You happy now?'

He put his head to one side. 'Yeah. Every man be tellin' me I ain't gonna get nothin' from you, every man between sixteen an' ninety five try, an' they all say you gon' die a virgin-' He ignored her outraged expression. '-an if a man be waitin' on you, he die a virgin too.'

'DID I TELL ANY OF YOU I'M A VIRGIN?' she yelled.

Luke's head snapped back.

'I DIDN'T TELL ANY OF YOU I'M PURE AND SINLESS! NONE OF YOU KNOW MY BUSINESSS! ANYBODY ASK ME WHAT MY BUSINESS IS?'

Appalled, he tried to interrupt. 'Woman, hush yo'-'

'DON'T TELL ME TO SHUT MY MOUTH! WHY, I COULD HAVE BEEN MARRIED AND WIDOWED, BUT YOU MEN JUST SIT DOWN AND CHAT ANY SHIT, SAYING I'M SOME ICE WOMAN!'

Luke stood up, nose to nose with her. 'WELL, I'M ASKIN' YOU! IS YOU MARRIED?'

'NO! AND I'M NOT A VIRGIN EITHER!'

156

'Agatha-Mae? Luke? What on earth y'all bellowin' an' actin' crazy 'bout?'

Neither of them had spotted Bea scuttling out of her dismal house, hands above her head. Drops of water gathered in her hair.

'Everythin' fine, Aunt Bea!' Luke lowered his voice and tried to withhold his laughter. 'She my family, but I know come Sunday she gonna be holdin' that Bible so hard it burn her-'

'Huh?' Agatha glared at him. Ignoring her anger, he put his hand on her waist. He felt her shudder.

'Shhh! She been hearin' every word we sayin'. Settin' in there strainin' her ears. She gonna be prayin' fo' God's guidance because her nephew in love with a woman who ain't no virgin.' Agatha looked startled, but he rushed on, pretending nonchalance. 'I feel sorry fo' the Lord, cause he gonna be all tied up hearin' bout her business.' He laughed. It didn't matter if she didn't say it back. Not yet. He had to speak. 'Don' be lookin like you don' know I love you. Every man in this town love you, but I'm the man stand fast the longest.'

She looked at him, expressionless.

'Luke, you sho' you ain't vexin' Reveren' Salisbury chile?' called Bea.

'No, Aunt Bea! Go on now! Rain catchin' you! We fine!'

Bea's head disappeared. Agatha was the first to sit down. She threw back her head and laughed. Luke took his seat and waited.

'I'm sorry I've been pouring lemonade down your throat...' she said.

He raised the glass. 'Well, I been drinkin' it. Taste good.'

'So are you mad I'm not a virgin?' she asked.

He raised an eyebrow. It wasn't a question he'd expected.

'Well, I be lyin' if I say I don't wish you was one, but you a beautiful woman. So I s'pose a man been tryin' befo'.' He smiled. 'An' you not no ordinary woman, so I reckon you let yo'self feel good, even if ain't no married finger.'

They sat. He searched for something else to say. His statement of love lay between them, like a boulder, and he wanted to be done with it for now.

'You hear those rumours 'bout the CORE boy?' he said.

She moved on her chair.

'What rumours?'

'Some plannin' them CORE folks doin'. They was fixin' to cause some trouble Sat'day night so some white folks beat one of them boys, left him fo' dead.' He stretched. It seemed to him that she was watching him too closely. 'Alla the kids scared. Some funny feelin' on the air up in town. Like it gonna blow.'

She was silent.

'You ever speak to any of those chaps?' he asked.

'No,' she said. 'All those things are too hard on a body when you've got a growing boy to be worrying about.'

He nodded. So she was afraid. It would be good to let her see he was no troublemaker. 'Well, I reckon they crazy. Makin' trouble when there's no need fo' none.'

'You don't think there's any need?' she said. Her fingers drummed against her top lip.

'I never care none 'bout Jim Crow. Seem to me that white folks an' niggas don' need to be eatin' shoulder to shoulder like they family.'

She didn't reply.

'They said nobody kin fin' the body,' he continued desperately. Something was wrong, but he didn't know how to change the flow. 'Maybe they push him in the swamp. Wouldn't be the first time.' He leaned forward. Perhaps she would play along with gossip. 'You know what I'm thinkin'?'

'What do you think?' she said.

'I think that CORE boy run an' somebody help him. Niggas roun' here know more than they sayin'. I think he at somebody place. Anybody hidin' him lookin' fo' trouble.'

She looked at him like she'd never seen him before. He kept trying: talk in the town, Tony's schooling, the weather, Bea. After another frozen hour he got up to leave, defeated. He tried to kiss her, but her hair made a dark curtain between their faces. Her indifference hurt him.

'All right,' he said. 'You gon' be hard with me?'

She scowled. 'You think you're going to lay down with me just like that because I'm not a virgin?'

He stared at her, shaking his head.

'Maybe everybody right, say I shouldn't care fo' you,' he said.

'Then don't,' she said.

'Tell me somethin' nobody don't know.' Winona sat in Tony's lap, touching his face. He thought she'd want to go home after the movie, but she didn't seem to care about the time. So they'd come here, to the water hole. He could tell by the position of the sun that it was nearing six. Goose pimples stood out on his flesh. The rain hip-hopped across the water, covering it with diamonds.

'Why?' he asked. He stirred, irritated with his body. It seemed attached to her every movement with invisible strings: she breathed, and he got hard. He wondered if she could feel him under her.

She put her finger in his mouth.

'You my man now, baby. We s'pose to tell everythin'.'

He pulled at the back of her head for a kiss, but she resisted.

'I was hopin' you love me, but I never know fo' sure.' She nestled against his shoulder. 'Tell me somethin' nobody don't know, daddy,' she said. 'Then I kiss you all you want.'

'What you want to know?'

'Mmmmm...' She looked into the sky. 'I dunno. I been knowin' you since the days you ain't talk to nobody...' She kissed his forehead. 'I feel so sorry fo' you, standin' there with yo' cute self, not talkin'.'

She rubbed her hands along his thighs. Tony sucked his breath in.

'Don' do that!' Her eyes flew wide. He softened his tone. 'Jes' that you makin' it hard to think, much less talk.'

She kissed him, sucking his tongue, then climbed off his lap. 'I'm sorry, sugar.' She began to undo the buttons of her blouse, her back to him. 'Jes' that-' She pulled off the blouse. '-I want to git to know you.' She stood on one leg, balancing, as her jeans came off. Her panties were white. She dived into the water hole.

When Luke left, Agatha took an axe to the chicken coop. She was furious with herself, and with him. Slipping his way under her defences with his false declarations. It was all a lie. *Hear them rumours? You ever speak to any of those chaps?* She gritted her teeth and swung the axe. The wood splintered. Rain plastered her hair and fell in rivers down her face. If they were coming, they'd have to tear the house down. If they knew it was her, they'd have to come and get her. They'd have to get her before she ran. She carried planks back to the house. Sawdust clouds settled on the furniture and scurried into inconvenient piles in corners. She sneezed, and paused to flex her arms. The middle of her back ached, but she wasn't going to stop.

She grunted as she lifted a heavy piece of plywood and prepared to nail it over the door. Water flavoured with fear ran trammels across the nape of her neck. She knew she was panicking, so she kept on working, her mouth uneven with nails. They were strong, heavy pine beams. Pappy used the best he could, even if it was just for chickens. *How them birds gonna feel inclined to pop out big eggs if they ain't comfortable?* he'd joked with her. *Birds like fancy residence too.*

Jamie laughed when he heard about the fowl coop, tickling her in his lap. *Look like those chickens are living better than you,* he teased. She rounded on him. *You tryin' to say my grandaddy place look bad?* He cuddled her. *Now you know I'm not saying all that.* She'd leaned her head against his chest, almost too big to be in his lap.

Agatha worked through the bleached, wet afternoon, and the house grew darker as she boarded the windows shut.

Words spilled out of Tony Pellar's mouth. Sterling sentences that whistled and fell away as the sun set, sinking behind the water hole and the dark brown girl standing in front of him, her thighs meeting, her whole body fascinated. He told her everything. Towards the end, she climbed out of the cold water and into his arms. She rubbed the tears on his cheeks into his skin, as if moisturising him. She rocked him and rolled him, holding his head safe.

Tony lay back, his head on her bare breast. He felt exalted. And light.

23

Chaz is home she's putting down her bag and hugging the walls and watching me out of the corner of her eye God I want to tell someone I want to tell another human being about my momma you see this is why I am insane this is why yeah it is her fault it's in the blood and Chaz is coming to me with the ropes asking *you gonna tie yourself* her voice is kind but I look into her eyes and they are rock steel she doesn't mean me any good she doesn't care about me and shit I have no evidence that I hit her OK I remember one time but it's not so bad as she says maybe that fool at the gas station been socking it to her yeah that's it

I'm shaking my head no while she's coming with the rope *no fuck you bitch I'm not letting you tie me up* and she is looking at me with those hard eyes *baby you know I'm seventeen right* she says and I'm in my corner looking at her *yeah so what* I say *well I never tole you that an I wanna tell you that* and she stops like she's not sure *I got to get some self respect for myself Tony baby I got to* and she sucks her lips in yeah I know what she's saying but the bitch better say it out clear and she's looking at me with her rock eyes *I'm I'm I'm* she says and I'm talking too *say what you have to say* and she says it finally *I got to go baby I got to have some self respect*

BAM I'm hitting her before she can tell me about self respecting herself ha what can I expect from an ignorant bitch *I know what you're fucking doing think I don't know you're leaving me for that stupid motherfucker* BAM it feels good to hit her again and again and again

my eye is burning *what the fuck* my eye is burning and Chaz is on her back underneath me and she's raising her nails again to scratch my eyes out and I'm thinking *no this is not the way it should be I should be*

161

able to do anything I want and I jump on her nearly bounce off the curve of her belly as she pushes me off

she pushed me off her wow she's hissing at me with her stone eyes and I'm hearing her yell and I'm amazed at the power in her voice

YOU GONNA BEAT THIS CHILE OUTTA ME YOU GONNA KILL YOUR OWN CHILE YOU KILL ME FIRST MOTHAFUCKA

I'm running and running and running and running and running and running I'm on the rails and I don't care my feet are fast past the third rail and I'm thinking *no she's not no she's not no she is not pregnant* and I can't get her words out of me like threads of acid whirling in my belly *you gonna kill this child kill this child kill this child* and now I'm still my throat raw I'm three inches from the third rail and I don't CARE

kill this child kill this child kill this child

little one I remember you

your name was Adele Morgan and I called you Addie Momma gave you her own last name because she never knew the name of your daddy and I was seven years old when you were born when you came back from the hospital in Momma's arms when she pulled back the blanket your face was like an old woman's and your eyes were shut tight and Momma was slow with you her frenzy calmed

you looked like her maybe she thought she had been born again because you were the beauty she could have been Addie you had her face and her skin and the same brown chalk colour Addie and you had no eyebrows hardly and you were beautiful

Momma was slow and yes I was jealous because she hummed to you first thing in the morning you know I think you made her sane and it was a relief because for a while she took her terrible eyes off me you know she was too busy counting your digits and powdering you and giving thanks for you and I was jealous but thankful too because you made her the momma I wanted there were no devils in the darkness when you were there

I played with you and Momma taught me songs *clap hands clap hands till Tony comes home Tony bring cake for baby alone* I nearly dropped you once but Momma caught you and I was ready for the sharp side of her tongue but it didn't come *just mind* she said to me and

I read you the Bible in the days when I was getting ready for the Easter evening at church I was the star performer because Momma decided it was a recital of thankfulness for you and for me yes for both her children and I had three months to prepare and the minister said I would make my Momma proud

I am black but comely o ye daughters of Jerusalem as the tents of Kedar as the curtains of Solomon look not upon me because I am black because the sun hath looked upon me I have compared thee o my love to a company of horses in Pharoah's chariots thy cheeks are comely with rows of jewels thy neck with chains of gold do you remember Addie do you remember me practising those words over you as you cried you know I was helping Momma more because she was staring at the wall and I was afraid once more dang I was afraid

the darkness hunted her I could see her trying to fight it as she became fast and furious again she was biting her hands and counting the nickels on the table and you know I think she was scared we would starve and I got the palm of her hand too many times to count over and over because of one missing nickel she would sit in the bed with you at her breast and me leaning against her this was the way she wanted it yeah she wanted both her children in attendance and how could I have known Addie how could I have known baby I would change it if I could I was a little boy forgive me

I passed you to her from your crib *time for baby* she said we did this every day several times a day and I wasn't allowed to look when she took her nipple to your mouth that was nasty but I was curious that day I wanted to see her feed you because she made such happy noises so when Momma said *look away Anthony* like usual I looked away and looked right back again

her chin was tucked into her neck and she was watching your face it was pressed into her warmth and you jolted as she pressed you to the teat I thought it was normal how would I know but then Momma looked across at me and the devil was in her eyes scratching to get out and I knew something was wrong *Momma* I said *Momma please* but she took her other hand and pressed it over my mouth and I thought she was going to do it to me too Addie I'm sorry I thought she was going to make me jolt and struggle too like you and I was scared as the flesh on her breast puckered and her left hand pressed you to her while she was looking at the wall you know she had her teeth in her bottom lip and her right hand was pressing me into the bed and mashing my teeth against my lips and I was trying to breath through my nose but you wouldn't have known how to do that Addie no you were too young to save yourself

afterwards she laid you down and put her finger to her lips *shh* she said *shh she sleeping with God* then she went to the front door and screamed I think she was screaming for the weight of her heart and later the police came and they said it was alright *very sad* they said but nobody at Church told them the Devil rode Momma at night that was private business they took you away and I waved at the door and your pillow was cold and wet and I could smell the milk and Addie you were so little when they took you away dead

oh the church sisters were proud of our Momma they said it was such a sad thing but the tragedy made her pull together *sometime the Lord know what He doing at least Sister Morgan taking strength to mind the boy look how be dressed all nice ready to recite for his sister and she gone to Heaven two months ago*

I climbed onto the stage and all I could think of was you Addie because I knew and Momma knew and you knew and nobody told and the police don't care about a little baby girl with a poor momma who couldn't love enough I stood on the stage and there was a scrape on my knee I was wearing red shorts and the pianist readied his fingers he was short no more than five foot and he kept his fingernails long and the minister was patting Momma's knee *Sister Morgan lookit how your chile gonna make you proud*

the church turned to me and waited and the Song of Solomon evaporated from my mind you know my head was damp from the rain outside because there was a storm with real lightning and I was counting to see how far away the electricity was because I thought God was making his terrible judgement ready for me and I couldn't remember the Song of Solomon my mouth was dry as a drunk ocean and Momma saw I couldn't talk so she's mouthing *improvise improvise* that big word she learned God knows where she learnt it for her beautiful Tony who was going to be a star and it was like the encouraging clapping went on forever I could see pink fans sandwiched between brown hands and pink fans dropped on floors and laps and the short pianist struck a single chord and whispered at me *start boy* while embarrassment and fear and your face stayed inside my head your face and the games me and Momma played with you

before I went to school Addie you would laugh up at me and Momma playing *clap hands clap hands till Tony comes home Tony bring cake for baby alone* and my mouth fell open and I improvised like Momma said and each traitorous word was a lock on her head each one condemning her to the place where crazy people go

Addie was a little girl she dressed in blue and green
and all the funny neighbours said that she was peachy keen
one day Addie went to sleep she did it good by counting sheep
when she woke her pillow was soaked and that was all I seen

people were shifting and smiling doubtfully *what a clever boy you know what he talking about* and Momma was rising from her seat and I knew she knew where the nonsense rhyme came from but she wasn't moving fast enough and maybe she wanted to get caught maybe she thought someone could help her with the devil and the fairies because I couldn't and she was on her feet too late because I was yelling as loud as I could yell

NO
THAT'S NOT ALL I SEEN
MOMMA HURT ADDIE MOMMA HURT ADDIE
SHE A LIE SHE A LIE
MOMMA KILL ADDIE
IT WAS HER

I ran off the stage as the church looked at my Momma and that was why I didn't talk to Agatha Addie I didn't talk to anybody because I talked too godamned much already but NO I'm not sorry I told I'm NOT sorry I think that all lives however short must be told Addie tell me am I crazy just like Momma because you know it's in the blood do I fuck around like my momma or like my daddy because you know it's

165

in the blood and would you have been crazy too Addie or would you have been our redemption

24

Agatha looked down at the sleeping boy. His eyelashes looked like feathers against his cheek. She'd fallen asleep before he came home, too tired to worry anymore. Tony had put a sheet over her and taken off her shoes. She couldn't help smiling at the irony. *So you boarded up the house and left the front door open. You let somebody take off your shoes. You looking to die girl.* She'd slept badly, half-waking, conscious of the floor, then sloping back into her lack of dreams. Over and over again. But when she woke up, she was calm. She looked at the boards. If the night riders knew that she was hiding people, they wouldn't have sent Luke Brown. They would have come themselves. And if they came, they would find a bare house. They were going. She didn't care where. She'd helped them all run, and now she was going to do it for herself. And her child.

Tony opened his eyes and looked at her sitting on the edge of his bed.

'Hey,' he said.

'Hey,' she said.

He looked at her suspiciously. She looked normal. The house had been a surprise. Boards reinforced the doors and covered the windows. Agatha, in the middle of the sawdust, sleeping next to the still damp couch. He was glad she slept. His head was too full of Winona. His sweetheart. He'd known that she was right the moment he found himself wanting to tell her about Adele's death, about why his momma was in an asylum, about the speech and the song and the guilt. In the end, it was so easy. She'd cried with him and held him close.

Agatha caught the spectre of a smile at his mouth. There was something different about him this morning.

'I'm sorry I brought Mikey,' he said.

She shook her head. 'You should be saying sorry, but there are too many sorrys in this house right now. You alright? You look tired.'

'I'm good,' he said.

'Tony, I'm not sending you anywhere by yourself. I don't even know where Eleanor is. You just have to promise me you're going to be wise.'

He nodded. 'I promise.'

'You know I feel like I'm your momma, don't you, child?'

He moved to her and hugged her. She spoke into his shoulder.

'I've got a new plan.'

He grinned. 'You always got a plan.'

'This is a new one. How do you feel about going to New York with me?'

'What?' His face broke in half. 'What you mean?'

'I want to go up North, back to New York. Get a job. It would be good. You could get a better school...'

He moved away. Winona. Mikey. She couldn't want to leave.

'No, he said.

Agatha tried to smile.

'It would be good. You've got to understand. I might be in trouble if we stay here...'

'NO!' He buried his face into the pillow.

As Susie Dixon watched barely-grey water swirl around the sides of Mrs Miller's bath-tub, she wondered why the woman made her scrub it twice a day. It was never dirty. The Millers hardly bathed. She'd been jealous of the bathroom ever since she'd first seen it, with its yellow bath mat set just so in front and the yellow daisy-scattered curtains at the window. She could live in this bathroom, just this one room, and feel happy.

She stood up and rubbed her wet hands on the front of her dress. Her hips ached. She'd worked for the Millers ever since Pearl turned three months old, and she was sure that the maid before her had died of drudgery. Mrs Miller laboured nearly as hard as she did checking on her help. Susie lifted the mat and scrubbed underneath it. This was the first time she'd been left alone in the house. She thought of venturing into the den and turning on the TV, but rejected the idea. It would not do for Mrs Miller to arrive home to the sound of *Bewitched*.

Rooster wasn't happy about the job, but she tried to ignore him. The sound of her voice seemed to whip him into long monologues, soaked with self pity and alcohol. He was intrigued with his daughter, counting her toes and tickling her tummy until the child cried. He ignored Daniel, even though the boy adored him, watching him stagger from room to room with happy eyes. Susie followed her husband, picking up the things he knocked aside. She was glad that his mother stepped over to watch Pearl and Daniel in the days. Rooster spent his time drinking and talking to different parts of his wasting body.

She heard the front door slam. She tiptoed into the hallway and put her cheek against the cool, high-shone banister. She listened to the angry voices. The Millers never stopped fighting. The fights were usually funny. She didn't know white folks could cuss so much.

Mikey sat up, rubbed his eyes and looked around the room. It looked the same as it had yesterday, yet not the same: yellow, red and white book spines stared at him with moral indignation. The Sonic Satellite yo-yo curled up on the shelf turned over, yawned, and declared its intention never to whistle again. The King Kong model shrugged one small, hairy shoulder. *What do you expect?* it seemed to say. *All this nastiness.*

He rolled back on the bed and tried to decide whether it had all been a dream, Rosie on him, her mouth on him, and in the end an incredible release that bucked his body across her tired bed. He was confused afterwards, wanting to sleep and wanting to hold her.

'Time to go,' she said.

The Coach drove him home, steering with one hand, patting him on the shoulder with the other. Mikey kept his chin up, but he would not look at the man. When he got out of the car in front of Miss Ezekiel's yard Coach David winked, just like Timothy Crampton.

'I knew it wasn't nothin' a little pussy wouldn't cure,' Coach said. 'I won't be gettin' no note next Monday, boy, you hear?'

The car pulled away from the house, tyres scraping through the

169

dust. He told Miss Ezekiel that the Coach had kept him back to give him a physical. She was not pleased.

'Don't that man know I excuse you from all that? You too fat to be runnin' around,' she said.

He muttered something, his head whirling. He couldn't decide whether he was happy. He felt absurdly pleased with himself, yet fingers of nausea gave him the hiccups before he fell asleep.

Susie put her hand to her mouth. She was listening as hard as a body could listen, and she still hadn't heard enough. *You never hear that,* a voice whispered in her head. *Naw. You never hear that. He say he goin' to Agatha-Mae house.*

No he didn't.

Yes, yes he said so, Mizz Miller tellin' him she ain't gonna let him go.

'Susie? Where you at, gal?' That was Mrs Miller's voice, coming from the hall. Susie stepped backwards.

'I'm in the bathroom cleanin', Mizz Miller, ma'am!'

'Come down here, gal!'

Susie hurried to the stairs. She muttered under her breath. 'Bitch mus' think I got wings to fly when she call.'

'You talkin' to me again? Gal, I said come down here now!' Susie descended, nearly tripping over her own feet.

Mikey looked at Timothy Crampton in astonishment. The bully was talking animatedly to him, thumping his arm.

'Boy, you a genius! I never know a girl turn roun' so fast!' He lowered his voice. 'I don' know which boys you done it fo', but I got some buddies interested. Some of them want letters fo' they girls, some of them wanta get some girls. So I was thinkin', since my daddy a businessman an' all, we kin make some money. I tole 'em you write them the kinda thing you wrote fo' me. We split the money fifty-fifty, since I gotta find the guys. You don' know nobody.' He rubbed his hands together, gleeful, 'Whaddaya say, boy?'

Mikey tried to register the words. It was the first time anyone at school had asked his opinion.

'Whaddaya say?' Timothy was nearly dancing with excitement.

'Yeah.' He tried to think. He would have to ask Tony, of course, but Timothy couldn't know that. 'You tell me what you want.'

Timothy thumped his arm again. It was getting sore.

The girls were on her as soon as she arrived. Questions rained down on her head. Bethanne Collins was at the front. Her best friend. Her face puffed with excitement.

'How far you go, girl?'

Winona shook her head. All night self-hatred had crept into her bones, nibbling at the marrow. How could she have known it was such a big secret? She thought Tony would say he was shy. That was why he hadn't talked. Or scared of being in a new place. They could have called him sissy and had done.

'How far you hafta go to fin' out?'

'Second base,' she said.

The laughter, bitter as virgins' tears, scattered around her. Bethanne's face loomed up to hers.

'So tell,' she demanded.

Winona hesitated. She couldn't. It had all started as a dare. A pleasurable one. Bethanne grabbed her hair. 'We waitin',' she said.

Winona told.

Agatha walked down the main street. She was late for Miss Ezekiel's, but she didn't care. The woman was evil, and today was the day she would quit. She'd wait until Miss Ezekiel stepped out and then she'd use her pretty blue Princess phone to call her old college. Just like that. Get her job back. Then she would quit. Politely.

She twisted her mouth. She should have known Tony would feel bad. He had friends here, but he would have to understand. She'd leave him to get used to the idea, and they'd talk again tonight. Job or not, they would go tomorrow. All she had to do was pack and keep calm. *Nothing's happened to us yet,* she reminded herself. *I'm going to buy Tony some clothes to wear in New York City.*

'Girl, you lookin' fine this morning!'

She looked across at the young black man. He sat outside the five and ten, chewing gum. She reckoned that he was no more than eighteen. She could be his momma, but she supposed that didn't matter. Well, not quite his momma. *You're not that old,* she reminded herself.

She walked past her young admirer. He wore the sparkle in his eye like it was a gem.

'Mmmmm-hmm! Like that strut, lady.'

She slowed and stared at him, her lips twitching. 'Boy, you mind how you talk to your elders.'

He tipped his hat as she moved on. 'Never mean nothin' by it, ma'am.' He kept on twinkling.

On Temper Street, she thought of Pappy. It had been Temper Street as long as she could remember. They'd played a game with its name when she was a little girl. *Who lose their temper on Temper Street? One angry ant, vex 'cause it rainin'.* She could almost hear his voice. She would join in: *Who lose they temper on Temper Street? One angry ant, vex 'cause it rainin'. Two big bears, cussin' bout marriage.* Pappy had tried to frown, but didn't quite make it. *What you know 'bout cussin' an' marriage, chile?* Then, conspiratorial: *Don' talk so loud. People be sayin what a preacher doin' playin' Devil's games?* She was seven, looking at him adoringly. *Not no Devil game, is it, Pappy?* He corrected her. *Say 'It's not a Devil game, is it?'* Folks *don't know better. They think the Lord care 'bout things like that.*

She knew that her Pappy had a personal connection with the Lord, so she didn't worry. *Yo' turn, Pappy! Yo' turn!* He tickled her, and picked her up, her bare legs hanging. *Now, lemme see if I can remember. Ah, yes. Who lose their temper on Temper Street? One angry ant...*

She sang it under her breath as she walked into Mr Cooper's bargain store. 'Who lose their temper on Temper Street?'

Mr Cooper, turned towards her, a pleasant expression on his face. 'Every time you come in here you singin' that song, Agatha,' he said.

She laughed. 'Coop, every time I come in singing, you tell me I'm singing.'

'What kin I do fo y'all today?' He shook his finger. 'Don' tell me. That boy of yours want mo' pencils an mo' paper.'

'You've got that right. Boy gets through pencils like I don't know what.' She flicked her hand through the shirts on sale, two for five dollars.

'Coop, will you take off a dollar if I buy four of these shirts?' She held up a green one. 'This boy is going to start thinking about dating soon and I want him to look good.'

'Well, now. I don' know bout *that-*' Mr Cooper stopped mid sentence.

'What's the matter, Coop? Talk of a deal steal your tongue?' She looked up, laughing. Mr Cooper was known in Edene for his stinginess. She stared at the man's face, puzzled. He looked as if something had stung him.

'What-'

She felt the white man before she saw him. He was standing behind her. Too close to be friendly. She felt him breathing. *How did he get up on you without you knowing?* The thought died in her mind and was replaced by one word. *Run.*

She didn't run. She looked over her shoulder.

She had never seen him before. He was sucking his bottom lip, his face inches from hers. His jeans and blue shirt looked new. His hands hung loosely at his sides. A bunch of muscle twitched in his neck. Her nostrils flared. He smelled of lilac talcum powder. There was something terrifying about it A big, masculine man, smelling like a woman.

Agatha shuffled closer to Mr Cooper's counter, trying to increase the distance between them. Mr Cooper's face was almost comical: a mixture of anger, astonishment and fear. White men called to her on the street sometimes. But none of them, except Jamie, had come up on her like this, with such ease, such arrogance. Such intimacy.

'What the hell do you want?' She heard her voice shaking.

He didn't reply. He moved forward, no more than an inch, closing the gap between them. She was aware of the power of his thighs and the anger inside her.

'Get off me!' She twisted to face him, pushing at his chest as she moved. The man rocked back on his heels, but kept his place. His expressionless eyes did not leave her face. He put his arms on either

173

side of her, resting them on the counter. She tried to duck underneath one, but the arm sloped lower, like a heavy bar. She rose up and he moved forward again. His hips were a breath away from hers. She could hear someone singing outside. The noise sounded very far away. Her head swam. She was overpowered by the lilac smell.

As swiftly as he had come, the man moved backwards and away from her. She clung to the counter as he walked through the shop door. Stung by anger, she followed him, hitting the exit in time to see him move down Temper Street and then off, into a side shop.

'You bastard!' she yelled. 'You bastard!' People out shopping stared at her. 'You-' She stopped, aware of them and how hollow her voice sounded.

'Agatha, you alright?' Mr Cooper touched her arm.

She whirled to face him.

'What the hell do you think? You're not worth shit, letting that boy come up on me like I'm some whore he can-. Damn, Coop- you never did nothing- you never- you could have-'

She stopped. What did she expect? What did she want him to do?

'I take that dollar off those shirts,' he said.

He searched the room for Winona. He knew there was a shit-eating grin plastered to his face, but he didn't care. She must be out, fixing her hair or something. He wondered if she was as nervous and as happy as he was. He'd run nearly all the way to school, trying to forget what Agatha said, then stopped a mile out. It wouldn't do to arrive all nasty and sweaty.

The teacher was late again. He crossed the room and sat in his seat, next to Crow Turner.

'Hey,' said Tony. 'You see Winona?'

'Naw,' the boy retorted.

Tony raised an eyebrow. It wasn't like Crow to be in a bad mood.

'What wrong with you?'

'Nothin' wrong with him, Tony Pellar.' Bethanne's hips bumped his desk. She smiled cruelly. 'Maybe somethin' wrong with *you*.'

Tony looked around the room. All eyes were directed at him.

'Ain't nothin' wrong with me.' He looked up at her, perplexed.

His chest quickened. 'Where Winona at? Somethin' wrong with Winona?'

Bethanne leaned forward, her breasts in his face. 'Naw. She out back. She prob'ly fraid you comin'.'

'She my girl, she ain't gonna be 'fraid of me. Why she gonna be-' He shrugged. 'You jealous, that's what. Jealous she my girl.'

Bethanne ignored the comment. 'I *ask* you what wrong with you.'

He felt irritation. Maybe she and Winona had a fight. That was it; that was why the quiet loomed. There'd been a down and dirty cussing match. 'Girl, move outta my face,' he said.

'Whatcha gonna do, Tony Pellar?' She dangled her hands in front of him. 'Whatcha gonna do?'

'I don' hit girls.' He spoke scornfully. 'Git outta my way. I'm gonna fin' my woman.'

'Crazy boy. Crazy boy. Crazy boy. Crazy boy.' She laughed.

As if they had been waiting for a sign, the chant spread over the class, like rain. Bethanne Collins beat time with her fist on the bench,

'Crazy boy crazy boy crazy boy crazy boy crazy boy crazy boy.'

Winona stood at the door, swaying to the dirge. She answered Tony with her expression. Scrambled emotions. Fear. Shame. Defiance.

Bethanne cackled. 'Crazy boy! Yo' *girlfrien'* make five dollars today. Second base an' you spill yo' guts!' Tony didn't hear her. All he could see was Winona's lovely face as her lips opened and she joined in.

Agatha counted her breaths as if she were at school. Layers of bright clothing dotted the bedroom floor. She sniffed the air. Pappy's smell was gone. Under her yard clothes, she found what she was looking for. The gun felt solid in her hand. Pappy had taught her to use it when she turned eleven, Jamie behind them, teasing her. She was a good shot. Jamie told her she had a merciless eye.

She put the final piece of Tony's clothing into the big bag. She put the gun on top of the drawer.

Mikey spotted Tony on the front porch before he came through the gate. His book bag thudded against his shoulder. Two new pads of

paper shuffled inside. They could make their fortunes writing. Timothy
had six, maybe seven boys lined up, just waiting. He'd have to
interview them, of course. Talk to them about what they liked about
the girls they wanted, the girls' best features. Then he could tell Tony
and he'd make it sound good. He squeezed his eyes shut and opened
them. He'd be good at it. It would make him popular. He and Tony,
why, they'd have money all the time. He could even go back and give
Rosie some. Not for doing it, no, he didn't want to do that again. Just
for herself. She was too skinny.

He hit the porch, panting.

'Tony, where you an' Agatha get to? Mizz Ezekiel raisin' hell say
she gonna fire Agatha if she don' see her today, an' the day nearly
done. I never say I was comin'. I got good news! Timothy say he gonna
set us up in business-'

Tony did not look up.

'Hey! You never hear me?' Tony still had his school clothes on.
Agatha never let him play around in them. 'Where Agatha at?'

Silence.

'Tony?'

Silence.

'Tony!'

Tony raised his head. Something about the drag of his body looked
familiar. Mikey ran his hand through his blonde hair.

'You- you not talking?'

Tony tucked himself into a knot.

Inside the house, mosquitos sang. Agatha slept.

25

I stayed down on the tracks in the dark crying for my sister and the long silences I stayed down there and cried for my unborn child and when I came back Chaz was gone but through the candlelight I saw the neat piles she left they were perpendicular piles of apples and Oreos and Doritos and Chitos and chips and Butterloaf and oranges and Saltines and Wheaties and cornflakes and Eggo waffles even the syrup they're good defrosted I swear and Twinkies for quick energy that was the heavy bag she had

I sat staring at the food and my mind was empty then I realised what it all meant I remembered Addie and that was why Agatha came she came to tell me to remember Addie and with the knowledge I sagged into the darkness and I couldn't stop smiling this meant that she was gone and I was free it was an adrenaline rush baby and my mind ran liquid with plans I would go Topside and find Chaz I would be a baby daddy I would have lunch with Mikey and be a baby daddy and the sleep took hold of me and lulled me in its arms and the trains sang *she's gone she wasn't bad she's gone she wasn't bad*

I feel like I've slept for fifteen minutes I'm lying here with my eyes closed liberated thinking *I'm free Agatha will never come back*

I'm opening my eyes

GOD THE ROOM

there's yellow liquid hanging from the beams it is two inches deep on the floor I'm sitting in a pool of the stuff and there are droplets on my HANDS I'm soaked in despair up to the waist like a black island in a yellow ocean it's like regurgitated cornmeal you know when I first

177

saw the stuff flow from Agatha's feet it looked like liquid but I guess I was wrong

I can see through the dark because whatever it is that the bitch left on my sleeping body is GLOWING lighting up the room IT'S LIKE SHE PISSED ON ME *is it hot is it cold* I'm reaching down pressing a finger into the spatters of it across my CHEST it's like putting my hand to a warm sponge the drops on my chest run towards my finger as if it's a magnet and they're disappearing and I'm retching *where did it go God let it not have gone into ME* but I can't stay sitting forever I'm standing up watching it SLIDE down my body and disappear again I'm walking forward in it up to my ankles holding my breath as I wade through clumps of it and all it's doing is gleaming and disappearing as I touch it she was in here she climbed all over me BREATHING

I'm walking around the room watching it fall away into some secret void I can't see reaching up to the steel beams and touching it and watching it spring back from my hands the room is getting darker and darker as if someone is blowing the lights out and when it's all gone I'll be left in the dark with her

the light is going

going

going

gone

26

Susie Derkins walked the room, rocking her daughter. Daniel slept on a mattress in the corner. She grimaced, scraping a patch of raw flesh on her lip. She hated this grey room in this grey house, where dust bunnies hopped over the wounded floor. Pearl looked up at her with identical eyes. They wept phlegm. Her forehead felt hot and dry.

'Hush baby. Hush baby,' Susie said.

The request was unnecessary; Pearl was an unusually peaceful child, and illness didn't change that. Susie wished she would cry. There was something eerie about the child's stoicism. She'd hurried home as fast as she could. She would ask Mother Dixon to stay on and then she could run over to Agatha to tell her what she'd heard at the Millers. But Rooster's mother was gone. Chaos and silence greeted her at the door. Rooster sprawled across the floor, his liquor-laden snores bouncing off the walls. She found Pearl lying on dirty blankets, moaning quietly, her tiny eyes scaled shut. Milk, long dried, sat in white patches across her face. Susie gently pried her eyes open and squeezed fresh milk out of her breasts to clear the mucous. She cleaned and changed her. Daniel woke up and even though she'd promised to wean him she put her cracked nipple to his mouth, wincing. The little boy smiled and drifted back to sleep.

She saw what had happened. Rooster must have put on a good act. She could almost hear him, with his hypocrisy and sly comfort: *Everything fine, Mamma. You don't trust me with my own chillun? You run home and I fix 'em up. They momma soon come.* Then he must have set to drinking. Mother Dixon was easily fooled. Susie couldn't think why. Rooster must have been full of shit and sin long before he had first tried to impress her, that Tuesday morning three

179

years ago. The day after her first fight with Benjamin.

Susie stepped over Rooster's quiet body and walked onto the porch, jigging Pearl. If only she would sleep. She could feel the thunder coming.

Fifteen men marched three abreast, curved proudly under the night. Dirty white hoods obliterated their pale faces, eyelashes crowded through eye holes. Below, the rhythmic material sucked at their nostrils. Back and forth breaths. One man sniffled and brought a hand up to creep under his pliable mask, but their leader frowned. The man with the cold snaked his arm back down to his side and wrinkled his nose.

Clancy Miller led them. At these times he felt most like a man. Strength, purpose, movement. He ran his fingers through the red-brown hairs that nestled at the neck of his robe. All was good in the world. It seemed to him that the crickets, the mournful sound of an owl to the left, all these things cheered them on. It was a cold chorus.

In one hand he carried a clumsy torch, the end soaked in kerosene. In his pocket, matches bumped against his thigh. Their small rattle kept time.

Miss Ezekiel paced the kitchen. She swiped at an imaginary piece of dirt on the table. Nine o'clock and Michael not home. She would give him a piece of her mind, no, three pieces, when he arrived. *Jes' like a boy,* she thought. She should have known not to take on a boy at her age. Why, everybody had told her. *Find some other relative, Charity,* they'd said. *Don't the boy got no other kin?* Well, that was the reason why she'd brought Michael to Edene in the first place. To find family. She had always felt sorry for Mikey's father, even when he'd told her not to come back to his house. She was ashamed. She'd tried her best to control Allison, but the child was wilful from the day she was born. She was almost frightened when her daughter began to walk. Always in things, too inquisitive, wanting to wear the brightest colours, sing the loudest, only baby songs, but why did she have to bellow? She'd pleaded with the Tennyson boy to leave Allison alone. Her daughter spent all her time breaking men's hearts.

180

She still recalled the day she'd crept up to his home, when she knew Allison would be out in the town, galivanting, almost ready to have the man's child, still not keeping her tail quiet. He was scrubbing the steps, and she was choked at her daughter's audacity, letting her man work like a slave. She tried to explain that something was wrong with Allison, that she, Charity Ezekiel had nothing to do with it. Allison needed a firm hand. He should either marry her and try to control her, or leave her be. He kept staring at her, arguing quietly. He loved Allison. He wasn't going to leave her with a baby. He hated men who did things like that. And Allison didn't want to get married. She said *that* was slavery. Miss Ezekiel shook her head. He was such a good, strong man, so respectful and calm. *Look how she have you cleanin' the house like you not a man*, she'd told him. *She takin' yo' manhood.* He laughed, low. *You don't understand*, he said. *I thank God for everything, Miss Ezekiel. I thank God for Allison, and for my child that's nearly born.* His face was filled with a strange kind of light. *It feels good, Miss Ezekiel. I came all the way from Edene, and I'm still alive.*

When she leafed through his personal papers and found his request for her to care for his son, she thought of the name again. She remembered him leaning against the thin tree, telling her where he came from. She could remember how the bark was dappled with white patches. Edene. What with him muttering about the Lord, first she'd thought of the Bible. Then he'd made it plain: *I was born in a place called Edene.* As she worked her way through his house, his clothes, his pots and pans, she thought hard. Edene, North Carolina. That was where she would find family for the boy. What choice did she have? She had to do her best for Michael. So they'd come. It wasn't easy. The father hadn't left much money for his son. But they'd come, her heart full and eager to find Tennysons in Edene. They would be good people, gentle, like Michael's father. She saw the scene in her mind: rows of Tennysons, a grandfather for Michael, maybe aunts, uncles, cousins. Other womenfolk, who could help her raise the boy. But she'd failed. No-one in Edene had ever heard of a Tennyson. She asked everybody, fighting back tears at the blank faces. How could she have believed the ravings of a mad man? He wasn't quiet or good. He was crazy on God's love. And in the name of his craziness, she had changed her whole life. Adam and Eve in the garden of Eden. That was what he'd meant. Him and her daughter, in the garden of innocence, Allison pulling him into God's wrath with her wicked ways.

She poured herself a cup of milk. Imagine, Michael Abraham had her up in here, past any decent body's bed time, worrying. Well. He would be sorry when he came home. She gripped the cup and sighed. The boy needed a firm hand. She didn't know what she would do when he arrived. But she was sure of one thing. The time to be consorting with niggers was well past. She would make sure he knew that. Starting with that Anthony boy. She would get rid of the gal working for her; she was a bad influence on her grandson.

Miss Ezekiel raised her head. Someone was knocking. One-two long, one short.

Agatha stirred on her grandfather's bed. She sat up slowly. The room was dark. The only light came through the gap she'd left at the window. Around her, the white bed shimmered. The ball of gristle in her chest hadn't gone away. Groggy, she put a hand between her breasts, as if she could hold the feeling. She'd never been afraid like this.

'Tony?' she called.

No answer.

'TONY!'

A silence, then: 'Agatha?' Her heart dropped even further. It was Mikey's voice.

'Mikey?' She struggled to her feet. She had been thinking about him as well. She didn't want to leave him with his miserable grandmother, but she had to choose between the boys. She couldn't take Mikey with her and at least he would be safe in Edene, even if he wasn't loved. *That can kill someone too*, her mind whispered. She pushed it away. Maybe she could write to Mikey when she and Tony were safe. What time was it? She called out. Her voice cracked.

'Mikey, where's Tony? What are you doing here?'

Mikey appeared at the bedroom door. He looked miserable. 'I been waitin' for you to wake up,' he said. 'I came- Tony not talkin'- I come in- he not talkin'- he won't talk- I been tryin'- never want to wake- he not-'

She put both hands on his shoulders and willed him silent, but Mikey hiccuped in distress.

'He not- I tried- everythin'- try some jokes- ask him- he not- look like he- somebody say somethin' to him- what you- what you gonna-'

'Mikey!' She shook him. 'Stop. Where's Tony?'

Mikey gulped air. 'Tony stop talkin' again,' he said.

Agatha ran across the living room. Her head ached. Maybe the white man in Coop's store had touched him or hurt him. *Suppose they beat him,* she thought. *I'll kill them if they hurt him.*

Tony sat on the porch. He rocked, his eyes fixed on the floor.

Susie moved back into the house. Pearl's eyes were round, the slime unrelenting. Susie fought back tears. Everything hurt: her back, her breasts, the arches of her feet, the base of her spine where Benjamin had once kissed her. Her mind flickered to their meeting at the house a year ago. He'd turned from her. He blamed her. Agatha said keep going, keep going back if that's the one you love. *Maybe something lucky will happen,* she whispered, as she took Susie in her arms. That was Agatha. Strong, but not afraid to be happy. Not afraid to touch somebody.

Daniel turned on the mattress, and she sat down next to him, shifting Pearl onto her right hip. Daniel whimpered and smacked his lips. Susie stroked his face. All she needed was her boy catching what Pearl had. As she touched the child, Clancy Miller's words darted into her head. She'd tried so hard to hear everything, but his voice had been too low: *Gonna... Agatha ... it's set... that Salisbury gal down in... old preacher land... we goin' down there... tonight's the night.* If she hadn't heard the reference to an old preacher she wouldn't have trusted that she heard Agatha's name.

Pearl moved under her arm. She held her breath as the child closed her eyes. Maybe it was nothing. Maybe Clancy Miller was just sassing Mrs Miller, telling her he liked coloured meat. That he liked Agatha. She shook her head. No. He was a cruel man, but she'd never heard a white man boast of a coloured woman in his wife's face. No. And to name her? No. It was something else. She thought of the baskets of Agatha's cornbread. Agatha crying with her when Daniel was born. Agatha cursing out Rooster, the only person in the whole County not afraid of him, even with his crippled self.

Pearl opened her eyes and regarded her mother solemnly.

'Oh, Pearl! I need you to sleep! Close yo' eyes!'

The baby whimpered.

Susie picked up a blanket and clumsily tied the little girl to her chest. She took a deep breath and hoisted Daniel onto her hip. Pain stabbed her back. She bit her lip. She had to go. Agatha deserved her own babies one day.

She looked up as her husband entered the room.

'Oh, you stop snorin'! Looka here, I gotta go see Agatha. I ain't gonna be long.' Red Rooster Dixon nodded. He leaned forward and pinched her thigh. Susie cried out in surprise. Rooster smiled.

Miss Ezekiel glared at the man standing in front of her door. He grinned ingratiatingly, revealing a gaping hole in his mouth where three teeth were missing. A fourth curled upwards, as if someone had peeled it back. Now she had the proof. Imagine, Michael staying with the hired help, and this white trash at her door telling her he'd seen her grandson with his own eyes, up on Agatha's porch, merry as the day was long.

'-So I was thinkin' I should hurry on here an' tell you myself that yo' boy with them niggers. Neighbourly-like. Unless you send him there, which case I'm beggin' yo' pardon.'

Miss Ezekiel looked down her nose. 'When you see him, you say?'

'Not more'n ten minutes ago, ma'am. I was goin' home to my supper.'

'Down past Edene? Then how you get here so fast?'

The man gesticulated behind him at the shiny red car in her drive. 'I'm doin' some drivin' fo' The Wilsons.'

Miss Ezekiel drew herself up to her full height. It really was more than a body could stand. This no-good man cavorting the night away with the Wilsons' automobile.

'Well, I know the Wilsons. Very well. I'm gettin' my hat an' you

184

gonna take me to get my boy, hear?'

'Saul's the name, ma'am. Saul Bowkett. Miss Ezekiel, you sure you want to go down…'

She waved her hand. 'Boy, if the Lord righteous in yo' life you not afraid! Jes' set there.'

Agatha took Tony into Pappy's bed with her, singing to him, fighting her horror. Mikey stood by the door.

Tony stared straight ahead as if he was blind. His head lay on Agatha's chest.

'Honey, you talk to me, now. You talk to Agatha. You talk for Agatha like you did that day. There's nothing you can't tell me, baby. Tell me what happened. Are you afraid of New York? What is it? Tell Mom-' She fought back the word, shocked at herself. It might hurt him more. 'Tell me. Tell me what happened, sweet baby.'

Tony stared at the window. Agatha had put three planks against all of them, leaving a small triangle that let the light in.

'Please, Tony. Please say something.' said Agatha.

Mikey sat down on the edge of the bed. He sniffed.

Agatha cursed herself. This was her fault. She should have made him talk about his life. Should have been harder, insisted. Then she would understand. Nothing could hurt him if she understood. She should have known better. If she'd told people about Jamie, if they'd understood, if Eleanor had seen what she and Jamie had meant, it would have been alright. But she had run. She hadn't explained. She looked into Tony's shuttered face, helpless. Yes. If she had talked about Jamie, somebody would have understood their mistake, and it would have eased her heart. This was her own selfishness. That was what locked this child down again. What could she expect, him living with a woman who kept secrets? *He's your mirror,* she thought. *If you don't talk, and you're a grown woman, how's he going to trust his own voice?*

'Tony, talk to me. Tell me what happened,' she said.

'Agatha…' Mikey's voice was puzzled, but she ignored him.

'Tony, please, please, please-'

'Agatha… somethin' burnin',' said Mikey.

She turned and smelt it too. It smelled like her cigarettes, a hundred fold. Like a barbecue. As the smell thickened and spread, the ball in her chest rose up, thudding against her throat.

She could feel a question inside her: *Hysteria or calm? Choose one. Choose one.*

She chose.

She pushed Tony aside. The gun lay on top of the drawer. Her hands felt enormous, like frog-pads. She squeezed her dead fingers around the gun barrel; felt Tony get off the bed. Then Mikey's voice, the spur she needed.

'Agatha, what you doin'-'

She twirled as he spoke and was across the room before he could get another word out, her arms heavy across his chest.

Rooster struck Susie once, but it was enough to knock her backwards across the room. Daniel flew out of her arms as she fell, and she moaned as he hit the floor. He made a strangled sound as all the air left his body, then whooshed back in. He screamed.

Susie crawled towards him. Her panicky breaths sounded too loud in her ears. Underneath her, Pearl moved her arms and finally, began to cry, joining in with her brother's sobs.

Rooster crossed the room in three strides. He picked Daniel up before Susie could touch him and flung him onto the mattress. The boy bounced, his screams rising to a crescendo.

'Rooster!' She was on all fours. 'Rooster what you-'

'You ain't goin' out to see yo' fancy man!' Rooster bellowed. 'Come sit on this bed! You ain't goin' nowheres!'

Susie closed her eyes. All thoughts of Agatha swam up to the fat moon outside, forgotten.

Agatha walked through the front door and onto the porch. She held Mikey as if she would never let him go, one arm across his throat, slightly bent at the waist. Tony watched Mikey's face become the colour of his eyes. His whole body was a question mark. Agatha's lips peeled back from her teeth. The gun was cocked at Mikey's temple. She stepped forward so they were illuminated by the lamp on the porch.

'WHO'S OUT THERE ON MY LAND?' she yelled.

The men came upon her house like phantasms, swooping forward silently. Tony couldn't see where their blazing torches began or ended. They made no sound, but stood, a line of folded arms and white cloth, yards from the porch. Agatha didn't wait for an answer.

'LOOK GOOD! I'VE GOT THIS WHITE CHILD HERE AND I WILL SHOOT HIM DEAD IF ANY OF YOU SONSABITCHES COME ANY NEARER!'

Mikey moaned.

'IF YOU DON'T GET OFF MY LAND I'M GOING TO KILL THIS CHILD!' She yanked Mikey's head up and back. 'YOU SEE HIM? THIS IS MISS CHARITY EZEKIEL'S KIN! HIS NAME IS MICHAEL ABRAHAM TENNYSON! AND I SWEAR I WILL BLOW HIS BRAINS OUT!'

'Nigger bitch, you ain't gonna kill no white boy.' Clancy Miller's voice trembled with rage. His head came forward in the darkness, hood billowing. 'YOU AIN'T GONNA KILL NO WHITE BOY, NIGGER!'

'I'M TAKING THIS BOY INTO MY HOUSE! IF ANY OF YOU MURDERING BASTARDS HIT MY PORCH YOU'RE DEAD AND SO IS HE!' She glared at Tony. 'Get inside!' Tony obeyed her.

'I'M GOING INSIDE NOW!' Agatha backed up swiftly, pulling Mikey with her. Through the front door. Slamming the frame and then the sturdy pine door. Hours of Pappy's labour. She thrust Mikey into the middle of the room and slotted the planks into their niches.

Mikey crouched down by the sofa and clung to its scaly leg. His blonde head pressed against a nail. He felt it cutting into his skull. Tony stood in front of him, rocking back on unsteady soles.

They watched Agatha.

She handled the weapon as if it were something precious but forgotten, a leftover posy from a love affair gone sour. Her face pressed against the board on the front window, her eye set to a crack. Tony stared at her, breathing fast. Suddenly, she looked different. Her father's shirt clung to her breasts. Thick sweat revealed her nipples and clung to her neck. It was the colour of a peach. He'd never noticed that the down on her arms was golden brown instead of black like her hair.

She moved, and the shirt parted, revealing a smoky dip at her waist. Her stomach was beautiful. Curved and mysterious. He shook his head, hotly ashamed. And there, like a tiny devil, the whisper in his head, maddening him: *But she not yo' momma. You could see her like that. Ain't nothin' wrong if you see her like a girl.*

Agatha listened to the air. Momentarily satisfied, she swung around. They watched the gun see-saw.

'This will keep them quiet for a while. Nobody's coming in here right now. We've got time,' she said. 'I boarded up the back, so even if those fools try to break in they'll cuss some. Mikey, I'm going to need you close to me, so come over here. Tony, you make sure you keep your head down in case these sonsabitches think of something stupid-'

Neither boy moved.

Her voice rose. *'I said,* come over here! Tony, I said *sit down!'* She stopped.

'Oh. Oh...' she said.

Tears fell down her face. Tony closed his eyes. When he opened them, she was back. Just Agatha. Crying. Suddenly the fear rushed at him. How could he think of her like that, nasty like that, with the men at the door? *You really crazy,* the voice whispered. It died away from his brain, giggling and giggling.

Agatha folded her feet underneath her and sank down, facing them, her head inches below the window jam. The gun clattered to the floor. Mikey jumped.

They all stared at each other.

'Please.' Her voice was small. 'Please. Please don't be afraid of me. Please. My boys. Don't be afraid of me.'

They stared. In the distance, they could hear the night riders yelling. Agatha's voice caught, like Bea Brown's washing on barbed wire.

'I never meant to scare you. Please. I just want to tell you something. Tell you both something important. Please.'

Mikey crawled forward. He settled against Agatha's breast, drawing his legs up. His hand crept to her shoulder and then to her cheek, as if to catch tears. Tony glanced up at the window. There was nothing to see. He dropped to his knees and crept to the other side of her. She was his mother. He wouldn't think about her like *that*.

Her arms closed around them both.

'I need to tell you a story,' Agatha said. Her voice was soft. 'Mikey, you told me your story, and that's good. When you talk out, it's like a big stone on you gets lifted up.' She pinched his nose gently. 'Didn't you feel good after you told me about your daddy and your momma?'

Mikey nodded.

Agatha looked at Tony. 'I know you can't tell your story, Tony. I can tell that it's too soon. But you're going to tell it one day. And I'm going to show you there's no shame in speaking it out. Telling everything.'

She began to talk as if it were a sunny day. As if they were sitting on muslin grass. As if the telling of it was something she had practised all her life.

27

I am by myself I have never been alone before I am always filling up the space around me distracting myself from me yeah me in the middle of bubbling crowds and Paco Rabanne and raw silk and twirling arms and loud music SUCH a social butterfly

I've been reading and reading and you know what I don't even see the words anymore I heard her call to me an hour ago I walked up the tunnels breathing and listening for her and saw a trickle of yellow and felt her presence she darted behind a rusty drum just near enough for me to see her big eyes and there was a curl of mischief and sorrow tied up in each one

I'm saying *you coming for me bitch then come for me I'm here I'm here* I wasn't afraid anymore and she peeped over the drum and I heard her whisper *tell my story baby tell my story and I might not rip you*

it is dark Chaz is gone and there are no more letters I am touching the ones already here light a candle for myself cut my index finger on the paper edge

remember the time you and Agatha saved me from Timothy the anger jumped off the page I remember the look on his face when they were slapping his belly I have never seen someone so humiliated but I was afraid I didn't want to get into white people's business but Agatha didn't give a shit NOW I have her in my mind in a calico print dress all smooth against a tree branch with a deadly aim biting her bottom lip and I was like *whoa where you learn to shoot lady someone taught you good* and I remember the morning I spoke to her because she was so angry and frustrated when they slaughtered those children then we sang freedom songs all the way down the road can you imagine the guts the irreverence that took SHE WAS NEVER AFRAID I wondered for a long time why she didn't have a man there were so many sniffing around and all this woman had was all these people filling up her grandfather's house and her home was heaven for tortured souls and she didn't make hardly any money but there was always something on the table and she wiped snotty noses while the people who were running just took and took from her but those were good times too we ignored the fear and hid it in the spices she added to the pot we made it stretch to all the bellies of the people running under the cover of night to the North to something else to another existence but there was no one for Agatha sitting on the porch dreaming there was no one to give her any sugar or touch her

do you hear me Agatha I'm getting it right at least it's a start it's been 30 years I know it's a long time to wait but we starting girl

who's afraid of the soul snatcher not me not me not me because it always calls in Agatha's voice not me not me not me and she breathes and she breathes and she breathes and she breathes not me not me not me who's afraid

I'm trying to remember her I'm trying to play a game she used to play it was a parlour word game like Truth Or Dare her grandaddy taught her *who lose their temper on Temper Street* angry Agatha admonishing me for my absence bold Agatha baring her beautiful breasts coy Agatha caring for civil rights workers devilish Agatha damning my soul eccentric Agatha easing my entrails fucking Agatha frowning when I wouldn't speak gorgeous Agatha giggling at her gawking admirers happy Agatha hearing me holler ill tempered Agatha imagining my death joyous Agatha jumping the trains kinky Agatha I wonder if she ever got kinky with her old man I can feel the heart of the story coming hey hey and then will the bitch go away this isn't bad remembering I thought it would be worse but

it's fun

28

Charity Elizabeth Ezekiel raged. Fury made her body a splendid thing. Torch light turned her arms the colour of an old wedding dress. Battered ivory. Her shouting cut through the night and the testosterone. The men caressed their guns and shifted uneasily. Her finger darted in Clancy Miller's face.

'Clancy! Clancy Miller! You ain't gonna take no guns in there an' hurt that chile! You crazy? Y'all crazy? Huntin' niggers make you crazy? You ain't goin' in there, you hear me? *You ain't goin' in there!*'

Clancy's hood fluttered at his shoulder.

'Now, Mizz Ezekiel. You know we all respect you, but this is man's business. You gotta trust us. You need to go on home now. Ain't nothin' gonna happen to yo' kin. The White Knights know better than that.' He beckoned to a tall man seated on the grass, picking at his boot heel. 'You! Go on and set up your boys by the door there. Three a side. You other boys over there go 'round the back an' see what you can do about the back door.'

They started forward, but Miss Ezekiel blocked their path, her hands on her hips. She glared at the tall man in front. 'Ben Harp. Yes, thas Ben Harp in that sheet, ain't it? I know the shape of yo' behind anywhere, an' you still stinkin' with that lavender mess! I know yo' gran'mamma! I know you ain't gonna take no gun near any house with my boy inside there!' The man tried to step around her, but she put a hand in his chest, then up to his face, snatching. 'Don't you move, Ben Harp! Over my dead body you gonna do this thing!'

'God damn!' Ben Harp tore his hood aside. His blonde beard was turning white. He looked at Clancy. 'Maybe she right, Clance. Ain't no sense messin' this up. I ain't come out here to kill no white boy.'

192

The other men murmured agreement. Clancy glared at them.

'What in hell wrong with you all? Ain't nothin'! Ain't nothin' but go inside an' get one little stinkin' nigger bitch! She ain't got nothin' but one gun, prob'ly can't even aim, much less shoot! You gonna let one nigger bitch stand before God Almighty an' His judgement?'

'It don't have to come to that! It don't have to happen like that!' Miss Ezekiel tried to look at all the men at the same time. She wanted to fit her frailty and her age into their eyes. She felt desperately afraid. She'd seen this before. Blood boiling over, eyes curdling, frantic, uncompromising muscles straining with gun butts. Screaming and crashing. She'd seen it too many times to let it happen with her grandson in that house. She wondered how long their respect for her would hold them off.

Clancy was the problem. If he saw her fear he would knock her down and step right over her. 'Clancy, you send one of these boys to get the law. If that gal done somethin' wrong, they deal with it. Get Sheriff Cole down here. He come if he know I'm here!'

Clancy rolled his eyes. 'Why you out here anyway, Mizz Ezekiel? You some nigger lover?' He grinned at the small crowd of men. Necks stretched. Somebody cracked their knuckles. Encouraged, he raised his arms and spread them wide. 'Maybe Mizz Ezekiel forget she was raised a good Christian! What your boy doin' up here? He a nigger lover? I seen him with that bitch-'

'Ain't *about* no nigger. This boy could be your chile. He my family. Get Sheriff Cole!'

Clancy Miller smiled. 'Ben, Get them boys-' He shook his head as Miss Ezekiel opened her mouth again. 'We ain't gonna do nuthin, ma'am. I jes' don' want that Salisbury gal to run nowhere. I'll wait fo' Cole.' He grinned. 'Cole a man who understan' the workin's of the Lord.' The men around him chuckled. 'Cole is Klan.' Charity Ezekiel turned her face to Agatha's house. It looked small and defenceless. She began to pray, her soundless lips moving.

Agatha told them that her grandfather was a good man. Very silent, very soft. He was afraid of life, and as a result, he was afraid for her, his only grandchild. When she was a little girl, she walked with him from room to room, their fingers touching. He gave Agatha to Jamie because he wanted her to be safe.

Jamie was nineteen years old the first time she saw him. It seemed to her that Jamie had been in her life forever. She remembered him from the month she turned ten, coming home from school and finding a white man in her grandfather's house. He sat at the table. Pappy made dinner. She sat on a tall stool, drank the fresh milk that her grandfather put before her and stared at the man. She felt her grandfather watching her, but she was not embarrassed. Pappy let her do things. She'd never seen a white person in her home.

He was tall. His hair was very dark. It brushed his shoulders. His arms and legs were long. His mouth reminded her of ladies wearing lipstick. The shape of his face looked strange, his cheekbones exaggerated slashes in his face, as if someone had inserted steel under the skin. There were dark circles under his eyes. She thought he looked like a boyish girl rather than a girlish boy, sitting there watching her. He leaned forward, and his breath smelled like syrup. *What's your name?* he said. Agatha looked at her grandfather. He nodded. *If you in mah grandaddy house you should know mah name,* she said. Jamie smiled. *Guess I do,* he said. She grinned, delighted that he was not angry. Her teacher told her she was a too clever and loud to be a lady.

What mah name? she said. *Your name is Agatha-Mae,* he answered. *What yo' name?* she asked. *Jamie Campbell,* he said, patiently.

She grew bored. She left the men in the kitchen and walked into the living room. She liked looking at the pictures on the walls, in their ageing, hand-carved wooden and tortoiseshell frames. Her favourites were the pictures of her grandmother and her mother. She could see that she had her mother's mouth, and that her mother had her grandmother's chin. But she and her mother were not the same colour. Her mother was Pappy's colour, reddish brown like the earth. She, Agatha, had her own colour. And her own hair. No-one else had hair like hers.

When Jamie said goodbye she was ready for her supper. She ate her greens, meat and some bread, sitting at the kitchen table where he'd been.

She saw Jamie nearly every day after that. She became used to it, even as she learned the rules of her community: don't matter if Mr Charlie wicked or evil or not-so-bad or pay a good wage or don't pay a good wage. Coloured and white don't mix. She came home from school, did her chores, ate supper, went out into the fields - a small sack of money in her hand - and paid her grandfather's men their wages. He sold corn and some tobacco, and they preserved the garden produce in big jars that were too heavy for her to lift. She chopped tomatoes and string beans, fed the two cows, Elementary Jones and Prizewinner, the three pigs, Summer, Spring and Fall and the mule, Peanuts. And at night, Jamie sat on their porch. When coloured folks came calling, he disappeared into the living room, and read the Bible until they left. Then he picked up his unfinished glass of lemonade and resumed his talks with her grandfather. They talked about the Bible. The seasons. Town news. And all the time, Jamie's eyes followed her.

As she got older, she felt his eyes in a different way. At twelve, she surprised herself by stuttering when he greeted her. She was thrilled and annoyed at the same time. Her ability to trade witticisms and insults became sharper as her breasts grew. She began to shut the bathroom and bedroom doors as her grandfather observed her through the rites of her life: baptism, breakfast, new shoes sometimes, sit with yo' knees together, you a lady. Her teacher bemoaned her sinning ways and intoned the old saying: kin of a preacher was always the worst.

Jamie's name became a song on her tongue. Every day after school, she walked through dust, humming it. His cheekbones became the melody of her still-innocent thoughts. She found that she could hum his name exactly two thousand times before she reached the steps, keeping her head down, only peeking when two thousand was sung and then, oh glory, he was in the chair as always, that evening and the next, his grey eyes sweeping and seeing and crooning her name.

Gone were the days when he held her in his lap, got down on the floor to play jacks, sang old spirituals, his pleasant tenor making the corn whirl and the watermelons tremble. She didn't run after his cigarette smoke circles anymore, sticking her plump fingers through them, lead grey like his eyes. Her fingers lengthened, graceful sweeps of skin and bone, topped with nails that she scrubbed clean, hoping he would smell the good soap. She back-answered him as he ignored her adolescence. She stuck her chest out so that he could see, but he only asked her why she was walking so funny, and if her back hurt. It didn't occur to her that he was too disinterested, too bored, too indifferent - as her nipples sat up straight and took notice of the world - for it to be real. For the first time, she felt self-conscious about her face, wishing both sides smooth.

One night, exhausted by her efforts to make him want her, by her irritation at herself - after all, this was Jamie, old white boy Jamie and she knew that there could be, would be, nothing, and what did she want anyway? - she decided to give up. They were all sitting on the porch and she said she had homework as her belly itched and rolled and her thighs met at a place that threatened to eat her alive. As she stood up, Pappy averted his eyes. He turned away from her. Jamie's face flushed. *What wrong with you?* she snapped. She looked at her grandfather. *Pappy, you sick?*

The old man looked and glanced away again. When he spoke, it was a tone he reserved only for field hands: *Chile, clean yo'self!*

She followed Jamie's eyes downward. The blood spread arrogantly across the skirt wrapped around her thighs. She was frightened. The girls whispered about monthlies but it seemed a vague, unguaranteed promise. She'd decided it wouldn't happen to her. She couldn't move. Jamie would think she was nasty. Then she broke, and ran from the porch, angry at her grandfather's voice and hurt at the downward tilt of Jamie's face.

She scrubbed furiously at her sodden thighs and set the skirt in cold water. She wished for death. Tentatively, she put her fingers between her legs. They came away bloody. When she accepted that she couldn't stem the bleeding she calmed down. It wasn't the gush she'd wondered about, nor did it flow from her like a river.

She found an old shirt, tore it into strips and made a clumsy pad of material for her panties. She organised more strips, destroying three garments. She didn't know how long the scourge would last, and she felt the need to be ready for anything. She knew she wouldn't leave her room until it stopped. She wouldn't look at anyone. The knock at the door, she was sure, would go away if she didn't hear it. But his voice joined the knock, calm, deep, like singing, like his low whistle over the hedge, testing to see if they had company who would ask questions, *why this white man here? What he want? Reverend you crazy?* She was the one who whistled back if the coast was clear.

Agatha? It was he. *Go away,* she said. She gathered the strips, and shoved them under the bed. *Go away. No,* he said. *Let me help you.*

NO! She couldn't have him in the room. Nevertheless, he pushed the door as she knew he would. She realised that the circles under his eyes had lessened over the years, but was that because she had been so young and he had seemed so tall?

He sat on her bed. *How do you feel?* he asked *I'm fine.* She gave him her back, praying that the crimson wouldn't fly onto her fresh dress. *Don't feel bad,* he said. She'd never heard him awkward. *This the first time you get that?*

Mmm-hmmm, she said. She wouldn't cry. This was Jamie. He was a fool anyway. Why the hell did Pappy have him up in the yard? She would ask him to ban Jamie. He was never to come back. She would find out why he came, and whatever it was would not be enough, and she would pout and cry until he was banned.

His hands turned her to him. She thought that he wasn't so tall and that his eyes were as bright as they'd always been. He made her lie on her bed and patted her hair. He told her all he knew about the blood That it would always be with her, until she was a very old woman. It meant she could have a baby on the day that she wanted one. He didn't know how she should take care of herself, but she should speak to a woman, a teacher, one of the church ladies. It might hurt her, but she should put heat on her belly, like his sisters.

Agatha went to sleep with his fingers in her hair, in the shelter of his breath. She slept and forgot about all that she would change in her face. She never knew that Jamie traced the shape of her body with his hands, scooping ghostly kisses from her lips and her elbows.

29

I am lying on the damp floor and all I have to do is concentrate I remember going home with the chant in my ears when the kids said I was crazy crazy and I was shutting down again and my mind said *let's not talk huh let's never talk again* and I remember Mikey standing in front of me but I couldn't hear what he was saying yeah he was scared I see your face brother I don't blame you for being scared because I was rocking like my momma

back and forth back and forth then Agatha's thighs were in front of me *baby who hurt you* she said Mikey's voice was small *he not talking* she put her warm hands on my shoulders *what's the matter baby*

when the night riders came I wanted to cry at her voice she was talking fast but sure like she rehearsed the words in her mind before and all the time my back was tickling and I'm thinking *they're coming in here* imagining what they would do to her *will they hit her or beat her when they come am I big enough to put my body across her maybe if Mikey and me get on top of her they won't hurt her he's a white boy they won't hit him and I can take the licks*

why is she telling us about blood don't she know the night riders wait for her why is she telling us about bleeding it's nasty only girls do that and what was it like when she stood up on the porch did it drip down her thighs or did she leave puddles

don't make me remember the scent of you Agatha don't make me remember my nose in your neck and the tortoiseshell frames on the walls and the stains on the couch and the black room and the bobbing lights outside and Mikey's breath reeking with fear and his hands pale in the strange light you know he held one of mine in both of his and around us your arms were so warm yes I loved you once

I'm retching into the darkness I DON'T WANT TO THINK ABOUT HER BLOOD or holding hands with Mikey no I DON'T WANT TO AGATHA DON'T MAKE ME REMEMBER

30

Tony shifted in Agatha's arms. Mikey opened his eyes. She'd blown out all the lamps and stopped speaking.

Agatha felt their tension spreading down her arms. She couldn't hold the minutes. But she had to tell it all. She knew what the men outside would do to her.

Mikey sneaked a hand out towards Tony. He took it. They looked at her, waiting. Agatha began to talk again.

She woke up to a note by her bed. It made her smile through breakfast, her grandfather trying to slide shame-laden phrases through her happiness. He shuffled, glared at her, and asked the question twice: *Jamie make you sleep?* and when she nodded, it was not enough: *Agatha, Jamie make you sleep?* There was more regret as she tripped down the front steps. *I'm sorry ain't no woman in the house,* he said. She laughed. Stroked the note in her pocket. *Sho' they is, Pappy,* she said. That was what Jamie had written.

You are a woman.

The word held such sweet promise. She could hear herself, talking to her teacher: *I'm not a lady, but I'm a woman now.* Her tongue had weight and substance on this new day, with this new body. She touched her face as two girls caught her up on the road to school. The strange marks didn't matter after all.

Jamie didn't come to the porch that night. Surprised, she walked around the house. He always came. Even when Pappy was called to a sick bed. She and Jamie would sit laughing together and when Pappy returned their merriment eased the smell of death or pain that walked slowly behind him. When they were alone, she asked him the question closest to her heart: *Why you come heah, Jamie? Why you come down heah?* She couldn't count the different ways he side-stepped the question. With a quiet smile, a well-placed pat, a story that made her sides hurt with mirth, and when she really insisted, a glare that made her feel insignificant. She tried sulking but he laughed at her.

She fretted at the door, looking back over their fields waiting for his whistle. Now that she was a woman, surely she was old enough to hear the secret.

The flowers she'd put in her hair on the way home closed and fainted onto her forehead. She had arranged them like the white ladies did, and she wanted him to see them. Her hair, she thought, was better than the white ladies anyway. Its spring and density held the stalks in place. They didn't fall through golden gaps.

Pappy called goodnight from his bedroom. It seemed to her that his voice was hurt and musical. She knocked on his door and stepped back at the expression on his face. He glared at the dying flowers. She realised that he was waiting for Jamie too. *Why he not comin' back, Pappy?* she said. *I don't know,* he said. She stamped her foot. *Then why he come? Why he come an' set with us like we all the same? He know we ain't the same! Why he come? You all readin' the Bible alla the time! He come fo' that, 'cause you a preacher?* Her grandfather looked at the flowers as if he wanted to rip them out of her head. *Agatha, I'm findin' you fresh these days!* She snapped back: *If I'm fresh you never raise me no other way! Chile, don't back talk me like you the Lord Hisself. I don' wanna heah no more! Been a long day!*

She looked at him. All this because of Jamie. Pappy wasn't an angry man. Even when she was four years old and dropped his Bible in Peanuts' sour mash on purpose; even when she was six and told him that she didn't need to go to school to learn to read; even when she stayed at Miss Polly's yard for two days and he was tearing up the whole County trying to find her. She pushed: *Why he come, Pappy? I ain't movin 'til you tell me.*

The slap made her stumble. *Don' ask me!* She put a hand up to her face. The slaps continued, his workman's hands scraping her cheeks. The dead skin on his palms caught on her birthmarks and pulled free. *Don' ask me!* She was driven to her knees, the grey of his beard

201

flashing past the corner of her eye, and the slaps became fists, rolling against her skin. *Don' ask me! Don' ask me! Don' ask me!* Sobbing, she tried to crawl away, finding her voice *Pappy!* and it was finished. There was only his church voice left, unquestionable, untainted in its righteousness: *Don' ask me.*

She searched the neighbourhood, dodging bad breath, leers, white eyes. She knew nothing about his life, save his last name and the small-town clues that he'd provided. She didn't know where to find the Campbell house, but she could walk the town in two hours. Eventually she was directed north, and came to a blue porch where she dug her toes into the front yard dirt. A coloured woman looked up from where she swept the ground. Agatha tugged at her plait so hard that it stopped hurting. *You know Jamie Campbell?* she said. The woman looked at her: *What you want with Mr Jamie?* She didn't know how to lie, and swayed, saying nothing. The woman took pity on her, hoping that gossip would be greeted with gossip. He was gone. Up North. They were all proud of Mr Jamie, so bright, gone up to learn in New York. He wasn't coming back, she knew that because she reckoned it took a man some years to learn the law. All the Campbells took law. *Jamie gone up an' all I know is that his momma rejoicin', see he makin' up for that no-good son they had befo', never amount to nothin'. An' you know I'm right outta a job heah 'cause they followin him up there.* When the woman saw the pretty, high-yellow girl stamp her foot, she shook her head. *Don' vex, gal,* she said. *He never mess with you none? Tell me a pretty gal like you don't gone an' ruin yo' chances an' you expectin'?*

At home, her grandfather sought her fingers with his once again. Sour sweat fell from him onto the clean board floors. Pappy tended his men and harassed his crops and preached the word, and all the time he watched his granddaughter mourn Jamie Campbell like a death. She sleep-walked through her lessons, pleasing them all despite her glassy eyes. She graduated Valedictorian and began to pray and apply for college. Pappy was comforted to hear his words in her mouth. He was ambitious for her: *Book learning is the only way out fo' anyone of us with pride, goes double for a Negro girl.*

Agatha spent summers with her aunt in Mississippi, cleaning tables for take-home money. Customers fell in love with her impertinence, grabbing for her hips and higher. The big cook, so large that he had to enter the kitchen sideways, bellowed threats when he heard her annoyed shrieks.

Stories of her mother poured from her family's tongues. Her mother would have been proud of her. If the Lord had spared Anna Salisbury a day to look at her child she would have been so happy. Her aunt tried every cold cream and home remedy on her face, fussing: *We gotta get you married to a man with money, chile, an' you don't want to be scarin' that fine man when be roll over on his honeymoon mornin'*. She quarrelled back: *The man ain't gonna be blind, he gonna see my face when he gimme the ring* but the tireless attempts went on. Agatha kept trying: *Ain't no man on the road tellin' me I'm ugly* but Aunt Nell would have none of it. The men on the road were looking to disgrace her, not marry her. Finally, Agatha got angry: *My gran'pappy say ain't nothin' wrong with what the Lord make right, so I don't wanna heah no mo'*. After that, her aunts and cousins quieted.

The seasons disappeared. She wrote her grandfather long, lazy letters to tell him how the college and the girls were and what she learned. He travelled up for her graduation, and when she peeked from behind the curtain, between the brown legs of her graduating class, she saw that he was crying, without shame, near the front. Afterwards, he was on her: *You ain't comin' home?* No, she said. *I've found a job teaching. I'm not comin' back South.* Her voice was straightening, and he liked to hear it. He said: *You forgive me, Agatha. You a good girl. You go to the Lord an' you done forgive me?* Her confirmation did not hurt her. The beating had been years ago. She marvelled at how quickly she'd forgotten Jamie, in between harmless kisses. As long as it took to bob her hair and whisper about those dirty girls who went with white men for the price of a drink and a laugh. She didn't tell anyone about Jamie, and she saw the bitter lines in her grandfather's face melt.

She taught Mathematics. As she marked term papers, she thanked God that she was no longer in a small town with its hypocrisy and rage. She was happy. Flirtatious, but not unseemly; thinking about who she should be wife to. Harnessing young minds.

203

Six lectures froze her brain, her arms full of papers, struggling for the door key, and there he was, a smile in each eye, the shadows like yesterday. *What's your* name? Jamie said. She dropped the papers. *If you at my door you must know my name,* she said. They laughed and chased Mary Ellen's A and Brad French's C all over the road. Inside her room he looked at her books, curtains, crockery. She was ashamed at how small it was, but proud that he could find no dust. Surely he was a lawyer now, with his heart full of grand things. He made her sit down, and dashed out, came back with good hot food. He dropped a dish, and they skidded on rice grains. She told stories about her students and saw how much older he was. He told stories of the courts and saw how much older she was. They didn't talk about why he was there. She was afraid that questions would drive him away.

In the early morning the clatter of conversation finally ceased, both of them lying side by side on the day-bed that acted as her couch. She ached from the good wine and the bad thoughts and his hair was too close not to touch. He put careful kisses on her face, each one burning her skin, leaving a gentle imprint. His lips were slow. Over and over again he put the tiny kisses on her face, as if she was precious, and each one was proof. His tenderness made her gulp great breaths of air. He placed his palm on her right cheek and self consciousness swamped her.

Why is your face like this? he said. *Pappy never tell you I was born like this?* she asked, trying to smile. *They say my momma was distressed at birth. I had a caul on my face. They usually come off easily, get buried under a tree, you know the tales. This one left me scarred. Pappy says the midwife was surprised. The caul was fine and pretty, my face underneath was-* Beautiful, he said. She laughed. *Your sweet mouth. I was going to say strange. No,* he said. *No. Tell me about your momma,* he said. *What do you know? Nothing,* she said. *She was a wonderful young woman with my sassy mouth and she died in childbirth.* She stirred. *That's it.* He raised on his arm and looked down at her. *You look as if you fell asleep on a piece of lace. Like it imprinted its pattern on your face.*

Agatha nearly cried. She did cry when he bent between her thighs, scooping moisture from her with his tongue. She held her breath to concentrate on the stroking, moving towards a place that was so mystical and sensitive that tears were not enough. She pushed her hips into his face. She bit her lips and dug her fingers into his scalp, pulling him closer in so she could rub herself against his mouth. Jamie came up and tangled his teeth in her hair. His fingers slipped inside her, rubbing against sensitive grooves, finding places that stretched her legs wide.

The smell of her filled the room. Her nipples hardened, left side, right side, then back again. Jamie's eyelashes crumpled against her flesh. He held her hand to feel her heartbeat and then he held her hand to make her feel him. She gripped him too hard and he made her slow down. He watched her while he entered her, moving so slowly and so surely that she was forced to let go in streams of heat and breathing, amazed that he could fit, and all the time he murmured *you like how that feels?* and *yes* she breathed and there was another inch and *you like that?* panting against her cheek until she became savage *YES YES I LIKE IT* and she pulled him the rest of the way. He waited until he was sure she knew him inside her, until she became angry, hitting his shoulders and begging him not to be still, and then he pulled out, pushed in, pulled out, hips circling wide and then in again, harder, as she began to scream. She screamed until she heard his laughter against her temple *I want to stop it I can't stop* she gasped *stop then, baby, stop and laugh with me* so she laughed, still climaxing, so tired that all she could do was cling to his back.

He brought a jug of water to the bed and sprinkled it on her brow. She slept, but he woke her for more. It was only when they heard students calling to each other outside that they moved into dreams.

Agatha let the boys sleep, listening for sounds outside. An hour had passed, and the night riders had not yet marched.

31

I didn't want to hear *why she telling us this nasty stuff why she telling us her private stuff she says we gotta keep the memories alive why she telling us* she never gave no details yeah she told us that she made love to him but she never told us what his dick looked like she never told us if she came or not but honeychile looked like she'd want to come like she'd need to come LIKE SHE'D DEMAND IT

Agatha she was the only mother I ever had and I don't want to think of her spreading her legs but she loved somebody and somebody loved her back and Mikey's nails are deep in my hand I can see the confusion in his face and she was sweating it all collected on her top lip and I jumped because the gun was near my feet and it reminded me of a snake waiting and heavy and she saw me and she kept talking but she moved it away from my legs because she knew I was afraid I tell you Agatha knew a little boy's thoughts yes she did and we tried to listen to her do you know how hard it is for the average person to listen I mean really listen it's so hard for a man your mind's always dancing on some shit in the present yeah settling on the now as people talk to you if a man ain't got a pot to piss in a nigga to cuss or a woman to want he concentrates on his own breathing the rush of his own blood but he doesn't listen you know we tried so hard that night

I wanted to pull the sides of the house around us like a shield *they coming Agatha what you doing about it why are you talking and talking about love and this white man with his grey eyes*

I'm eating fucking Oreos I'm cramming them into my face I'm shouting through the saccharine *where you at now huh where you at*

now I'm remembering and you're not with me you coulda been with me why am I
    alone
    with this

32

Agatha woke them up. She shook occasionally in the telling, as if the memories had been closed inside her for too long. Mikey touched her face. Tony kissed her cheek.

In the halls, students and lecturers commented on the change in Miss Salisbury. Her usually cheerful face was now so happy that they whispered it could only be love. Male teachers exchanged looks of regret. They waited for the first appearance of the man and the wedding announcement. No-one that joy-struck could be doing anything less than planning her honeymoon.

She heard them and didn't care that they knew. She saw the staff room faces brighten as she entered. Her friend Eleanor, who taught history, demanded to meet the man who was rolling her eyes up in her head. There were invitations by the score, more than even she was used to receiving. Campus couples vied to be the ones who first invited Miss Salisbury's boyfriend to dinner. Everyone knew that the honour would fall to Eleanor.

Agatha and Jamie hid together. Classes and court were tiresome and they chafed at the responsibility. He arrived, a familiar knock on the door, and she was there seconds later, grinning, swept up to him, a flurry of arms and skin on the floor. They examined each other's bodies with minute precision. One morning he groaned into her ear: *I feel like I'm dying.* She clung to him, understanding. It was if a layer of her skin had been removed. Sometimes the intensity of their lovemaking was so unbearable that she burst into tears: *Oh God Oh God Oh my God.*

But soon she noticed that he only came to her at night. The taboo of their different coloured skins skirted under their lover's whispers like a warning: *I told my friend about you, but she doesn't know,* she said. *Don't think too much,* he said. *There will be an answer. At least we're not home, this is New York. I know white men with Negro women.* Yes, she said. *I do too. But they're sad women, and they never get to meet their lover's mommas.* He was silent, then: *Of course you'll get to meet my momma.* She smiled: *Really?* She didn't say what she wanted to say: *I never met your family once when I was a little girl.* She hoped that something had changed.

They went to Eleanor's small brownstone in Brooklyn, self-conscious and excited, out as a couple for the first time. They rode in Jamie's gleaming green car. Agatha took Jamie's left hand in both of hers. He knocked with the other. Hayward, Eleanor's husband, pulled it open, smiling: *Agatha!* He tried to conceal his surprise, and they tried to pretend it wasn't there. *Pleased to meet you, Jamie. Ellie, they're here, come out of the kitchen, girl!* Her friends shook hands, pretending. As the men walked the hallway into the small front room, Eleanor hissed: *Girl, what you doin'?* then fell into the meal's ritual, taking coats, filling glasses full of wine and plates full of aromatic food.

Jamie regaled them with stories of court and Eleanor and Hayward laughed at the right places. Agatha sat there and remembered how she felt the first time she came face to face with white teachers. How afraid she'd been that her work would not come up to some absurd white standard. She thought of the pleasant but formal relationships she had with white faculty members and the dreadful nervousness she felt the first time she stood before an integrated classroom. Jamie kept up with the jokes and Eleanor laughed in spite of herself. Agatha thought about the fact that Jamie was the only white person who had never felt white to her. He didn't feel black, but she was not resentful, or scared of him, and that was what white was: fear. And if she wasn't afraid anymore, what colour was he, and did it matter? Jamie complimented the food, his hand never moving from her arm.

Finally, it was not his colour that made Eleanor angry or Agatha weep. It was his absence. As the relationship moved through passion and asked for comfort, she found that it was not there for the taking. Jamie disappeared for days. First time became second became fifth

209

became tenth and even though he came back, with his maddening, soulful smile, she began to die inside. She asked him over and over to include her in his life: *Why do you leave me, baby? What? 'Cause I'm coloured? Because you're ashamed? What is it?* But all he would do was hold her, ten days growth of beard on his face, his eyes weary, the fatigue of something he would not explain deep in his bones, saying *No, no, it isn't your colour. It has never been your colour.* He came to her bruised, his eyes inward-looking, sat in her two rooms and asked forgiveness with his slow, enigmatic stare. *Please be with me,* he said. *Please lie down with me.* Agatha sat on the other side of the room, desperate, angry, afraid. But too soon the maze of him moved her and she soothed him. Fell into the tangle once again.

Frustration followed her through the classrooms, and stalked her through their thirsty sheets. He peeled her open and twisted his tongue into thick knots inside her. He made her rake her nails across the long roll of his back. She divided his body into a grid of tiny squares and placed a kiss in each one. He knelt at her feet, arms locked around her waist, and examined her vagina as if he were committing it to memory. They watched each other masturbate. She felt that they were perverse angels together. She could not say no.

In their first winter she slipped on grey ice in her excitement to tell him that she was pregnant. He lifted her so high that her head brushed the ceiling. He gave her a soft toy, but by the time he returned an empty fortnight later, she'd seen the hospital walls. The ice was thick on the streets as her body rejected the life inside her and spread it over her sheets and floor.

When he knocked, Agatha was past caring about his bruises. She couldn't forgive the world. Nobody could understand. Not even Jamie. She rose: *I'm going for a walk,* she said. She needed a long path through the snow to lose the ache. She could see the heavy white through the window. It seemed vast. She thought that she would lose herself, catch a few snowflakes, distract herself. Her body felt empty. The baby had taken her heart and her lungs. She would find out where her baby had gone.

Jamie saw that she wouldn't return. He held her. She struggled, wanting to pack the snow inside her. She punched his face and scratched him. She was strong. He held her brutally. When she tired, she leaned against him, his back to the door.

He wrapped his body around her and, inexplicably, began to laugh. It was like wine. She began to fight again but Jamie kept laughing, gently, softly, inviting her. He put his mouth to her mouth and the laughter bubbled over his lips. It flowed out into her, filling her with thick bubbles that burst and caressed her face, her throat, orange-hot liquid flames. Agatha became so full that she gasped, and the liquid overflowed, back into him. They stood at the door for most of the night, switching the warmth back and forth, giggling and crying. He told her she should wear her hair up and never feel ashamed of her face. She told him he wore terrible ties, dipped her fingers into the shadows under his eyes and licked her nails. They giggled more and got drunk on the orange laughter. *I know the emptiness,* he said. *I know how you feel. That's how I've felt all my life. Please,* she said. *Please tell me what makes you feel this way? I don't know,* he said. *It's always been there. Emptiness. Perhaps I am mad.*

After the baby and the orange laughter he stayed longer. They walked the New York streets, bouncing forgiveness off the buildings. She pretended that he would stay. Their connection was deeper, their love even stronger, and his admissions of emptiness would lead to promises. When he was gone again she sat with Eleanor. She promised her friend that she would leave him, that things would change. Hayward skulked past, apologetic and embarrassed. Eleanor had made the right choices. Eleanor knew that her husband would return - and when. Eleanor questioned her: *Is he married? I see that he loves you, girl. But maybe he's married. You think that? I don't know, I don't know,* Agatha said. *I know he loves me, I know he belongs to me. It's something else. I don't know what it is! He's always been like this!* Eleanor frowned. *Always? How long have you known that man, Agatha?* Agatha stared at the floor. *Since I was a girl,* she said. *I've never loved anybody else, I don't know how to be with anyone but him.*

The pain disabled her. The Dean called her to his office. *Best you take time off,* he said. *You're a good teacher, but I cannot accept your private life affecting your work.* He was kind. She took time. She played with knives and long pins. Eleanor came to visit and took her home when she saw the intricate task Agatha had begun. The lacy fingers on her face were red lines. She'd cut open each inexplicable scar.

She slept most of the time, waking and then forcing herself to sleep once more. She vomited the soup that Eleanor fed her. Consciousness was too painful.

One afternoon she woke to Jamie's shouts. She dragged herself to the door and into the hall. He was trying to push past Eleanor. Hayward was at work, and there was no-one to help. Eleanor tried to pull her away, but Jamie grabbed her hands and sat at her feet, hugging her calves. He began to cry and to tell her the truth.

'Sheriff, I'm so glad to see you.' Miss Ezekiel clutched at Sheriff Cole's shirt. 'This here thing is crazy! These boys sayin' that gal done some thing, stirrin' up them niggers. I don' care 'bout that! But my grandson inside there, you know my Michael, an' that gal got a gun to his head like she wanta kill him! What you gonna do 'bout it?' The Sheriff regarded her calmly. Piggy eyes glittered above his fat cheeks. 'Well, now, ma'am.' He patted her arm. 'This gal work fo' you, right?'

'That's what I been tellin' you!' Miss Ezekiel shivered. The night was getting colder. She'd already refused two offers of robes from the men. 'What you gonna do 'bout my boy?'

Sheriff Cole rasped his thumb across his chin. 'That depend on what that nigger think about fire, ma'am,' he said, 'Cause she gotta come out. That gal is a criminal in the eyes of the Lord and in the eyes of the law.'

Miss Ezekiel looked at the torches. They were blazing again.

33

I must have slept like Agatha did when Jamie hurt her you know
flowing in and out of consciousness yes I made myself go to sleep and I
dreamed and in the dream I was not Underneath I was in a clean bed
my man was leaning over me with coffee and doughnuts there were big
windows and fluffy clouds

he's going away as I wake up *no no I want to be with him let me
stay where it's clean and light*

Marcus raises his hand and his fist is full in my face he's pushing my
head back against the wall YOU BASTARD I CAN SMELL THE
BITCHES ON YOU

cookies are smeared in my beard I'm trembling and I'm awake

I'm looking out of the window on good old Greyhound and there
are people rushing back and forth feeling the Southern summer it's so
hot and I am the last one off the bus but I don't know who I am looking
for and then I see her in between the embraces between cousins and
aunts and between the grandchildren saying *what you bring me* and
their Mommas cuffing them *you say hey to your Grandma like you got
manners* and her hair is on top of her head it's pulled up in a white rag
and she is reaching up to touch it

she is standing shoulder to shoulder with the men and she is all in
white *I never seen a woman in white except for weddings* and her
white dress is blowing and the bottom of it is playing in the dust but
not getting dirty *how she do that* and I'm climbing off the bus and this
woman is moving towards me I see that her face is funny but oh so full
of light and I'm stopping at the bottom step and behind me the driver
says *boy you not getting off* and I step into new life an untrodden dirt

213

road and she is the only one looking at me her smile is the widest I've ever seen and her hand is reaching down to my head which is all messed up because Cousin Eleanor didn't even cut my hair and while I'm thinking that her hand is soft on my cheek she is tracing a line down my face and the tenderness there well it's like she loved me before she saw me

I look up into Agatha's face and there are delicate lines scattered on her skin and I'm thinking *how you get to be so pretty* while she's kneeling down in the dirt and the white dress to face me and her hand's stroking my face

hey Tony she says

she is holding me in this place Underneath and I can feel our tears running down her fingers they're laced in my fingers she's holding my hand there and now she's holding my hand here the woman I loved the most

God I hear you Agatha

I am the storyteller

34

She spoke rapidly. Her voice was almost cold. She had to finish, and then she would give herself up. The boys would know the story. It would still be alive. Mikey would know the truth. Tony would know he had to speak the truth.

Jamie sat on Eleanor's hallway floor. His tears dried, but his eyes continued to cry. Agatha stood very still, looking down at him. She closed her face as he painted pictures in the air between them.

He had not lived in his parents' house since the day after Agatha's first menses. The Campbell home was criss-crossed with rules. They were invisible traps that sliced at the ankles. Ignorant visitors tripped over promises. Promises not to say the wrong thing at the wrong time, to not reach for a plate other than the one designated, to not dare speak in the hush that was a Campbell tradition, to not scare the silent men and women inside the walls with boisterous jokes.

At supper time the family sat around the big table, Jamie's father Eliott at one end, his paternal grandfather, Paul, at the other. On the left hand side, his younger sisters, Faith, Hope and the incongruously named June perched in identical chairs, dressed in identical button-up dresses. Their grandmother sat next to them, at hand for spills and hiccups. Eliott placed his sons on the right hand side of the table. It was correct, he often pointed out, for his boys to be on the right. They would become men who would follow in the Campbell footsteps, all the way to the law courts. Eliott loved the law, its order and rhythms were as inexorable as himself. Jamie's mother, Eve, never sat down. Despite their maidservant, Eliott Campbell found it fitting that his wife serve her family, like his mother before her.

Jamie's father believed in sharing, and he did so every evening at supper time. When Jamie was older, he realised that it was not the rules nor the tip-toeing of his mother that made him hate his father, but the fact that the man was so boring. Eliott described the courtroom beams and judge's chair every time he tried a case. His days were humourless, colourless, repetitive. He punished them with his days, all silent except for the clink of deftly-moved dishes, all quiet except for Paul Campbell, full of nostalgia for his working past, and Peter.

Peter was the only Campbell who refused to be still. He was the only person who could interrupt Eliott, eagerly asking his father for more details. He loved his father, and he wanted to be a lawyer more than he wanted anything else. Jamie looked forward to his brother's excited outbursts. They were miniature rebellions across the table. Peter told jokes that made his sisters choke, earning them their father's glare.

Everybody in Edene knew the stamp of a Campbell man. It was amazing. The girls looked like their mother, the boys like generations of Campbells before them. The genes were strong and brooked no argument. The tilt of the jaw, the unruly hair, and especially the smile. They were slow smiles, twitching at the base of the chin, spreading carefully, coaxing the mouth crooked, dripping into their dark grey eyes as if God had stopped by and poured honey in each socket, spilling down the whole face. They said that a Campbell smile stole your heart, but it came like a rare flower, once, perhaps twice a year.

Peter first saw the girl out of his bedroom window. She was small and quick, with dusty blue shoes. Her face was fine and broad. There was something about her that made people want to take care of her. She parted her thick hair in the middle and wore it in a long plait down her back. All of her body, arms, legs, face, seemed burnished and rubbed to a dull glow. And she smiled, an effortless smile, an easy smile that broke into huge, whooping chuckles and snorts that were totally unladylike and utterly irresistible to the boy in the window.

Peter loved her. This girl who passed every morning at seven, surrounded by her friends, with her lunch money clenched in her fist.

Peter with his tall self, his broad shoulders, shoulders that up to the moment he saw the girl laughing, had easily held all the duties and responsibilities and expectations of his family. Suddenly, the pretty girls that were paraded through his home, pushed forward by Acheson County mammas anxious for the first son's hand, were dull.

He kept his feelings close to his heart. When the knowledge became too big, he began to whisper its details to Jamie. His seven year-old brother didn't understand, but he was proud that his brother told him his secrets. He listened to his brother's determination. He would speak to this girl and he would kiss her lips one day. He was stubborn. First-born. Used to getting what he wanted.

When the smiling girl saw Peter loitering around the five mile walk from her school, she was afraid. The tall white boy looked at her so intensely, as if he knew her. She hurried past him, her eyes on the track. On the third occasion he said hello to her and she mumbled a greeting in return. She wanted to tell her father that the boy was following her, but she knew her father. He had no fear, and he would get himself into trouble if he talked to a white family. She'd seen her father talk to white men as if he were their equal, and their faces scared her, bent and misshapen at his arrogance. Her father was fiercely protective of her. He didn't even allow coloured boys at his gate.

Peter told Jamie about each victory: the way she pushed the sun out of the way to see his face. How her mumbles became clearer and more confident. One morning he picked a yellow flower from the backyard and cradled it in his hands, waiting to give it to her. He told Jamie how her face shone when he handed the flower to her. He said: *I brought this flower to show it how beautiful you are.* She hurried away, but not before he saw her pleasure. She put the dying flower in a cup of water in her room and the next day, when Peter called to her, she left the path and went up to him to share her smiles. She didn't go to school that day, but walked in clumsy, happy silence as he took her into the woods. He picked handfuls of flowers and trickled them onto her head, making her sneeze. She told her teacher that her father had extra chores for her and she could only come to school three days a week.

By the end of that summer she began working for Mrs Campbell. Peter tried not to hover. He became as silent as his family at the table, trying to catch his lover's eye without betraying them both.

By August, they lay together in hidden places in the woods, and by their second summer, the girl grew fat and round. Peter told Jamie their plans. He was saving. They would run away, hop good old Greyhound and disappear. In love and careless, he forgot that whispers were shouts in their home. He didn't know that the promises his little brother made, over and over, not to tell, never to tell, crashed to the ground and crept into waiting ears. Her name fell down the stairs: *Anna-Mae. Anna-Mae. Anna-Mae Salisbury.*

Agatha's face cracked open. Revulsion ran rivulets into her open mouth. Jamie held onto her legs. Confused, Eleanor looked from one to the other. As the words formed on Agatha's lips, Eleanor leapt at Jamie. Her hands beat harmlessly on his back.

That's my momma name, Agatha said. *My daddy is your brother? You my... you my... Jamie... you...*

I'm your uncle, said Jamie. He held onto her hands, and Agatha looked at the bandages around each of his wrists. *I'm your uncle,* he said.

Eleanor screamed: *You lousy sonofabitch! You sick bastard! Get outta this house! Leave her alone!* But Agatha shoved her away from the man at her feet. This was it. Finally. A tattered answer.

Tell me the rest, she said, *then I never want to see you again.*

Jamie followed Anna-Mae on her morning walk, giggling at her swollen belly. The August sun shone down on him, streaming boiling gold across the lawns as he moved behind bushes and buildings. Peter had asked him to look out for her while he was gone for the day, and that was what he meant to do, but his brother had warned him that she would be mad if she saw him. She said that Peter fussed too much.

Anna-Mae's stomach bounced as she walked, as if she'd swallowed a huge balloon as a prank. On the town roads, young boys yelled and fried eggs on the sidewalk. The old joke. Anna-Mae's stomach was covered with green and yellow cloth. Jamie followed her as she walked through the woods, humming into the wet grass. She looked funny but she was still the most beautiful woman he had ever seen.

He was puzzled when the man walked towards her. The man was

still strong, with very white hair and hands. Jamie opened his mouth, but the greeting died in his throat. He watched the man punish Anna-Mae, placing well-aimed blows in her stomach, tearing at her breasts until blood soaked her blouse. He stared as Anna-Mae rolled in fear, boots in the small of her back. He saw bruises burst from her dark flesh, her nose flatten against her cheeks, her tears and vomit and cries staining the grass and sinking into the earth. He watched as the man laughed with each blow. The man's hands tore at Anna-Mae's hair. He spat on her. Finally he urinated on her silent body, then walked away, like a hard worker at the end of a shift.

Jamie came forward from the protective trees. Anna-Mae's hands fluttered on her belly. He bent over her as she gave birth. He lifted the baby and tried to show it to her. They were so alike, and she might be comforted.

Her eyes stared into the blue sky.

He picked up the baby. He walked, stumbling, but he didn't fall. People with black mouths and eyes stared at him, making him frightened. The baby cried. He looked down into her crumpled face and walked faster. The umbilical cord bled onto his pants. Eventually, two women rushed up to him, their questions beating his brow. He gave the baby to them and told them who she belonged to.

His home was as silent as ever as he limped towards it. He'd cut his foot on a stone. He stopped at the wooden gate and looked up at the house. He sat and waited for his brother, who was out of town with their father. Peter hadn't wanted to go; Anna-Mae's time was too near.

Jamie sat at the gate and wondered if his mother was washing his grandfather's shirt in the sink. She knew what to do with evidence. She was a lawyer's wife. He waited for his brother. He wanted to be the one to tell him.

Peter saw him first, whimpering through the dusk. His arms were tacky with the blood and mucous that had dried on his skin. Peter shook him: *What happen?* he asked, low. *What? Anna-Mae have the baby? Something happen to the baby?* Jamie stuttered. He was tired and terrified, and his mind would not register the old man who sat in the living room, back and forth in the rocking chair, like he'd done nothing. Peter shook him savagely. He looked into his brother's face and whispered as their father came up behind them.

Grandad kill Anna-Mae in the woods, he said.

Jamie told Agatha that he'd never forget his brother's face when he heard that Anna-Mae was dead. It seemed to fall in on itself. And because of the stamp that played across all their faces, it seemed to him that the man who shook him and shook him and shook him was not his brother after all, but his grandfather.

Jamie began to scream. For the first time in three generations the Campbell house became a place of noise.

The swearing and shouting went on late into the night. Eliott ordered his mother and wife into the house and strode across the big blue porch, swearing alternately at his eldest son and his father. He couldn't believe that his father had set on the girl without discussion. It was unnecessary. He could understand the anger, first child out of his grandson by a nigger, but who would care or notice? It was as old as time. He yelled in Paul Campbell's face: *Peter's not a fool, daddy! If he get himself some nigger pussy there's no harm! He knows what his life is gonna be! It'll take more than a nigger gal to mess him up!* The old man yelled back: *You expect me to sit here while my own flesh an' blood give me a nigger great-gran chile? I knew you wouldn't do anything, so I took it in my own hands!* He thumped his knee for emphasis. *My own hands, boy! They can still take care of Campbell business!*

Eliott glared at his son. *What's this dead girl's name? Amy-May? Anna-Mae? Who's her family, boy?*

Jamie looked at Peter. He was huddled on the steps, hugging himself. He had not said a word since his face had changed. None of the anger and noise seemed to register for him, until he heard his father call his lover's name. His voice was thin and clear. *I loved her daddy. I loved that little girl. An' her name was Anna-Mae. She work here, an' I know you never even seen her.* He nodded, as if that would make it real. *She work here, daddy. An' I loved her.*

His father stopped, mid-tirade and stared at him. Then: *Well, you a fool. And your grandaddy was right to deal with her.*

Father and son stared at each other. Afraid, Jamie stepped between them. Peter didn't move. He said: *Nothin' you say don't make no difference, Daddy. She's dead, and I'm alive.* He stared at Jamie, beseeching: *How can I be alive?*

Jamie saw the thin, grey man before anyone else. The man stood in the middle of the yard, looking at them. He wore a pressed, starched suit. He looked as if a sigh would push him to the ground.

I would like to speak to Mista Campbell the Second, Arthur Salisbury said. His enunciation was perfect.

Jamie's father moved forward. *What do you want on my land?*

The Reverend Salisbury stood very straight. His grave eyes were wet and fixed on Jamie. *My name is Reverend Arthur Salisbury. I come fo' my chile.*

Eliott Campbell glared at him: *What you say, boy?*

Arthur ignored his tone. *I come fo' my chile,* he said, as if it were a simple thing. He spoke with the kind of voice you would use to teach a very small girl. *I come fo' my chile. An eye fo' an eye, the Bible says. You take my child, I want one of yours.* He moved his eyes back to Jamie. *I want yo' blood promise.*

Agatha's grandfather had revenge for the death of his daughter. As Jamie Campbell, nine years old, stood watching the old man curse his family, their generations and their blood, something inside him calmed. As Arthur Salisbury was pushed, kicked and beaten off their land, and he saw Peter beg for the old man's life, the old man who refused to fight, he thought of the child he'd held in his arms and the dying woman.

Jamie Campbell promised himself to Agatha Salisbury that night. Not in love, but in pain, in the echo of his grandfather's boots in Anna-Mae's body, the only thing protecting Agatha from fury. Surely the waste from his grandfather's body had burnt its way into Agatha's face. Paul Campbell's soft eyes had not stopped smiling as they murdered. They were the same eyes Jamie saw in every mirror he passed. By the time he was nineteen, his bedroom silent once again, his brother long gone, he'd learned how to shave without a mirror and he walked into Arthur Salisbury's house to keep his promise.

Mikey's eyes were wide. 'Agatha, you ever see him again? Thas why you don' wanta speak to Luke? 'Cause you love Jamie?'

Agatha pulled him closer and breathed his scent into her nose. Seconds ticked away. She slipped her palm under Mikey's chin and pulled his face up.

'Mikey, there's something I have to tell you. I know it's going to shock you, but you need to know. You listen to me, now. You trust me, don't you?'

Mikey nodded. Agatha traced his face as she spoke.

'I nearly fell down the first time I saw you.' She stroked his eyebrows. 'I wanted to run away from that house. Never look at you again.'

Mikey twisted in her arms. Shame rose in his throat, so hot that he felt as if he couldn't breathe. 'It's cause I'm fat. I know I'm ugly, Agatha. But you never say nothin', you never make fun-'

Her face contorted. 'Oh no, baby, no! It's *nothing* like that. You're a fine looking boy. Just that-' her voice dipped into a whisper, '-just that, my God, you are so alike!'

Mikey waited.

'I looked at you, baby, and I knew. Didn't make any sense. I told myself it wasn't possible. But there was no argument I could make. You have the same face. Oh, you're blonde, like your momma, but that doesn't matter. Jamie told me about that stamp, and the eyes, but I never thought I'd see those eyes again. I left New York to get away from them. I've loved them for twenty one years.'

Mikey breathed through his nose, still confused. Tony sat, open-mouthed. He looked at them, Mikey and Agatha, back and forth.

'I didn't need anything but his face in your face to know. But I didn't want to see. And then you told me about your daddy. Peter Tennyson and the names he called when he was dying.' She still whispered. 'What did he say while he was dying, baby?'

Mikey's mouth fell open. 'Allison... he was sayin' Allison. Thas my momma. He say he don't know if she dead, but he know he gonna see her some day in heaven.'

Agatha smiled. It was sad and bright. 'What else did he say, Mikey?'

Mikey began to cry. 'He say Allison, thas my momma name, an' he say Anna. Anna-Mae an' Allison.' He brought his fists up to the tears. 'He say he gonna see Allison an' Anna-Mae. He gonna walk an' talk with Allison an' Anna-Mae. When he get to the Lord. He ain't gonna be alive no more an' he gonna get to see them in a big white garden, with red roses an' good things, an' the Lord gonna bless all of 'em, when he see Allison an' Anna-Mae in the garden of Eden.'

Agatha lifted his face again. She smoothed the tears away from his eyes. 'Nice to know where my daddy went. Nice to know my little brother.' They looked at each other. 'You've sure got Campbell eyes.'

They clung to her as she thanked them for listening, even as the cold voices of the night riders echoed through Agatha's land. They heard the fire crackling. She told them she would always be with them.

'BITCH, WE KNOW YOU STILL IN THERE!'

Agatha wept as the boys tried to hold her. She twisted in their arms, the memories heavy. She began to wail. For Jamie. For the mother and father that she'd never known. For all she could have had.

'WE KNOW YOU IN THERE! WE GONNA BURN THIS PLACE DOWN IF YOU DON'T BRING OUT THAT CHILE IN FIVE MINUTES!'

Agatha's head came up. She stopped struggling.

'COME OUT NOW, GAL! WE GONNA BURN THIS PLACE DOWN!'

Agatha pushed their hands away. The voice on the wind was so familiar. She wanted him so much, now, at this time, when she told their story. He should have been there to help her tell it. It wasn't impossible that he could be there now, for her, when she needed him most.

'AGATHA SALISBURY!'

Agatha reached for the front door, laughing at the sound of Jamie Campbell's voice.

35

Gather around as I become the storyteller.

In the end I told it all. It had to be me. In this hell. In this heaven, kicking the needles aside.

We will never know why she ran to the door. It was as if she had no choice. She did not tell us. There were no final words. We were holding her. Trying to stop her. Mikey was screaming, but I believe she was ready to die.

The bullets spread red roses across her chest and her legs. Pushed her back into our arms like a moth, as if she was light. There was a sigh from the night riders as they saw her fall. The sounds came back to my throat as I pulled her clear. I was screaming, enraged, disbelieving, screaming no, no, no. It was Mikey who slammed the door and lifted the planks back into place. I don't know how he did it. For seconds there was nothing but breathing in that room and the sound of gun barrels on the walls.

Mikey cried. I couldn't. She poured across the floor, but her eyes were still alive. My arms were dipped in sticky rivers.

I looked into Mikey's face. We agreed in those moments, splinters raining down on us from the door. We couldn't let the night riders finish her, drag her, defile her. We knew it as the door buckled with their blows. Mikey reached up to the couch. She twisted, her mouth opening and closing, blood spraying onto my chest. She wanted us to hear her story. Not only to hear it, but to tell it. She wanted people to know she lived, who she loved and why. She wanted Eleanor to know. And perhaps somewhere Jamie knew she told their story too. It was a sick tale. A sad one, and one she could not change. She was trying to

224

tell me to speak, to always speak it out, and she led me into this filth to learn the lesson I had not learned. The lesson always comes back.

It was me who pressed the cushion across her face, past that skin, those scars, that tale. It was me who saw the alarm in her eyes and I know now that her fear was not for herself but for us. The price we would pay and the smell of our inevitable nightmares. I was thirteen years old. I leaned forward and I took the last of her life, and it is my guilt that has made her a monster in my mind.

Agatha shimmers in this darkness. Today she kissed my forehead the way she did at the Greyhound bus stop. Ran her fingers through my messed up hair, took scissors to my scalp. Told me she had a honey and lime kiss for me. And I saw myself reflected in her eyes: a little boy, alive, wriggling, giggling, clear innocence in his eyes. With raven lips, ebony eyes, tight jet hair cupping my forehead. Yes, she loved me before she died. I raised my head as the warmth of her disappeared. I stood and I straightened my back and I felt her power. And mine.

Tomorrow I will go and see my friend, Mikey. He was the best friend a man ever had. I think I will. Tomorrow.

Acknowledgements

My deepest love to Carol Russell, without whose belief and patience I would have become a blubbering wreck. Many hugs to Jenne, Paul, Soroya and Bobby for their faith, love and advice.

Thanks to Lynda, for trodding through North Carolina with me. To all my family, for gobs of money and affection. To my mother, for determination, and my father, for magic. To all my friends, who will forgive me for not quoting every single name again. My deepest thanks to Reverend Pickett, Dr Carl DeVane and Lieutenant Russo, New York Metropolitan Transportation Authority, for their help with research. Also deepest thanks to Jiton Sharmayne Davidson and Angela Royal for their sensitive critiques. Many thanks to Shane, for driving up hills and down mountains. And to Claudine, for thirteen years.

My apologies to residents of North Carolina, who will know that I have taken liberties with their beautiful state and that Edene is a figment of my imagination.